Jo Jackson was born in Birmingh̶̶ ̶̶̶̶̶̶̶̶̶̶̶̶̶̶ ̶̶̶wife
before becoming a family therapist ̶̶̶̶̶̶̶̶̶̶̶̶̶̶ ̶̶̶̶̶e of the most
vulnerable people in society. She h̶̶ ̶̶̶̶written one other novel, the
highly acclaimed *Too Loud a Silence*. She lives with her husband in rural
Shropshire.

By the same author

Too Loud a Silence

Beyond the Margin

Jo Jackson

To John,

Thank you for reading my book.

Jo Jackson

First published 2019
© Jo Jackson 2019
ISBN 978-09956094-0-2

A CIP catalogue record for this book is available from the British Library

Published in Great Britain by Apedale Press   www.jojacksonwriter.com

Cover image by Logan Armstrong Unsplash.com

Cover design by Derek Hall

Typeset, printed and bound in Great Britain by Imprint Digital.com

For all those who work to make
the lives of children better.

England 2016

'Christ. It's a girl.' I slammed on the brakes, came to a juddering stop and dropped the window. 'It's hell out there,' I yelled 'I'm only going to the next town. Can I give you a lift somewhere?' I saw her hesitate. Suspicion clouded her eyes. She wiped the rain from her face and shook her head.

'Hey, I didn't mean to frighten you, just it's filthy wet and there's nothing between here and where I'm going – about ten maybe fifteen miles.' Lashing rain on the cab roof drowned the opportunity for further explanation. A loud clap of thunder and she opened the door, threw in her backpack and hauled herself inside.

She was shivering, water dripped in pink streaks down her forehead. Her hand held fast to the door handle, her body rigid, as far from me as possible. I knew fear when I saw it. I tossed her a towel. 'Here, this might help.' I drove off, the wipers arcing across the windscreen. She dried herself and used the towel to wipe the inside of the window where it had steamed up.

'I've all this lot to unload. I'm heading for the timber yard on the Edge. Do you know it?'

A faint lift of the shoulders.

'What brings you to be in the middle of nowhere on a day like this?' She flinched and I cursed myself for being clumsy. Bewilderment contorted her face; she picked at the skin of her thumb.

'I live in town, work there.' Her voice a soft Irish lilt. 'I've been visiting … my grandma. Yeah, I've been visiting my grandma.' She stared straight ahead as she spoke.

I didn't believe her. She wanted me off her back. Not my problem anyway.

1

'A Northern Irish accent if I'm not mistaken. Spent time there myself but live across the border now on the west coast. This is a regular journey for me carrying timber.' I flicked my head indicating the load on the trailer. 'From Liverpool originally as you can probably guess.' I prattled on. It was working, she seemed less edgy.

A pretty kid or could be. Crazy pink hair shaved close, a fair Irish skin.

She struggled out of her wet jacket and put the towel round her shoulders. Below her T-shirt a red bra strap hung like a smile down her arm.

I could see her better without the black hoodie with its lurid purple lining. A flush of colour was brightening her face.

'Here, spread your jacket on the seat. It might dry.' About the same age Nuala must be. The thought so sudden. Guilt, remorse, grief, a flash flood of emotion. I tapped an incessant beat on the steering wheel to cover my agitation.

The girl stared at my hands then bent forward and helped herself to a row of chocolate from my half-eaten bar. She broke a piece for me and flicked it across the seat.

'Help yourself.' It came out hoarse and grainy. I grinned to lessen the effect. She looked startled, but seemed to realise I was cool with it, mumbled thanks and tucked into the rest.

On the inside of her arm etched in purple was a tattoo, **DAD**. A lurch of pain, the needle-sharp prick of jealousy.

'What does your dad think?' I wanted her to know I'd seen the tattoo. Her face flushed like she'd been burned, and I wished I'd never asked.

'I'm Joe. And you?' Her lips came together in a tight line. She forced a cough and stuck her feet on the shelf in front. Thin legs disappeared into laced boots. On the toe of one, written in white paint, I read FUCK and on the other, OFF.

She saw me looking. 'What's it to you?' she said and lifted a single finger in my direction.

'Okay, okay.' I held up one hand, relieved to see a smirk curl the edge of her mouth. I drove in silence after that, scared of my whirling feelings.

'I'll drop you here. Top of the High Street. Look, buy yourself a warm drink or something, dry off. There's a café along there on the left.' I put the twenty-pound note on the seat beside her. I didn't care if she knew I didn't believe her story. 'There's a bunkhouse too.

On the hill. Cheap but clean. Take care.'

The girl opened the door, hesitated then took the money and jumped to the ground. 'My name ... it's ... it's Jess,' she said with a forward thrust of the chin. 'Thanks.'

'Good luck, Jess.' Our eyes met before I had to turn away overwhelmed by a sense of familiarity. I fought tears as I watched her go, bereft at my emptiness. 'Damn you,' I threw it at her as she turned and waved before disappearing between the parked cars. I thumped the dashboard, upped the radio's volume and drove the short distance to the timber yard.

'Go well. Whoever you really are.'

Nuala
Ireland 2016

A few more hours.

Over there. Beyond the breaking waves, beyond the steely sea, to the place hidden in the mist. Thinking about it is a weird kind of freedom. No one knows I'm going. It's how I want it. Who'll miss me – Jess, Mrs Leafe? Reported as missing? Probably not. I'll be a statistic. Marked as a failure.

Disappearing will be the success.

The sand is damp. My bare footprints washed away by the waves, like I was never here. Has Jess guessed something's up? Tell her. No, don't. She'll give me a hug. Stop me. The jumper she gave me last week, brand new, told me her mother had given it to her. 'More you than me,' she said. The ten pounds too. 'Got lucky in the office sweepstake.' Bollocks. Social workers can't give their own money to clients. It's against the rules. Her problem not mine.

Flat and cool, my phone is an oblong in my hand. So hard to let it go but if I don't, I know they'll trace me. The screen saver – me and Ted by the river pulling faces, squashed together in a selfie. 'Your number, Ted, it's in my head, the only one I need. I'm coming.' I toss the mobile as far as I can. An arc of white, it drops into the grasping sea. Without it my palm is bare, my fingers long to curl around its shape. My hand is light.

Wind in my hair, freezing water, crashing waves, sticky seaweed. 'Yeah. FREE.'

Hiccup a sob before it gets to count.

I run in crazy zigzags back along the beach – there's no one can see. Collapse on my back, sand in my nails. I'm a marooned starfish. The clouds see. Blurry clouds. Don't cry.

4

It's a beach. There will be others.

England here I come. Goodbye Ireland. What have you ever sodding given me? Scars on my arm, a tattoo, that's what. Oh, and other memories …

Crouching in the corner. My dad slams the door. I'm in the dark.

Crying.

He doesn't come back.

Hungry.

Climbing onto a chair to reach the cupboard where the biscuits are. None.

Rubbish in the bin. A baked bean tin to lick.

Knocking, loud knocking, shouts. Wriggle under the bed.

DADDY. Daddy. Daddy.

Nobody.

Chew burned bits in the frying pan, the label off the bean tin.

Banging, shouting. The door falls in.

8th January 2005
Name: Nuala (name provided by another tenant) surname uncertain.
D.O.B. March 2000??
Last Known Address: 24, Feeney Street, Londonderry
Information received: Mother deceased. Father's whereabouts unknown
General Comments: The child is pale and undernourished. Scabs around her mouth (possibly impetigo). Bruises visible on arms and legs. She does not respond to her name or any other stimulus. Appears hungry and thirsty.

Me. Aged five. The scruffy handwritten note in my case file. Tore it out. Reckoned it belonged to me.

Who wrote it – Christ didn't they even know my birthday?

Get rid. Let go, leave it with the garbage.

It's me. Proof I existed before being 'In Care'.

The note. I'm keeping it.

2005

A red car and a fat woman. I hide my nose from the smell when she puts her arm around me; pulls me into her armpit. Shan't get out the car. She's tugging me, lifting me. Through big doors. Brown doors with a silver handle.

They give me milk. Don't want it. One sip, a little sip. It's nice.

Talking stops. They're watching me. Put the glass down and sit on my hands. They push it nearer, heads nodding. I lift the glass, drink and drink, without stopping. Only sloshy noises. It's empty. Sick comes. Over me, the carpet and the table full of papers.

'Call me auntie.'

'You talk soft. My mummy didn't.'

'Sleep tight, little one.' Auntie's put me in a cot with a blue teddy bear and a woolly sheep.

'I'm too big for a cot.'

She kisses my head.

I climb out and sleep on the floor.

Uncle's name is Mick. He's got no hair. He pulls faces, trying to make me laugh. Gives up 'cos I won't.

'Do you throw things?'

'No, Nuala. Throwing things isn't good.' His face goes funny, so I don't tell him Daddy always threw things.

Auntie's thin with squashy boobs and a cross on a chain round her neck. She has pink cardigans and big pants. She hangs them on a line to dry next to mine.

'Nuala, eat your tea then you'll grow up to be a big girl.' She said it last night and tonight.

'I don't want to grow up.'

'Course you do.'

I don't like stew. Don't like nasty carrots. I move them round and round in my mouth. Make slapping noises. Spit out a black slimy thing.

'It's a mushroom!' Mick's gone red. 'Swallow the bloody thing.'

'MICK.' Auntie's cross.

He throws down his knife and fork and takes his plate to the kitchen.

Good.

They buy me a bed, it's in a bedroom next to theirs. It's a funny house with no stairs. I can't get out of the window because it's locked.

'Don't lock my door.'

'Keep you safe, Nuala. We're close by.'

'I want my door open.' Cry and can't stop.

How will my daddy get in when he comes back for me?

*

'Is Daddy coming today?' Auntie's lips go thin. She's bangs a pan on the work surface.

'Stop asking me. I've told you, Nuala, Daddy can't care for you. It's why you're here, why we're looking after you.'

'Yes, he can. Yes, he can.'

'And stop screaming.'

'Will he come tomorrow then?'

I'll tell her about the beach. Then they'll know.

'Wake up, wake up. Mummy won't wake up.' I shake her. She smells.

'Make her wake up, Daddy. I don't like it when you and Mummy go to sleep for a long time. Teddy doesn't like it when I put your needles in his arm.'

'Don't, Daddy, don't cry.'

'She's dead, fucking dead. FUCKING DEAD. And stop yelling. STOP BLOODY HOWLING.'

I stop.

Then we go to the beach.

'Daddy, Daddy. You can't see. You can't see.' On his shoulders, holding his hair. I'm giggling, hands over his eyes; he's falling all over the sand. We jump the waves.

'My toes are freezing.'

'Crabs coming,' Daddy shouts.

I squeal.

'What's dead mean? Why hasn't Mummy come? Will she wake up soon?'

'Bloody shut it. Asking questions all the time.'

We have crisps and a drink sitting on the sand.

'Can I take my dress off, play like that girl?'

He throws me in the air, catches me, tickles me.

'Stop it. Do it again. I like it.'

My daddy is as big as a house. He's got ginger hair on his chest and the strongest arms. Sometimes he hugs me.

'I love you, Daddy.'

We go back to a different place. Daddy's friend lives there, but he's gone away. Mummy doesn't come. Lots and lots of sleeps go by.

'Where's Mummy? I want Mummy.'

One day he slams the door and leaves me in the dark.

Joe
Northern Ireland 2005

It drove me mad, either her noise, like the whimper of a chained dog, or her silence when she watched my every movement. Sitting with her thumb in her mouth, a dirty T-shirt of Bridget's hanging from her hand. Her blue eyes followed me. She could see inside my soul, exposing it to the light; she knew my thoughts, knew what I was going to do.

Bridget, dead. Two days. Dodgy gear, but we took it anyway, desperation or craving the driving force. She'd gone before I surfaced. No drama, no last gasp. I spewed my guts up watched by Nuala's empty eyes. Diarrhoea ran from me when I had no strength or will to get out of bed. She brought me water and with her child's hands wiped the vomit off my face. She tried to do the same for her mother, shaking her when she wouldn't drink the water, desperate for a response. Aged five. This was her life.

We'd never wanted a child; we were barely past being children ourselves. Bridget, wild and unruly, would disappear for days returning wrung through and exhausted. I never asked where she'd been. While pregnant she tried, succeeded mostly, to ditch drugs. I didn't try.

The baby had come. Black-haired with a tiny screwed-up face who for a few short days or weeks made us want to live a different life. I was the first to succumb to the old way. Persuaded by a mate, I was too weak to resist. Wanting to indulge. To feel the utter selfishness of having no one else to think about. I needed the companionship, the familiar world where questions weren't asked, where drugs were the only currency.

Bridget screamed at me, hurled obscenities at the baby who

made demands of her. She'd leave her to cry, until after a while, the child stopped and only chest-heaving sobs registered her need.

'I'm a slut.' Bridget's first words to me. The tilt of her chin defied me to say otherwise.

Measured against her I was no better. Our sex, primal and cruel, the bridge between shooting and smashing out. We hated ourselves. Shacking up together gave us someone else to hate more.

Love didn't bring us together, nor affection or lust. I saw her first in a bombed basement crouched by a fireplace trying to set light to a few sticks. Her fingerless gloves were rainbow coloured. She wore baggy pants with psychedelic zigzag patterns reminding me of a 'trip'; her bright orange top strident in the dinginess of the surroundings. Her hair fascinated me. A shaved head but for long thin dreadlocks sprouting from the back of her skull.

I wished the baby had died so I didn't have to feel guilty any more. Despite us she survived, and she grew, she demanded more. We kept moving. From town to town, one seedy dump to another. A dirty bed, a new supplier, no ties, no trace.

I went with a slut, got what no one else wanted, who no one else could handle. Bridget knew her life would be short. She either hung on the moon or crawled in shit. All her energy put into dying, fast and young. Giving birth to Nuala merely a pause.

I arrived in Northern Ireland a few months before the new millennium. First to Belfast, on the night ferry – when I had to flee Liverpool fast. But what had been an endless, empty stretch of water now felt too short a distance. I flitted to Derry where I could get involved. Plenty going on. I was a Catholic with enough anger to turn it in any direction. But a Catholic with a scouse accent. Having Irish ancestors stood for nothing. They didn't trust me.

Either side.

Shunned by Derry's inhabitants, ignored, abused, all of which I could take, but humiliated – no. I was around three years old when I learned if I didn't look out for Micky Joe McCurdy then no one else would. I fought my older brothers for the food on the table and learned to survive on scraps, read the signs when my stepdad came home from the pub and Mum got battered just for breathing. Hid under the bed waiting for the belt to come off. The streets were tough but join the right gang and you were okay. Show respect where it counted, be smarter than the next kid. Show you didn't give a toss about school, the cops, anything.

No one messed with Michael Joseph McCurdy.

Until Nuala. A baby meant nothing to me. The product of a basic urge, the need to master a feisty bitch. For days the child had no name, neither of us capable of giving it an identity. Then Bridget remembered her nan had been called Nuala. Her nan had brought her up, then a succession of aunties. Shared like a dose of gonorrhoea, she'd said. So, Nuala it was.

Sometimes I watched her. Her small face creamy-white in sleep, her mouth moving, shaping words in a language spoken only by the young. She frightened me. Needed me and I couldn't deal with it. She stirred something I didn't know existed. I rejected the responsibility, shook her when she cried, threw her into the cot when I craved a line. She began to smile when she saw my face, to curl her fist around my finger. The harder she tried the further I pushed her away.

'She's fuckin' dead.' I yelled at Nuala when she cried for her mum. I covered Bridget, not being able to see her meant she wasn't there. After two days, her stink became worse than the pong of damp and vomit. And need took over.

Nuala whimpered or she watched. Silence crept into the corners, wrapped Bridget like a shroud. I grabbed the child. Lifted her up, crushed her to me, shared our body heat, her skin touching mine.

I ran along the street, over the dunes to the beach and dumped her at the edge of the water. A wave running out of energy tickled her toes, she wriggled them into the sand, peeked at me and giggled. Take her into the water, submerge her until she lies compliant in my arms. Then let go, let her float with the tide and I wouldn't have to care any more. She giggled, giggled at me. I sat beside her and let the water tickle my toes too. She tugged off her dress and ran along the beach throwing it onto the dry sand. In just her yellow knickers she jumped onto my back, wrapped thin arms around my neck. I held her hand and leapt the waves squealing as ice-cold water streaked our bodies. I threw her in the air and caught her dizzy with laughing. The sun shone.

'My skin's being blown away,' her little voice called.

'It's the wind of the sea my little one. The wind that blew your daddy here.'

She was like an indoor cat a twilight child, a child of the shadows, her skin unused to sunlight and fresh air, flesh as white as limestone, bruise-coloured around her eyes.

'Daddy.' She tried the word, repeating it like it might disappear.

I gave her pop and crisps; she copied how I drank from a can licking her lips like I did.

We left the beach, fled from Bridget, went miles away, to a mate's room where we'd dossed before. He was absent someplace. Nuala became an inside cat again. She resumed her silent vigil, following me with staring eyes, sucking at Bridget's T-shirt. I opened a can of beans and tried to fry eggs. The fat burnt; blue rancid smoke made us cough. The eggs turned black and stuck to the pan. I scraped at the charred pieces.

She pushed her plate away.

'Bloody speak.' A million needles pricked my skin. I swept her plate off the sofa, hit the light switch so as not to see her eyes.

Slammed the door. Gone.

I ran from that room and its slamming door, not stopping until my head throbbed, and my brain begged for oxygen. Away from Nuala and her pleading eyes. My first recourse to find a dealer.

Slept rough. No money – no gear. 'Mates' melted into corners sensing the lunacy they saw as I clawed at my arms tearing the skin, blood oozing in rivulets. Withdrawal, my hell as I sat in the gutter, a hundred gutters. A vortex sucking me to a bottom I dared not reach. Nuala came to me. Just beyond my vision, her hand in mine. 'Let's go to the beach again.' A myriad of lights, pouring sweat, shivering, convulsions, screams inside my head, the pain ate me from the inside. She, the dullness, the dark, the pinprick of light, the warmth brushing over me like a butterfly, the grain of self-respect I hung onto.

I got lucky. Many succumb to the agony of dope sickness. She wouldn't let me go, hovered behind my eyes when I wanted only to die. Always there as the weeks became months, she was the reason I dragged my emaciated, exhausted carcase away from the city to a place where I could heal.

I told myself to find her, find where they'd taken her, but couldn't do it, knew I wouldn't cope. Finding her would send me back to a black place.

11

Nuala

Auntie gives me soft toys. I hide the blue elephant, stuff it between the wall and the back of the wardrobe. Make it disappear like Daddy. See if it comes back. I bury a woolly sheep in a smelly heap at the bottom of the garden where Uncle Mick puts the cut grass. I dig it up sometimes. It's green and slimy and one eye hangs loose on a black thread. It pongs. I rub it all over me, on my face, in my hair, between my legs so I can be horrible like sheep.

'Look at you. Why, Nuala?' Auntie's scrubbing my hair in the bath, hurting me.

They buy me a Barbie doll. It's got long hair and boobies.

I twist the head and arms and legs off.

'You've broken it, Nuala. You'll have no toys left. Can't you play nicely?'

'I am. Barbie's dead.' Auntie sits me on the sofa and gives me a biscuit.

They don't buy me anything else.

Elephant hasn't come back.

I'm dressed in a white blouse, a green jumper and a grey skirt.

'You're so smart and grown-up. Let's take a photo in the garden. We'll put it in your life story book'. She and Mick are smiling. They always smile when they talk about my life story book. 'Something for you to keep forever.'

I don't want a silly book and I don't want to go to school.

'Snotty botty. Snotty botty.' A naughty boy. Other kids say the same. They pull my hair and lift my skirt.

'I don't want to go to school.'

12

Mick's cross again. 'Always this palaver. She makes me late for work. Get in the car, Nuala.'

'I hate school.' I throw my school bag in the hedge. Auntie takes me back inside.

I won't have to go today.

She's holding my hand too tightly. Takes me into the bathroom and washes my face with a flannel.

'It's too hot.'

'Nonsense. It's hardly warm.'

I squeeze onto the floor between the toilet and the bath and bang the toilet seat up and down.

She walks me to school.

'Why do they call me orphan? Say my dad and my mum are dead?'

'Take no notice. Silly words. Learn to stand up for yourself.'

Auntie knocks on the classroom door. Eyes stare at me.

'Sorry Nuala's late.'

Auntie and teacher are whispering in the corridor, a hand and one red shoe are hooked round the door keeping it half-closed. I'm inside. All the eyes are giggling. Wee escapes, I hop to stop it coming.

Teacher's arm is round my shoulder and she's pushing me forward. Two red shoes walking. 'Come and sit here, near me, Nuala.'

I'm at the front. I've been bad.

Aileen McMullen says I can't play. 'You spoil the game.'

'I don't.'

'Do. Do. Do.' She sticks out her tongue. 'And you're a baby. Play with the baby class.'

I push her. Her head thumps onto the playground. My fingers scratch her face, digging into skin. Blood.

I sit outside the headteacher's room for the whole afternoon. Aileen's crying. She's a baby. She holds a white pad thing over her cheek.

'This isn't what I expect from year 2 children.' The headteacher's talking to both of us but she's looking at me. She smells like air freshener.

Aileen's mum has come to fetch her home, so she wails all over again. I put my hands over my ears and shut my eyes until she goes away.

After she's gone, it's only me, in the corridor. I wind a piece of wool from my jumper round my finger till it really hurts.

Auntie comes, her mouth is tight like she has no teeth. She sighs and grabs my hand when she leaves the headteacher's office. She's been in there forever.

We walk home too fast.

'My side hurts.'

She doesn't stop. She's not listening.

I trip over. 'Ow, my knee.'

'You're all right. It's only a little graze.'

'It stings.' I won't cry. She's dabbing my knee with cottonwool and puts a blue plaster on.

'You're nearly seven. Can't you learn to behave?' When she's cross, she has lines.

She gives me milk and cake. Her eyes are wet.

All afternoon Auntie's on the phone, talking about me. I sit on the floor and pull the fringe off the rug. Hum so I can't hear what she's saying.

I'm awake. It's dark. No television on downstairs. A runny feeling, warm round my legs. Wee wee. I rub my bottom across the sheets. My pyjamas stick but then they get cold. I want to be warm again. I tug the wet sheet off and hide it under the bed. The buttons on the bare mattress hurt.

Next morning Auntie's pulls the sheet from under the bed. It's a white monster uncurling across the carpet trying to bite me.

'You can bring it to the utility room and put it in the washing machine. I hope it was an accident.

'I'm disappointed.' It's what she always says.

I still have to go to school. I'm on a baby reading book. I want a purple one like the others. I jumble my letters and forget words. Uncle Mick thinks I'm a silly girl and must try harder. I stop trying.

I wet the bed every night because the warm feeling is nice. Poo is warm too, and soft. It squashes in my hand. I draw brown streaks on the walls of the bathroom, over the toilet lid and in the sink. I stamp it into the bathroom mat and wrap it in the towels. Not once. Lots and lots of times.

It makes me laugh.

It makes them mad.

'Nuala, there's a lady coming today.'

'What lady? Is she coming because I'm seven?' Auntie is packing my clothes into a suitcase with a lid. My tummy flutters. 'You said we could have a pizza? I haven't been bad today.'

'She's coming because … we can't …' Her head's shaking. 'You need counselling. Need someone to talk to.'

Don't want it, what she says I need. It'll taste disgusting like banana medicine.

'Why are you crying, Auntie? I feel poorly. Where's Uncle Mick?

'I won't talk to anyone, nobody.'

My bottom's full. Soft, gooey poo oozes into my pants. Stinky.

'Oh, Nuala. We tried … Go and clean yourself up.'

Brown on my hand, both hands. Rub and press, rub and smear, prints on the wall. Stick my finger near my nose and sniff.

When I come down, Auntie's sitting on the sofa. Her face has black streaks; she's dabbing a tissue on her lumpy eyes.

'Give me a hug, Nuala.' Her arm's a worm reaching for me.

'No. Don't want to.' I pull the throw over my head and she disappears.

A lady with an orange, dangly necklace comes. She pats my head, takes my hand. I get into a car. A blue car.

Joe

I left the city, my few provisions stuffed in a rucksack. I'd persuaded a wino huddled under a railway bridge to swap his tent for a loaf of soda bread and a beer. A truck driver gave me a lift across the border, told me of a place, recognised I wanted somewhere 'quiet'. 'At the mercy of the moon; only when tide's out can anyone walk across the sands. Cut off twice a day,' he'd said.

I looked over to the island, the shores washed by seawater. As the tide retreated and dawn broke, I crossed the strip of sand. Only shadows and marram grass saw me arrive. I walked to the far end of the island where Atlantic winds sucked the energy from the land. Stunted gorse struggled to survive, huge boulders slammed by winter storms made hollows and caves. The tent wasn't watertight, but it gave a little protection. I slept for almost twenty-four hours. A sleep undisturbed by dreams, undisturbed by Nuala's gaze. Next morning sand had piled against the doorway and the zip stuck fast. Those first few days I merely existed. I washed in the sea, shocked by the freezing water. Soon my limited supplies dwindled and forced me to venture to the island store – more a garage with a few tins and bottles on a shelf, a sack of potatoes on the floor, than a shop. The woman who served me bid me only good morning, asked nothing else. She locked the door with a key when I left.

Could she see what I was, an addict from Derry? Hair had grown on my once shaved head and a scant ginger beard fringed gaunt cheekbones. Inside I was fragile as a seagull's egg.

I couldn't climb to the high point on the island without stopping for breath. My limbs ached and heart pounded. I lay amongst the sparse grass, bare rocks and wind-blown screes.

I fantasised about heroin, relived the buzz of shooting.
Sometimes I cried.

The effort of it all was overwhelming. From the cliff tops I watched white water crash around the rocks below, the sea navy blue or violet or a swirling angry grey – always greedy. It would be so easy. The rush of air, the dizzying pull of gravity. The joy of nothingness.

Every day, I added a rock to a small cairn, marking another twenty-four hours I'd survived. Then I found it flattened. A broken monument. A pointless symbol. I cried to the gulls and hurled the scattered rocks down the cliff face, watching them fall, hit the water, swallowed by the sea.

A ewe emerged from a crevice, stared with mocking eyes. She stamped her foot, dislodging more stones. 'You. You did it.' I laughed so loudly she ran away, her skinny legs tripping across the cliff top. I'd forgotten I could laugh.

I explored the small island with its hidden places, avoiding farmers on ancient tractors, working in the fields. I'd only been here for two weeks but the space felt like mine. I resented visitors or walkers taking advantage of the low tide, ignoring their attempts at conversation.

Early morning was my favourite time, the blue sky streaked with grey, the air cold and fresh. Sometimes, as today, the rain fell, and I tramped in cloying mist. On the heathland I heard rather than saw the commotion. A string of curses from across the bog. Curses accompanied by the mournful sound of a cow in trouble. A bellow I recognised from my own well of desperation. I ran towards the sound, feet sinking into the soft peat, water seeping around my ankles. A cow struggled in the mire and with each lunge it pushed itself deeper. The size of the animal was terrifying, its huge eyes rolled back in fright. I could smell the panic as it bucked and struggled. I grabbed the rope from a man who coughed and wheezed with exhaustion. The man slapped the flanks of the animal, used words I didn't understand. Somehow after several attempts, balanced on tussocks of grass, I hitched the rope over the cow's neck, hung on, arms flailing wildly with each turn of the cow's head. The farmer inched back across the bog on his hands and knees and pulled himself onto his tractor. For about twenty minutes we struggled. The cow weakened; the rope taut to the point of breaking. 'Steady, steady.' I prayed it wouldn't snap. Slowly the cow emerged and with a brutal kick to my shin it freed itself from the foul-smelling muck. I collapsed onto the soft ground, head in hands, splattered with cow muck, peat and brown stagnant water. In my face, my eyes, my mouth. Freed from its lasso the cow ran off, its belly and legs caked in mud.

My leg felt broken. I tried to focus.

'Can you walk? She's a devil is Bella when she gets a mood on her.'

I raised my head, seeing the man as though through gauze. A hood pulled tight around his face, he wore a thick jumper on top of a fleece, baggy corduroy trousers tucked into fur-lined boots.

'Will you come and have a bowl of stirabout and a clean-up then?'

The farmer helped me to stand. He only reached my shoulder and I steadied myself on his rounded back.

We didn't speak as he drove the tractor back to the farm. In the farmyard, sheds and a long low house were all in states of disrepair. A green door hung on only one hinge and slates from the roof lay smashed on the ground. Hens ran squawking from under the wheels and a goose, its neck outstretched, advanced as I limped from the tractor. The farmer aimed a kick at it and its loud honking brought a woman to the farmhouse door.

Small and bent, she flicked a duster at the two of us and tutted as she disappeared inside. The farmer put out his arm. 'Best wait.' His voice thin, cracking like ice cubes. He pushed back his hood; I saw the crooked nose, the crumpled tissue face, brown and mottled, white wisps of hair plastered to his head.

He's old. They're both old.

The woman appeared with a bowl of warm water and some carbolic soap. She gave us each a rag and a towel.

'It's a disgrace you are, Jack O'Shea, bringing home folk in that state.' She shut the door and left us in the drizzle to clean ourselves. My leg throbbed; I rolled up my trouser leg.

'It'll be a good un that,' Jack's observation. 'Don't mind her, the wife. We're not used to visitors.'

I hobbled into the kitchen behind Jack and sat at the wooden table. Jack's wife stirred a pot on the range with birdlike hands. The room hot, steam from the kettle misted the windows. 'You'll be taking off them filthy clothes too before you gets your breakfast.' Her voice trills. 'The both of ye.'

'I'd better just go.' I could smell the bog on my tracksuit bottoms, could also smell the hot food.

'Woman, leave off. The lad's helped me out. Saved Bella, the daft bugger. Give him summat to eat, Mary.'

I peeled off sopping socks, ashamed of their unwashed state. Jack's wife picked them off the floor and hung them on a hook over the range.

A simple room, thick stone walls and a slate floor with a faded rag rug. A wooden frame occupied one corner and on it a mattress and cushions. I supposed it acted as a bed at night and a sofa in the daytime. A dresser displayed simple crockery.

'It's always been enough for us.' Jack had seen me looking. 'We don't need much.'

I nodded. 'Have you ... how long ... I mean, has this always been home?'

'Aye, and m' father's before. M' brother Amos, not interested in the farm. Wanted to join the merchant navy. "Not room for two of us on the land," he used to say. He wanted to see the world. He did too. Came home on leave one time and died in his bed, a massive stroke.' Jack poked a finger toward a door off the kitchen. 'Only forty-eight. I reckon he had a tough life, wild living an' all.

'Lived here for 83 years. Married Mary – can't remember when – a shy young thing, eighteen, prettiest girl in the west of Ireland.'

Mary looked at me, her face shrivelled like a stale apple. Hands on hips, her small feet buried in furry slippers. She shuffled across the floor and disappeared into the next room. Drawers were opened, banged shut again. She came back with a pair of overalls and a knitted jumper, held it in front of me checking it for fit.

'Mary.' Jack pushed himself up from the table. A bread knife clattered to the floor. 'Not ...'

'Hush your tongue, Jack. Them's your brother's. The lad's freezing cold and half starved. It's time. Time, Jack.'

Jack withered, clutching at the edge of the table.

I put on the borrowed clothes. The old couple stared into the fire. The jumper was coarse, knitted from wool in shades of blue and grey, the colour of the local sheep. It smelled musty, unused. Dressed, I stood awkwardly before them, hands by my side. Mary put an arthritic claw on her husband's shoulder. Jack shrank into his chair. He fumbled to fill a pipe. I watched him struggle, then took the pipe from his shaking hands and filled it for him.

When we were both in dry clothes, Mary put a bowl of porridge and a jug of cream on the table. 'What shall I be calling you, lad?'

'Joe. Joe McCurdy.' I said it without thinking. Shouldn't have given myself away. 'My stepfather's surname; made to use it. Born Joe Morgan. Joe Morgan's good enough for me.' It sounded lame.

'Aye, and Joe is good enough for me.' Jack met my eye. 'Best be eating that porridge an' all.'

I relished every mouthful of the hot oaty meal and scraped the bowl clean. I hadn't tasted hot food for a long time, its warmth slid down my throat. Mary refilled my bowl and poured cream on top, my protest brief and weak.

'Eat it, boy. Sure, and I can nearly see your bones.' Mary stood over me, watching.

'I've … I've been ill. I …'

'No need for explanations here. I see all I need to know.'

'Where you from then?' Jack puffed at his pipe.

'I've been sleeping …'

'I knows where you been sleeping. Over yonder, far end. I meant where you from?'

I put my spoon beside the emptied bowl. 'Liverpool – but an age ago.'

'Aye.' Jack nodded. 'Aye, lad.' A puff of pipe smoke curled between us.

'You best be having a lie-down befores you go anywhere else. Rest the leg.' Mary pushed me in the small of my back. 'You're done in. Get yourself a decent sleep. Come on, you can go next door.' Jack muffled a cry, his hand across his eyes.

A doorway led into a small room; Mary beckoned and shut the door leaving me alone. A single iron bed against the wall, green mould spreading upwards from the floor. I opened the window to let fresh air into the damp-smelling space. Rusted bits of car engine and part of an exhaust cluttered the surfaces. A screwdriver, a wrench and a box of screws were on the table as though the occupier might return at any moment.

I lay on the bed, resting for a minute, giving my leg time to stop throbbing, trying not to think of Jack's brother the dead sailor. It was three hours before I woke.

No one was around, I let myself out.

Back in the tent I lay with the flap open. Restless – yet satisfied – pleased. Content? I couldn't name the feeling. Lonely too. The two old people, this is their place, every hillock, every cove, every tuft of grass – a sense of permanency. Longing grasped me. This morning I had done something for someone else. Helped them. I wanted to grab hold of this moment, keep it, remember it.

I didn't want Nuala with her piercing eyes to come and take it away.

Nuala

The blue car smells of sour milk. 'Where are we going? Why aren't we there?'

The lady with the necklace is a social worker, but she's not driving, a man is. No more houses, only green fields and trees.

'See the sheep. Look, a tractor,' she says.

I'm not a baby.

I'm in the back. They're in the front. Her hair is black, her scalp coloured red under the hair where it's scraped into a brown plastic comb. Dye has stained her neck. I think she didn't have time to wash it off properly, had to dry her hair, jump in her car and rush over to remove me. Auntie used to dye her hair too.

'We'll take you to a nice new home – somewhere I think you'll be happy. Lots of space to run around and maybe a dog or some cats …' Her voice shakes. She twists her neck round and smiles. She's got white teeth.

I screw up my eyes and she's blurry. She talks to the driver and leaves me alone.

'Where's my daddy? I want him?' I howl. I'm a wolf.

'Stop screeching.'

I splutter.

'We'll have some sandwiches soon. Would you like a drink of juice?' Her voice is all soft and creamy now like melted ice cream.

'I want a wee.'

There aren't any toilets. I crouch by the roadside; the steamy liquid forms a little puddle under my shoe. She's pretending not to look.

I'll run away. Find Daddy. Live with him. My thumb bleeds where I chew the skin.

'Nearly there. I think this is it.'

We turn off the road and bump up a track. The car falls into holes full of water and swerves around like on the television programme Uncle Mick used to watch. The driver says a naughty word. Tall trees, close together, dark tunnels where monsters hide; I shrink lower in my seat. The car stops, the driver lets out a loud breath and leans his head on the steering wheel.

'What a godforsaken place this is.'

Why is he cross? I peep. There's long, cut tree trunks stacked like a stairway to the sky, a crumbly, frowny house and lots of sheds, Scary banging noises. Shut my eyes again, cover my ears with my hands, grab my knees.

'It's only a sheet of metal banging. Don't be silly.' The social worker with the red scalp is getting out of the car.

It doesn't seem the kind of place where my daddy lives.

'DADDY.'

A woman opens the door. I look at her through open fingers. A streak of grey, she stands with her hands on her hips. She isn't smart like Auntie. A grey cardigan over a grey jumper and a pleated skirt. She has slippers on her feet with a ruff of fur, the colour of rats, around her ankles. Her hair straggles across her face in stripes.

'Whatever is that noise?' Her voice is grey. 'You must be Nuala. I'm Bernie. You'd better come in and stop shrieking or you'll scare the birds from the trees.' She claps her hands; a group of black birds rise squawking behind the house. Louder than my shriek.

Where can I sit? There are three soft chairs. The grey lady gives me a stool with tiny legs and a picture of a dog's head stitched on the cover.

'Sit next to the fire.'

Flames are crackling behind a guard. Real flames escaping up the chimney.

'I'm too hot.' I wriggle my bottom while trying to stay still. The grown-ups are talking. A table with a brown cloth is against the wall; above it is a picture of some mountains and the sea. I can lift the corner of a rug with the toe of my shoe; the fringe flops over. I pull it straight before anyone tells me off. There are socks on top of the fireguard – six. Thick, rough socks, two blue and four brown. They must be a giant's socks.

Sometimes they stop talking and look over. It's raining, a pitter patter on the window. The orange curtains move but I don't know how. I can see white clouds pushing into a patch of blue. Nu, Nu: I hear Daddy call and I jump to him, high as the sky. We sail on the cloud of cottonwool.

'Well goodbye, Nuala. I'll come and see you in a week or two, see how you're settling.' The social worker gives me a quick hug, her string of beads sticking into my cheek.

The car disappears down the track, bump, bump, bump. Daddy's cloud has gone. I won't find him here. I kick the grey gravel, shiny and wet. By the house is a barrel and water drips into it from a pipe off the roof. Drip, drip, I count until I get to ten then sit on the front doorstep picking at a thread on my shoe.

'Come in, shut the door, keep in the warmth.'

The grey lady tells me again that her name is Bernie. 'Will you remember?' She makes me say it several times over as if it's difficult. 'I've bought you a colouring book, and some pens. You can sit at the table. Don't get pen on the cloth.'

On the first page there's a clown riding a bike, and then a spaceship with a child astronaut in it. I flick through the book to where a starfish lies stranded on a beach. It's waiting for the waves to come and rescue it. A boy with a bucket is walking along the sand. I scribble him out with a black pen, so the sea will find the starfish first.

'That's good colouring, indeed it is.'

I jump. A giant hand with black hairs smooths the corner of my colouring book.

'Hello, Nuala. Pleased to meet you.'

The giant ruffles my hair. I bury my chin in my chest and see his huge feet wearing socks just like the ones drying on the fireguard. He plonks himself on a chair beside me. 'Oops, forgot the newspaper.' He stands again and arranges paper on the seat before sitting back. He makes a squashy, crumpling noise as he fidgets on the chair.

'Don't want to be in the bad books, do I?'

It doesn't sound like a good place to be.

'Have you got a face or is your head a ball of hair?' His fingers walk across the table like a spider. He picks up a blue pen and colours in the sea. I peep at him through strands of hair. He wears a thick jumper like his socks; the striped collar of his shirt is half in and half out. He's so big I can't see where the door is. It's all right, he's not a scary giant, I colour in the sky and he hums a tune as we scratch away with our pens.

'Hello, Bernie.' He has a laughy voice. She's in the kitchen. A kettle's whistling. 'Nice smells. I'm hungry. Bet you are.'

'Who are you?' I whisper it, not looking up from my colouring.

'Well, it depends on who you want me to be. You can call me Robert – the name my mother used to call me and what Bernie calls me sometimes. Or you can call me Rob, which is a bit shorter, or Big-un, like all the men at work do because of me being ... big!'

My giggle burbles; he stretches across and tickles me under my arm making me squirm.

'Looks like Big-un is the name you like best then. Good, because I like it too.' He puts his finger to his lips as Bernie comes through the door.

'Now, Nuala, you must pack away the pens, we need the table set for tea. First, we must have a little chat.' She sits opposite me. She's wearing a flowery pinafore. Her eyes are blue glass. Big-un stops colouring; holds his pen like a lollipop.

'We only have two rules in this house.'

'Perhaps leave it till after supper, Bernie. The kid's shattered and I'm starving.' He leans back in his chair and rubs his belly.

'No, let's be clear from the start then we'll all get along.

'Two rules. Rule one, you do as you're told and when we say no, we mean no. Rule two, you eat everything you're given on your plate.'

I don't want to eat anything. My tummy is ready to explode like it's filled with pop.

'There. Simple, isn't it?' Bernie's hands reach across. The starfish is grinning at me and wish I could swim into the sea with it.

'There is something else, Nuala. Your social worker told me what's been happening ... and about the soiling.'

I drop my head onto the table, my elbows stick out like wings.

'Here there is only one place for poo and that's down the toilet. Do you hear me? Down the toilet. Look at us, Nuala.'

A bird is cooing outside the window and the clock ticks on the mantelpiece. I wait. Don't breathe, they'll go away. They haven't gone. My chest hurts, I sob in air. When I peep Big-un is nodding, long slow nods,

'Yes, in the toilet,' he repeats. He is making long, pointy movements with his finger. 'In the toilet.' His face crinkles as he smiles and gives me a slow wink. I decide from now on my poo will only go down the toilet. I nod, copying Big-un, and he claps me on the shoulder.

'We've got a winner here, Bernie. Now please can we have some food before I fade away and slip through the cracks in the floorboards.'

I giggle.

Big-un's plate comes first. One, two, three, four, five fat sausages on a pile of mashed potato with a heap of bright orange carrots. I feel sick, sag in my seat, hold my tummy, pick at a hole in my faded jeans. Bernie slides my plate onto the mat in front of me. I peep; one small sausage, a spoonful of potato and three round pieces of carrot.

'You can have seconds, thirds if you want, but you have to eat it all. Rule two, remember. Help yourself to gravy.' Bernie pours water for me from a jug. Beside my place is a red-checked cloth in a silver ring. What's it for? Hers is green and Big-un's blue. 'They were my mother's, these rings, so they must be at least sixty years old. Imagine. Put your napkin on your knee. It will keep your clothes clean.'

She pushes the gravy jug towards me.

'I don't like gravy.'

'What did you say, Nuala?'

'I don't like gravy.' Louder this time.

'That's all right. Lots of children don't like gravy, it's why I didn't put it on. Eat the rest while it's hot.'

Do they mean it? They are both tucking into their food.

The sausage smell tickles my nose. A bit, just a tiny slice. It's warm and yummy. I'm hungry.

It's all gone.

'Nuala and I would like one more sausage each please, Bernie.'

I hadn't dared to ask. Big-un's eyes are smiley.

'Sponge pudding with custard or you can have an orange?'

I can't choose so Big-un chooses for me. 'Sponge pudding, I think. This little lady has had a long day.' He covers my hand with his big hairy one.

Bernie lays out my pyjamas and hangs my clothes in the wardrobe.

'Am I staying here?'

'Yes. If you want to.'

I think I want to.

She tucks me into bed and gives me a quick kiss. She smells of sausage. The sheets are cold and tight. A quilt made of coloured squares covers the bed. Some have flowers. There's another with giraffes. I like it the best.

Big-un comes in and sits on the bed.

'What's that noise? Why are my curtains moving? Is something there?'

'No, nothing at all.' He lifts the curtain. 'Just the night and the wind having fun, playing hide and seek with all the creatures in the wood.'

'Do they like hide and seek?'

'It's their favourite game.'

'Are there any foxes?'

'Sure are, and rabbits and mice and squirrels and moles. Shall I tell you a secret, Nuala? I'm not so good at the reading and writing but there are two things I do better than anyone else in the whole world. Do you want to know what they are?'

'Yes.'

'I can chop down trees, big, big trees and I tell really good stories.' He pulls the quilt up round my neck.

'Once upon a time there was a little girl who came to live in a wood. To start with everything was scary. She was a pretty young girl and her name was …'

'Nuala,' I whisper.

'That's right. Wait a minute, I can hear something.' Big-un's hand is round his ear.

'What?' I can only hear swooshing trees.

'Listen. Hold my hand, come with me.' In the bedroom next to mine, Big-un gets on his knees and heaves a big bag from under the bed. Inside are comics and books.

'Can you hear it?'

I stand close to him. I've got jelly legs.

'Shh. Listen.'

He pulls out a blue rabbit with red trousers.

'I thought so.' He's talking to the rabbit. 'Did you make a whimpering sort of noise?' Big-un is serious. 'Rabbit says he's lonely and wants a cuddle. He wonders if you would like to give him one. Since my son grew big and grown-up and went away to England, Rabbit has had no one to love him. He's very sad.'

I climb back into bed with Rabbit beside me.

'Robert, let the child sleep. Turn off the light and give her some peace.' Bernie's voice reaches us from the kitchen.

'I don't like the dark.' I don't want him to shut off the lamp.

'Another thing I'm good at – forgetting to turn off lights. Bernie's always telling me off.'

He pulls a funny face then kisses me on the forehead and waves as he reaches the door.

'Sleep tight, little one. See you in the morning.' He cocks his head to one side and puts his hand to his ear again. 'It's Rabbit. He says he's cosy and happy.'

'Hello, Rabbit. I love you.'

Joe

I must move on. I like the isolation, but can't live like this forever, in a damp, cold, leaky tent, being hungry. I'll go to Cork where no one knows me. Find work. I know what the game will be. Another city. Another fix. Always expected to die from drugs. Like Bridget, a life choice. Somehow, I'd survived. In the torture of withdrawal, I'd made promises – as others do – if I lived, I'd make my chances count, every hour would matter. Promises as easily torn as a weak vein.

My leg still ached from the cow's kick. The bruising had turned purple, red and mustard-yellow. I saw it as a badge to be proud of. I began to notice things – the incessant call of a cuckoo, the way the waves sounded hollow as they crashed into the gully below the cliff, the taste of salt in the air and the popping of the seaweed when I trod on it; how the clouds can cover the moon embracing me in darkness. A warm dark, not the swirling pit of black that used to drag me into a tunnel with no end.

I walked across the dunes and into the dip formed by the low hills. Jack was working on a fence, an insignificant figure in the landscape's scale. I reached him, took hold of the sledgehammer and, swinging it in an arc, banged in the post. Together we restapled the barbed wire and stood back to survey the job.

'Mary said you'd come.'

'I wanted to return the clothes. Say …'

Jack raised his hand. 'We been talking, Mary and me. You'd better come to the house. Hear us out before you go saying things you don't want to.'

I carried the tools and we walked across the field with its spongy grass. Mary was in the yard scooping handfuls of feed for the hens from the bucket at her feet. 'Here you are then. Been waiting for you. Make y'self useful, carry m' bucket over to the shed.' She kicked at it with her foot.

In the kitchen, she set a mugful of tea in front of me and put thick slabs of meat on to fry. The aroma of the cooking made my stomach cramp with need.

'Have you showed him, Jack?' Jack shook his head. Mary prodded my arm and handed me a plateful of ham and eggs. 'Well sure, you can't be living in a tent for ever. Seems like you need us as much as we need you. What do you say, lad?' Both were looking at him, Jack's knife and fork raised in the air, Mary with the frying pan in her hand.

'I'm hardly a lad. I'm twenty-seven. I came to say goodbye.'

'Huh,' Jack snorted. 'I'm eighty-three so you'm a lad and you're a daft eejit if you think running for ever's goin' to solve anything. Will you come and see, then decide?'

Mary and Jack took me across the yard one on either side. Head and shoulders above them, I still felt like a little boy being taken to school by proud parents. Jack's fingers were clumsy with the bolt on the gate, it lunged sideways on a rusty hinge. He pointed. 'Over there. Better than what you've got.' He shook his head, struggling with the words. 'It's yours, lad. Can't give you much. Food and a roof over your head, bit of pocket money. Help us around the farm like.'

A small cottage sat across the field, ivy covered most of the front, I could see a green window and a door. The old couple, wearing age like a mantle, waited, Mary with weepy eyes and Jack with his chin stuck forward, his face in a pout.

'Door's open.' Jack took Mary's hand and they wandered back to their house supporting each other.

I shouted after them. 'Don't do this to me.' My eyes moved from the receding figures to the cottage, its dirty walls melting into the grey of the morning. Choked with anger I clung to the gate to stop myself running. Damn them for being old, for being needy. They were nothing to me. Gusts of wind tugged, sculpting the sparse trees into asymmetric shapes. My mind whirled like the frenzied leaves. Cloud shadows swept across the bog and engulfed the cottage. My headland, touched with sun, lay in the distance, the rebuilt cairn visible on the skyline.

29

For a day and a half, I mooched across the island. To the north it flattened, the waves ran shallow across the mud flats. Seabirds pecking at the pickings on the shore, swept screeching into the sky, like paper planes against grey clouds. Drawn back they gathered in noisy groups preening themselves, drying their wings when sun broke through. I envied their freedom. Below a hill I stumbled on a place where piles of stones formed the outline of a small church. I used to go to church as a youngster, made to by my mother. Older and I'd rebelled, gone missing on a Sunday. She said I'd be damned to hell; I still preferred to play with my mates. A surprise, therefore, that this sheltered space felt special. The quiet brushed over me. Wildflowers grew, yellow and purple. Beetles and ants moved through the grass and an early butterfly rested near my foot. The place spoke to me creating an atmosphere I wanted to be part of.

I avoided the farm, vowed not to go there; saw Jack in the distance fiddling with the tractor, peering underneath, stumbling as he tried to straighten. I knew I could get it started in minutes. I fought the panic, recognised the fear rooting me to my vantage point.

Dreams, wheeling like the birds, tormented me through the night. The tent sides slapped above my head threatening to suffocate. Take a look at the place – stay till I've fixed the tractor – just for the summer.

Gorse and brambles arched across the path to the cottage, branches of a tree scratched at the window. No one had seen me come. I turned the door handle, it wouldn't yield. 'No welcome here then.' I used my shoulder and wood scraped across the stone floor.

Something made me pause, one foot over the threshold. I called, 'Hi ye,' into the empty room. 'Hi,' louder this time. 'You daft bugger.' A dead blackbird lay on the floor, a few feathers over white bones. 'No one's lived here for ages.' I said it out loud to convince myself. I banged on the stubborn window frames, wedged open the front door, then sat on the step letting in the fresh air until the cold seeping from the stone became uncomfortable. Inside I ran my hands over the rough walls, saw where soot had fallen like black snow onto the grate. Peat bricks, dried and crumbly were in a basket beside the hearth.

Fire, flames crackling, light shooting into the room. I spread my fingers imagining the warmth. On the floor was a rusty screwdriver and a stirring stick beside a tin of whitewash, a dried paintbrush balanced on its lid; on the wall a line where the painter had stopped work. 'Were you a farmworker too? Are you coming back?' Only cobwebs waved in the breeze.

'I can't do it.' I burst into their kitchen. Mary sat in the chair by the range, Jack puffed at his pipe. Neither looked up. 'I can't. I know nothing about farms. The cow the other day scared me stiff and sheep, well, sheep are ...' Mary rose slowly and took the kettle from its ring. 'Aye.' Her sigh soft as the steam.

'Once I used to drive a truck,' I sank into a chair, rubbing at my scalp. 'It's all I can bloody do.'

'Aye, well, looks like I got lots to teach you. Best we waste no time and get on with that fence.' Jack thrust his feet into his rubber boots and pushed a pair towards Joe. 'I reckon these might fit.'

Jack took me into the shed. 'I'll gi' you a hand later. Take this stuff over to the cottage, make it more comfortable like.' Under a tarpaulin was a jumble of furniture spattered with chicken poo where the hens had roosted. The old man paused. 'You're a good lad, Joe.' Watery eyes spilled over before Jack yanked at his hat and thrust a box of staples into my hand. 'This rate, rain'll be in before we get started.'

Later we loaded the tractor trailer ready to take the furniture across to the cottage. A sofa, a stick-back chair and a table with three good legs and one that needed fixing. Hauling on a bed frame Jack told me to fetch the mattress and blankets from the spare room in their place. I knocked on the door of the farmhouse, crept in when I saw Mary asleep. Puffy legs bulged over too tight slippers. Her head had fallen forward onto her chest and she snored gently. Her bony hand grasped a feather duster.

I forced open the swollen cottage door. A fire had been set in the grate and a box of matches lay on the hearth. The floor had been swept clean and the windows freed of cobwebs. 'Has Mary done this?'

'Aye but she's done in. You must do the rest yourself. She wanted to ... See ... Well, anyhows it's yours now.'

I returned to dismantle my tent and pack the few belongings, a mug, a knife, a spoon and my tin-opener from where it lay on the crushed grass. Fresh air and a day of labouring had wearied me. A good feeling. Jack would be milking the cows. Only six, but a hard job at a day's end.

I climbed to my high point, looked back over the island, sat on a rock and listened to the pounding sea. Dusk, and a pale sun split the clouds as it sank into the sea. I added a stone to my rebuilt cairn and threw another into the chasm before descending the sheep path to the cottage. I'd stay until autumn, no longer. Far away the lights of the mainland were bright against the hills.

I startled myself awake, for a moment not recognising the unfamiliar surroundings.

'What?' I whipped my head round. A shower of fire sparks lit the gloom. 'What?' I listened. Nothing.

'Baby?' The name dropped from my lips, Nuala? Something bad was happening to her. The thought, an axe slicing through wood. 'Baby girl, is it you? Nuala, damn you. Let me be, leave me alone.' Her fingers curled into my hand. 'NO'. The room held its breath. The distant call of an owl became an echo in my head.

Once my stepfather made me sit in the outside coal cellar for a whole night. I don't remember what I'd done wrong, often there didn't have to be a reason for being punished. An owl had hooted then, its screech funnelling through the hole to hush my cries. Slowly I'd absorbed the sound, the owl became my link to the world. It called to me all night, kept me safe until daylight squeezed through the cracks in the wall and the lumps of coal became recognisable shapes again.

I stepped outside the cottage, my breathing shallow and timorous. A cold spring night, breaking waves a distant sound. Across in the farmhouse a dim light shone from a window.

I must let her go. Someone else will care for her better than me. 'I fail at everything, Nuala. I didn't want to fail with you.' I stared into the blackness towards the north. I can't see her, can't reach her. 'Baby.' The cry withered on my lips.

My days fell into a pattern. It began with the cows. Steaming, lumbering beasts I learned to summon. Creatures of habit they meandered from the fields pulling at grass along the track. In the yard they clattered and snorted waiting their turn to be milked. Their odour was earthy, primitive, dried manure hung on their flanks like tattered blankets. Bella, the cow I'd rescued, nudged me with a wet nose, saliva dripping from her mouth. Jack laughed. 'Aye, you'll soon be getting used to them. They detect you're scared. That's why them's bothering you. Show 'em who's in charge,' he said, slapping a brown, mottled rump and giving it a shove with his shoulder. Jack showed me how to milk them, but I was all fingers and thumbs and the cows restless in my hands.

'Don't farmers have machinery these days to do the milking? None of this palaver. Time to get modern,' I joked as I shovelled the cow pats into a heap, glancing across at Jack's shrunken, bent frame, the florid skin, the blueness around his lips.

'Aye, and I've heard that before.' The old voice checked and broke.

The farm was run down, but it kept Jack and Mary alive. 'The rhythm of the seasons,' Jack said. 'This'll all be here long after we've gone and after you've gone, laddie. You can't fight it, it's bigger than all of us. God's land.'

They never bothered me, never asked much. Sometimes Mary rested her hand on my shoulder. 'I've cooked your favourite to-night. Bit of stew to warm you through. You always liked it.' It wasn't me she was talking to, I let it go and tucked in appreciatively.

'I can see whoever lived in the cottage tired of painting the wall,' I laughed. 'Half-finished it is. Looks like they upped sticks and …' The kettle slipped from Mary's hand. It crashed onto the stone floor; splashes of hot water flecked her legs making her cry out. The water flowed from the displaced lid onto the rag rug. Jack didn't move, sat with his head in his hands. I eased Mary into her chair and put cold water on her legs to take the heat from the scalds, took the rug away and mopped the floor, righted the kettle and put it back onto boil. Mary told me to stop fussing.

'Sorry. I didn't mean …' I mumbled the words, not knowing what I hadn't meant.

I left them early, declining the customary cup of tea when usually they liked to tell tales of the island or to sit in comfortable silence, Jack puffing at his pipe and Mary dozing.

I couldn't face the cottage, not yet, so walked to the 'buried' church instead, needing its reassuring solace. Crumbling, weath-ered ruins hunkered in the quarried bowl. Mary had told me it had been buried in sand for hundreds of years until a parish priest had dug it out with the help of locals,

I lay on the damp grass counting the early stars. A year ago, I'd been on course to self-destruct. Much of the last twelve months were confused, lost in the hell my mother damned me to when, as a boy, I wouldn't go to church. I'd found this island, found a purpose. I hated that I'd upset Jack and Mary tonight however unintended. I wanted to protect this new-found sensitivity, as tender as an emerging leaf, afraid it might skitter away. I'd found two kind people.

And Nuala had found me. Images of her ran through my mind – her serious little face as she took her first steps, her sitting at the end of the bed watching me and Bridget, her snuffles as she slept, a wet thumb in her mouth. And the screaming. The screaming that stirred my rage.

The next day I went with Jack into the storeroom behind the cowshed and he pointed to a tub of whitewash high on a shelf. 'You'd better reach it down then and finish that wall.' His look silenced me.

I repainted the wall, painted the whole room. It only took two evenings. The fresh white walls, almost luminous in the dusk, brightened the space and the furniture in place made it mine. I'd do the bedroom and tiny kitchen another time.

Jack mostly had sheep. They wandered across the land finding grass on the heathland amongst the stones and the dunes. The lambs, born as I'd arrived, had grown into plump little things confident to wander further from their mothers. They marauded in gangs, reminding me of myself when I roamed the streets of Liverpool, unfettered and undisciplined.

As the summer arrived, we rounded up the ewes. Thomas the shearer came from the mainland, nodded to me and proceeded to remove the wool from the sheep with deft strokes. I was clumsy with the flock, herded them through the gates, but sometimes one would escape and race off in the opposite direction, leaving me to run after it, wave my arms and force it to turn around. Jack's old dog, Meg, her limbs stiff, watched me with her head on her paws. By the end of the day, tired and sweaty, the whiff of wool on their skin, Jack and Thomas sat on the bench; Mary brought a jug of stout and three glasses.

'Sit yourself down, lad. A grand day's work.' Jack pushed a glass over. The first pint drunk in silence, savoured. Thomas brought stories of other farms, of the successes, of the disasters. He talked of people meaningless to me, but Jack supped and listened shaking his head or chuckling to himself.

I slept that night with no dancing images of Nuala, undisturbed by a presence in the cottage; dreamt of sheep lying on their backs, their legs struggling and with a dazed expression returning to the field shorn of their wool.

*

I sang the words to *Mary in the Morning* as I pushed open the kitchen door. Mary always took my teasing with a smile, giving me an occasional flick with the back of her hand in response. A beautiful day, high clouds decorated a blue sky. I felt great.

'Where's my favourite girl then …?' The words died on my lips.

A young woman looked back at me. She was unpacking shopping from a bag. Bleach, toilet rolls, washing powder all littered the table. 'I'm away wishing my name is Mary, don't you know.'

'I'm after …' I tripped on the words.

'Aye, Mary you're after. I heard.' Her dark hair tied in an untidy ponytail, she tweaked escaping strands behind her ear. 'Will I do instead?' She put her hands on her hips, her head tilted to one side. A blush coloured my neck and I turned to go. 'Stop. It's okay. I've taken Mary to see her friend over on the next farm. They love a natter. She only gets the chance when I come and between you and me it's easier to get on when she's not here.'

I shifted from one foot to another, forgetting why I'd come, what I'd come for.

'I'm Aoife. I know who you are. You're Joe. Mary told me.'

I hovered behind the toilet rolls, a whisper of fear at the sound of my name on another person's lips. Exposed, I buried a sharp retort.

'Don't mind me.' Aoife picked up the shopping and stacked it into the cupboard. One of her eyes turned in very slightly and a brown blemish on her cheek rescued her face from being ordinary. 'Mary said I mustn't mind you and not to go badgering you about anything. I like a man with secrets.' She pulled a face as she stood on tiptoe trying to reach the top shelf. 'Come on, you can reach me down the jar from the top shelf? I've brought more candles just in case and it's where they keep them. Silly because they'd never find them in the dark.'

I righted the framed photograph she'd knocked over – Jack and Mary with a small child standing between them. I wondered who it was.

Her chatter gave me time to recover and I put the jar on the draining board. She stood beside me pert and petite. 'I come and give the house a good clean and stock up for them. Mary's sight's not so good. She can't see a cobweb, or mouse droppings when the little pests come in from the wet.' Aoife swept the floor. Dust jigged in the sunlight. 'Let's open the door, let in the fresh air. I'll be here until lunchtime so if you remember what you came for – come back.'

I wedged open the door. 'I will be certain to do that, Eva.'

'It's Aoife by the way, Eefa is how you say it – means beautiful, joyful.' She laughed, shooed me away with her broom.

I found Jack in the field, tinkering with the tractor, his breathing harsh with the effort. I knew about engines, had it started in minutes, I'd served my teenage apprenticeship, after dark, hot-wiring cars, taking them for a spin. Sometimes setting fire to them for a laugh. I winced as I remembered and the sound of the old man mounting the seat with a groan of pain made me feel small.

'This is a museum piece, Jack. You need to be getting a nice new shiny one.'

Jack moved off without a glance leaving me to regret my crass remark.

I didn't talk to Aoife again but saw her driving off and ran to the top of the sand dunes, watched until the car reached the end of the causeway and onto the road before disappearing around a hill.

Over supper Jack said, 'Why don't you take yourself across to the pub when tide's right. Reckon you could get fed up with the likes of us old 'uns.' I pushed meat around my plate and didn't reply.

Nuala

'Nuala, I've enrolled you in the village school. The teacher, Mrs O'Neil, is expecting you.'

My breakfast stares at me from the table but I'm not hungry any more.

'Come on, eat your cereal. You won't learn if you don't go to school.'

Shreddies, my favourite, today they taste like dry leaves. Try to swallow, only splutter. Don't cry. Sniff instead.

School. Why do I have to? Snotty botty, snotty botty. I remember what they used to say.

The door opens and Big-un's filling the space with fresh air and the smell of trees. He's looking at me then at Bernie.

'I'm telling Nuala about school. It's a nice little school isn't it, Robert? She'll make friends there.'

Clatter my spoon into my bowl, grip my hands together.

'It is, Bernie, but perhaps she doesn't have to go today. Maybe Nuala could start on Monday. What do you think?'

I don't have to go. Not yet.

'I came home to see if my favourite girl is awake yet and because I need a great big cup of tea. If Nuala hurries, finishes her breakfast and gets dressed I could take her to see my office.' He's nodding at both of us, winking at me. 'How's that sound?'

Shreddies and cold milk slide down my throat. What day is it today? Monday sounds a long way off.

'I'll ring Mrs O'Neil and tell her. Monday then, Nuala. A good day to start.' Bernie has brown tea-stain spots on her face. I like her pink scarf with squiggly lines. Better than grey. She disappears into the kitchen. She's dialling.

Get dressed quick. Yesterday's socks.

'Ready? Let's go, partner.'

I'm actually too old to hold hands but his are rough and warm.

'Whose bike is that?' It's leaning against the rusty blue barrel.

'Mine. Sometimes I go to work on it. Sometimes I walk and sometimes I use the truck. Can you ride a bike?'

I don't want to say no.

'Ugh. Have to teach you then. It's easy-peasy lemon squeezy.'

'Uncle Mick at my other foster home went to his office in a shiny silver car. He cleaned it on Saturdays. He wouldn't let me help.

'Why are you blowing up the tyre? Have you got a puncture?'

'Don't think so, it's just a bit soft. Won't be a minute.'

I peep round the back of the house. It's dark and cold. A metal bowl is full of water and leaves, a football floats on the top, dented and soft. There's a slimy dead creature on the ground, it's an old cloth. Wet drips on my shoe when I splosh the ball back into the water. My bedroom window has black wood round it; it's near the corner of the house. On tiptoes I can see Rabbit on the bed.

'Hop on then.' Big-un is ringing the bike bell. 'All aboard.'

The bar cuts into my bottom. He's going really fast, round and round in a circle. Grab his sleeve and hold on.

'Wibble-wobble, wibble-wobble. Aagh!' We fall off, Big-un sprawls on his back, pretending to be dead. Wee dribbles into my knickers but I can't stop giggling.

'Oopsy. Quick, don't let Bernadette catch us or I'll be in big trouble.' He pulls a funny face and more giggles come.

'There are a lot of trees.' We are walking under them. 'They're like tall soldiers.' When I look up, I can see the clouds moving. It makes me dizzy, like the trees are swaying.

'Yep, trees for miles and miles.' He runs his hand over the trunk of a very tall one. I do the same.

'It's sticky. Why do you cut them down?' My arms only reach a little way around the trunk, like when I used to hug my daddy's legs.

'Don't cut this one.'

'It's so people can have telegraph poles and furniture and fancy things for their gardens. We plant more though so they'll grow big and strong one day. Do you like trees?'

'I think so. Do you like trees?'

'Oh yes, I love them. As do beetles and squirrels and mice. See.'

Lots of crawly things are running around all over the place where Big-un has lifted a piece of bark.

'This is their home and their pantry; they don't like the light. Good, isn't it, nice and cosy. Would you like to be a beetle?'

I fidget 'cos it's a funny question. 'I wouldn't have to go to school.'

'Hmm.' Big-un replaces the bark on the log. 'Let me tell you something. My boys, Chris and Sam, attended the village school where you're going, and they liked it. They learned lots of things and now they are big and live in England, in London. They have good jobs and when they come back to see us, they fly in an aeroplane. Bernie and me, we've had other children, like you, who've stayed with us, they've gone to the same school. I'll tell you what I told them. If you're at school and anyone makes you feel sad, think of me sitting in your school bag. You only have to whisper, and I'll grow and grow myself until I'm this big.' He opened his arms wide until he was enormous. 'You won't be able to see me, but they will, and they won't make you sad any more. Remember, whisper and I'll be there.'

I hold his hand. We take a little path between the trees.

'Do you like my office then?'

'Where?'

'Here, all of this.' His laugh is as big as the forest. He bends over, throws something into the air. 'It's raining pine needles.' Leaves and twigs stick in our hair and on our coats.

'Look, Bernie, Big-un showed me how to whittle. You get a sharp knife. Be VERY careful and always push the knife away from your body.' Big-un said it like that.

'Robert to you, Nuala. It's more appropriate.' Bernie is knitting. She's not looking, just shaking her head. 'Should she be using a knife, Robert?'

'Oh.' I drop the stick onto the table. It rolls against the milk jug.

'Uh, uh.' Big-un wags his finger from side to side. 'She's a woodworker now, like my men, so I said she gets to call me Big-un if she wants to.'

'Yeah,' but under my breath so Bernie doesn't hear. She isn't pleased. I can tell. I'm keeping my stick under my pillow.

When Monday comes, Bernie walks me to school. I wanted to go in the truck. 'I can't drive and anyway the walk is good for you.' We don't take the track. We follow a narrow path through the trees. Fallen branches and lots of prickly brambles lie in the way. I jump the puddles and walk slowly. Bernie takes my hand and pulls me along.

'You don't want to be late on your first day.'

I do. I don't want to get there. Ever.

The school is like a barn. I don't like the high green-painted windows. It says BOYS over one door GIRLS over another. Children are running around, laughing and chasing each other. Bernie lets me hold her hand. Mothers, some with pushchairs, are talking. We don't stand near them. A girl with a red scarf stops her running and stares at me. I shrink into Bernie. I remember what Big-un told me and clutch my school bag close. A child appears from the school door and rings a loud bell. It goes quiet. The boys and girls push and shove into lines. The doorway's like a monster's mouth. They all disappear through the door marked BOYS. Why? Some of them are girls.

'Hello, I'm your teacher, Mrs O'Neil. You come with me, Nuala.'

Bernie's following the headteacher into her room, but she comes back and puts her hands on my shoulders. 'Remember you're a big girl now. I'll come back for you this afternoon.' She winds my hair behind my ear, turns me round and gives me a little push.

'Don't go.'

The teacher says, 'This is Nuala, she's come to join us. I want you all to be kind and show her where things are today.'

No one speaks. Teacher gives me a tissue. 'Blow your nose, dear.'

One of my laces is undone and trails on the floor.

'You can sit next to Siobhan. Lisa, will you sit at the back of the class this morning?'

'But Siobhan's my best friend, Miss.' Lisa clutches the girl next to her.

'You'll only be a few rows back.' Mrs O'Neil taps the desk.

The seat's warm.

'Baby.' Siobhan hisses, pinches me on the leg and turns her back on me.

At playtime I stand against the wall, hopping from one foot to another.

'Do you want to play with us?' Two girls are asking, I shake my head because I don't know what the game is. They go off. I really want to play with them.

I don't speak all day, though the teacher is trying to be nice. My tummy hurts. They stop asking me to do things.

Next day it's the same and for the rest of the week. I play games in my head. If I don't talk, they leave me alone. My tummy hurts all the time.

When it's my turn to read aloud the words gurgle in my throat.

'Nuala, perhaps you can read aloud next week.'

'That's not fair, Miss. We all have to do it.'

I sit down, my knickers are damp.

I never put my hand up in class.

Skipping games are fun but I stand and watch. No one wants to be my friend.

'You dumb or something?' A boy called Patrick dances in front of me surrounded by other boys. He's got a red face. They push him into me. I push him back. They all whoop with laughter and run away.

It's the end of my first half-term, we are in the headteacher's room. I am standing next to Bernie's chair. Mrs O'Neil is there. She's peering at me.

'She joins in with painting and craft work. Her writing has improved. She clearly understands. She seems to cope with the maths when it's set. Don't you, Nuala?'

'Why won't you speak to anyone, Nuala?' Bernie asks. 'She reads at night to us, loves reading to Robert, my husband. She enjoys books and stories.' She pauses. 'I think she relates to men better than women. I hope this not speaking at school is something she'll get over. It's not been a problem before; I've checked with the social worker.'

They babble on. I'm by the seaside on a warm day. I want to tell them, if Daddy was here, I'd talk to him, but it doesn't seem worth it because nobody wants to know.

The best bit of school is going home through the woods. Not walking fast like Bernie. She always gets home before I do. I dawdle and skip, balance on fallen trees and sometimes sit and wait for the birds to sing. There is a robin redbreast who hops near me. Beside a stream there's a favourite rock where I sing the songs from school.

'Elective mute, the school is saying.' Bernie is telling Big-un and the new social worker. I don't understand. 'Perhaps we should think about some counselling or a psychiatrist.' Big-un shakes his head. 'She chatters nineteen to the dozen when she's with me. Give her

41

time. She's a grand wee lass.' He gives me one of his winks and I try to give him one back like he's been teaching me to do.

I don't want to make him sad, but I won't talk at school because I don't want to. I want to be invisible.

Joe

I gave little thought to Jack's suggestion of going to the pub on the mainland. Let the idea sit there. Give it time to wither. I was used to the solitude, to my own company, to the safe boundaries of my new life.

But instead of withering it had grown, niggled away like an itchy scab. Crossing the causeway earlier in the evening my spirits had risen. I counted the marker posts and kicked at a chunk of polystyrene on the sand. Would it be a noisy place, young people laughing, full of eager chatter, vying for attention, flirting with each other? Loud music? Would Aoife be there? I hoped she might. She'd been back to the island, but I'd been busy repairing and rehanging a gate and hadn't been aware until Mary told me later. 'She's the daughter of Jack's distant cousin,' Mary said. 'Aoife works in the tourist office. Talks of going off to Dublin like all the young folk do. We'd miss her. Kind as velvet to a queen's skin.' I'd laughed at Mary's description so my disappointment wouldn't give me away.

I'd been on the island for months and never set foot in the pub. I hesitated outside the inn, walked past and sat on the wall staring out to sea. Only the Atlantic Ocean between me and America. The wind coming off the land dashed waves against the rocks. Plumes of spray careered away behind. Sand skittered across the beach covering the seaweed in grit. A plastic bottle rolled at my feet. My shaking hands made it impossible to light a cigarette.

Warm air and stale alcohol escaped as I opened the door. A bell tinkled above my head and conversation ceased. The sole drinkers, two men, studied me. I took a stool at the end of the bar. A fire flamed in the grate and I pulled at the neck of my jumper, unused

43

to the heat. Toby jugs hung from hooks on the low ceiling. Winking eyes and leery grins stared down.

'How are ye?' The barman slid a beer mat over. 'What can I get ye?' The men watched, waited for my answer. I pulled out a five-euro note. 'A stout will do me fine.' My voice reedy, I'd barely spoken to anyone except Jack and Mary in six months, got used to the soft mooing of cows, the bleating of sheep and the sharp cries of the seabirds.

'What name do you go by then?' The guy leaning on the bar asked the question. Next to him an old man perched on a stool, his back twisted.

I cupped my hands around the pint glass and peered into it.

A log slipped in the grate; smoke unfurled.

'Joe.'

No one spoke.

'Name's Joe.'

The men lifted their glasses in unison and took long swigs. The younger of the two lifted an eyebrow. 'Joe? Joe who?'

I didn't answer, flipped my beer mat between two fingers.

'Joe it is then. Bring the man a whiskey, Seamus. He's not looking so grand.' The two of them continued to drink their pints with the occasional grunt of conversation too low for me to discern.

I kept my eyes averted. The black liquid lying heavy, I licked the fringe of froth from my upper lip. Across the room from the bar wooden shelves housed a can of oil, ancient jars of jam, a stone hot water bottle and a Lyles golden syrup tin.

'Doubled as a shop once. Lots of pubs did.'

I wasn't sure who'd spoken. 'Makes sense.'

The old man eased off the stool, steadied himself against the bar, pulled a cloth cap from his pocket and thrust it on his head. 'G'night then.' He paused, about to say more, but patted my shoulder instead.

A draught of cold air blew more smoke into the room as he went out.

Only the two of us left; we could hear the bartender banging kegs in the cellar. My face flamed but my hands were cold as ice. I gripped the glass to keep them still. The silence hung heavy, I wanted to be away, leave my pint unfinished.

'Sure and sup it up, young 'un. Can't be wasting a good Guinness.' The man had read my mood. 'Will you hear me out now?' He flicked his head towards the window. 'See those hills?' Startled, I looked at the black shapes against the grey night sky. A blush of apricot hung in the saddle where the sun had set. 'Smooth, see, round as a woman's breasts. Took hundreds, thousands of years to get like that. Shaped by the wind. Shapes us all given time.' The man came across. 'Give it time, Joe, give it time. Word has it you're a good lad.' He extended his hand. 'Ronan O'Connell. Pleased to meet you.' As he opened the heavy oak door of the pub he turned, 'You'd best be getting back across the sand. Them tides can be as playful as a bitch on heat.'

I finished my pint and downed the whiskey in one go, feeling its burning heat. A good lad – I couldn't remember anyone ever calling me that, not even my mother. A good father, Nuala wouldn't agree. I sensed her, here in the corner of the pub. Her pale face, Bridget's dirty T-shirt in her hand, her eyes full of fear. God leave me alone, can't you. I tore my beer mat, swept the pieces to the floor and left the pub.

I thought I'd lain low. Slipped in with the mist. How could I have kidded myself? News of any kind here comes in fast as a spring tide.

It began to rain, a fine drizzle that shrouds the hills and blurs the outline of the bay. The pub lights bled into each other and grew faint. Waves staked their territory, washing the sand into ridges. Firm, but in places it moved beneath my feet, slowing progress. I imagined the water closing the gap behind me, affording me safe passage. I reached the island's edge, clambered onto the low dunes and looked back at the rushing water as it transformed the land-scape. The moon hung, a deflated ball amongst the clouds. White light illuminated the rocks and seaweed lay strewn on the tide line. The island settled. Those who lived on it, a handful of farmers, turned inward and kept their counsel.

Back home I went to bed. Jack had chuckled the day I first re-ferred to the island as home. 'Always good to have somewhere to call home.' He'd tipped my hat over my eyes and punched my arm. The bar had been passable, though a shock discovering they knew of me. Folk are nosy, but Ronan had been sound. 'The hills, shaped by the wind.' I liked it. Through the open curtains, dark clouds painted a mountain landscape back-lit by the moon.

'Nuala.' I listened to the creak of the beams, whispered into the dark. 'Sorry about being cross earlier but a pub's no place for you.' I wanted to see her face. An image of Nuala trying to waken her mother played itself like a repeating video, I closed my eyes to dispel it.

*

45

The lambs were shipped off to market in batches. I didn't like the job of separating them, having to choose the ones to go to slaughter. Their anxious cries, and bleating ewes, tore at me.

I accompanied Jack to the livestock auction, stood amongst the farmers listening to their banter, seeing their despair at the low prices. All the talk of foot-and-mouth and Bluetongue made Jack quiet on the way home; I knew him well enough to let him be.

Aoife was there when we returned. Mary fetched Jack a beer. He took it outside, stood leaning on the gate, watching the remaining sheep munching on the grass.

'Be off and see Aoife across the sand,' Mary admonished. 'There are times when we old folk need peace.'

'Where's your car?'

'On the mainland. Sometimes I like to walk across. If I've time and the tides are right.'

We'd been awkward at first. Aoife walked beside me, our arms sometimes brushing as we crossed the uneven ground.

'You're good to them,' I said to break the silence.

'I love them to bits. As a kid I used to come here every holiday – to get away – things weren't always so good at home especially after Mum died.' She paused. 'My dad. He drank. Not all the time but he would go on benders and we were all better out the way. I used to love it here. Such fun. The peace, when the tide comes in and cuts the island off. It made me feel safe – still does. I can't ever imagine them not being here. They mean so much.'

'It makes me feel safe too.' For a short while we sat on top of the dunes watching waves sucking at the sand. Clouds were building on the horizon.

We parted halfway across the causeway. I turned several times, watched Aoife head for the village. On one occasion our backward glances met, colliding with a jerk. I gave an open-fingered wave and stayed to watch her until she reached the mainland. Then I ran home as drizzle turned to sharp rain.

Nuala

'Who's your best friend? Who do you sit next to?' Bernie asks me on the way to school.

A shrug. 'Lots. Anyone.' I'm not supposed to lie but she keeps asking. It isn't really a lie. Only sort of. I've got lots of friends. Special friends no one else can see.

In the playground I've a secret corner away from where the other children play. I smooth the orange leaf I found and arrange it beside the others like the petals of a flower.

'Hello.' It's a girl in my class.

She places a leaf of her own beside mine. We make two flower heads side by side, bright yellows and reds. She collects sticks to use as stalks for our flowers, then the bell rings. I stand behind her in the line. Brown plaits, each with a sparkly band, hang down her back. She's holding two crumpled leaves; she gives me one and I put it in my pocket.

Her name is Ella. She sits at the front of the class and the teacher says things like, 'Can you hear, Ella,' or 'Tell me if you don't understand, Ella.' Her lips are funny with a scar below her nose and a wobbly top lip which dribbles. The other children laugh at her because she wears a plastic thing behind her ear and sometimes it whistles.

After school I watch her run over to her mother; they both wave, their hands like fluttering flags.

Bernie still comes to meet me. I wish she wouldn't. I walk a long way behind her, never get lost. Close to the house is a hidden place where there are trees with soft green leaves. The grass is long. When it's been raining the stream flows faster and I take off my shoes and

47

socks and let the water splosh over my ankles. Once I saw a deer eating grass. I didn't move for so long my legs hurt. Then it ran away, a white bottom bobbing through the trees.

My friends live in the wood and this is where we play.

Big-un told me about the fairies. 'Have you seen them?'

'Real fairies?'

'Of course. Early in the morning, or late in the day if you're very, very quiet – it's when they play.'

It's true. I hear their whispers and their tinkly giggles where the water splashes over the rocks. Once I found a ring of tiny toad-stools left in the rain. I lay on the grass and counted the raindrops, which are really fairy jewels.

Sometimes they leave me presents. One day I found a nut like a tiny bowl with a round hole. I leave them presents too. Half a pencil, a long, pointed cone or some yellow flowers from beside the school fence. I drew them a picture of Daddy and me and put it under a stone. Next day it had gone so they must have found it.

When I get home from playing, Bernie tuts at my dirty knees and pulls pieces of twig from my hair. She always hugs me. Not a warm cuddly hug like the ones Big-un gives me when I can smell wood-smoke and forest. It's a hug full of pointy elbows and bones digging into my cheek. Her boobs are squashy. I think it's the way a mummy must feel.

It's bedtime. Big-un and I are telling stories. 'Once upon a time there was a little girl.'

'You always start that way.' I snuggle under the quilt. He stops.

'Your turn,' he says.

'In the wood are lots of little people who live in the holes in the trees and there are big scary monsters who make loud noises to frighten the birds and make the butterflies flutter from the flowers.' He smiles. He's heard them too.

'If you clap your hands or sing, the monsters will go away. They don't like it when a little girl is happy. It makes them afraid and they run back into the dark places.'

Sometimes we kneel on the bed and gaze out the window at the black sky. The trees are like ladies in long dresses bending towards each other. They hush and sigh and screech with whiny voices. 'It's the wind telling stories to the trees.' Big-un says.

'Do you think my daddy can see the stars?'

An owl hoots. I want to un-ask my question because I think it's made him sad.

'Nuala, no one knows what's happened to your daddy.' The window is foggy from our breath and he rubs it clear. 'Your daddy was poorly. He needed to be by himself, so he could try to get better. I think leaving you behind was the hardest thing he ever had to do. When he looks at the sky, he sees the stars and he can see you, just like you see him.'

I squeeze my eyes shut tight, see shapes and colours.

'Has he got himself better?' I press closer to Big-un's arm.

'I don't know, Nuala. Can't say yes, can't say no.'

Ella's mummy asks me if I would like to come to her house for tea one day. 'She would, Mummy. She is saying she wants to.' Ella often does this. She tells the teacher when I want to go to the toilet, sharpen my pencil or need a new book.

'Let her speak for herself, Ella.' Mrs O'Neil says.

I don't though. The other children are used to me. If they need someone who can run fast, or they want me to hold the skipping rope, they let me join in their games now. I help Ella too – if she hasn't heard the number of the page then I open the book for her. I dig her in the ribs when her name is called and we have to stand in teams. If boys or girls make fun of her when her lisp is bad, I hit them or hide their shoes or something. They don't tell, not any more.

Ella's house has a yellow door in the middle of a row of other houses. It smells nice. For tea we have raw crunchy carrots and pasta with a green sauce.

'I don't eat animals,' Ella says. 'Neither does Mummy. My daddy works in the middle of the sea on a rig. Look.' It's a picture of a giant spider in the water. I wonder if her daddy eats meat. I want to tell Bernie I don't want to eat animals either but I'm too scared.

'Here you are girls, scones with strawberry jam.' Ella's mum has brought them to the bedroom on a tray and puts it on the bed beside the books we've laid in a row.

'We're playing libraries,' Ella tells her mum. Ella has a long shelf above her bed filled with more books than in the library at school.

'Perhaps Nuala would like to borrow some of your books to read at home Would you like to, Nuala? Bring them back when you've read them. Like a library.'

'Can I?' It comes out. I stick my finger between my teeth, feel my ears going hot.

'You talked.' Ella squeals, 'Nuala talked.'

'Yes. She did. Best friends always talk to each other.' Ella's mummy hasn't noticed my red ears. 'Let's have these yummy scones, shall we?'

Being with Big-un is my favourite thing. In the holidays I go to work with him. We go bumpity, bump along tracks in the truck or we follow paths the deer and foxes have made.

'That's fox's poo. It's got fur and feathers and tiny bones in it and it's really stinky.'

'Clever girl. You remembered.'

'And rabbits' poo is a pile of tiny balls called pellets. You told me.' I remind him in case he's forgotten. 'Please can we find the badgers' den? The sett, I mean.' I like it when he laughs when I tell him things. Timber lorries are grinding up the hill. They make a noise because the hill is steep. They're heavy and must use a low gear. The diesel makes me cough and Big-un lends me his handkerchief to cover my nose.

The men who drive the lorries know my name and I know theirs. There's Lee; he pulls funny faces. Ivor is old with a sore back. He makes yucky strong tea and pours it into metal mugs. He puts lots of sugar in mine but it's our secret. I like Matt best because he lifts me into his cab and lets me search on the shelf for a chocolate bar. We sit around while the lorries are loaded. When they leave, the drivers call, 'Bye, Nuala, see you later alligator.'

'Bye,' I shout back.

'Where do the tree trunks go?'

'All over the place,' Big-un says. 'I'll show you on the big map.' He lifts me onto the table. I'm as tall as he is. 'They go to lots of places in Ireland and on the ferry to England, Scotland and Wales.'

'To where your boys live.' I've remembered that too. 'One day I'll go to England and make lots of money.'

'Will you, pet? And why not?'

I think about Daddy. If I go to England will he find me?

Ivor's been here. He's just gone. Big-un's doing things in the office. Round the back of the yard I hear a squeak. Then another. A miaow. I crawl between the barrels to find where it's coming from but they're heavy and only my head squeezes in. I can see a pipe covered in green slime with water dripping from it. 'Oh, little kitty.' A tiny kitten's head is poking from the pipe. It's crying, showing me its white pointy teeth. 'Come here, kitty.' It doesn't move but keeps crying.

'Stay there. I'll get you out.' I wriggle backwards and run across the stony track.

'Big-un, Big-un. Quick. There's a kitten. The tiniest kitten in the world. It's stuck.'

I tug Big-un by the hand towards the mewing sounds. We roll the barrels away; they make a lot of noise and the kitten disappears further up the pipe.

'It's frightened half to death, poor little thing.' Big-un carries the rusty piece of pipe into where the men brew their tea.

'Hello, little kitten. Don't be scared.' I peer into the pipe and see tiny eyes. It has stopped mewing. 'Don't die. Please don't die. I'll look after you.'

Big-un pokes with a stick from one end. I'm crying, 'Don't hurt it, don't hurt it.' It shoots out like a cannon ball and I grab it to stop it falling off the table. Its fur is all wet and spiky. It has pink paws and a pink nose. I can feel its heart beating against my hand. 'Miaow, miaow.' It wants its mummy.

'Reckon this has come in on Ivor's lorry. A stowaway – jumped on when he had his back turned. Must have been terrified and cold.'

I hold it close to make it warm.

'Can I keep it, Big-un? Can I? Please.'

'Dunno, Nuala. Bernie's not fond of cats. It may not survive. It's very little.'

'Pleeese.'

'We'll take it home the while and see how it goes. Don't get too fond of it.'

The kitten is quiet, curled in the turned-up edge of my jumper. I'll keep her for ever.

Bernie gives me a shoebox for the kitten and strokes its head with her finger. Perhaps she likes this one. 'You can have a nice soft bed on one of Big-un's old socks.' It licks milk from my finger with a rough tongue, then takes some from a saucer and curls up in the box beside the fire. 'Can I sleep in here tonight?'

'No, Nuala. The kitten will be fine.' Bernie is using the voice that means she won't change her mind.

'Oh, but.'

I'm shooed off to bed, too late for stories. Kitten will be lonely all by itself without a mummy or a daddy. I know it will.

In the morning before it's light, I sneak through to the fire to see if the kitten's awake. It stands on its funny wobbly legs putting pink paws on the edge of the box. Yellow eyes stare from a black face. It mews. I lift it into my arms and creep back to bed where we both get warm and go back to sleep.

'Will Maisie always be mine?' The kitten comes when I call her name. She's on the windowsill trying to catch a butterfly trapped against the glass.

'Of course.' Big-un is typing on the computer using two fingers. 'I hate paperwork. It makes me grumpy.' He makes a sound like a lion, 'Grr.'

'No, I mean always.' I pull skin from beside a jagged nail. It hurts, and I suck my stinging finger.

'Daddy's got lots of animals.'

He stops typing. 'Has he, Nuala? How do you know?'

I laugh at his funny question. 'Because he told me.' Big-un rubs his hand across his forehead. Talking about Daddy makes him do that.

'Big-un, how long will I stay at your house?'

'What do you mean, Nuala?'

'When won't you want me any more?' I catch Maisie and whisper it into her fur.

'Come here.' He says in a squeaky voice. He's not cross, lifts me onto his knee and wraps his arms around me. I wriggle but it's nice. Maisie escapes and goes back to trying to catch the butterfly.

'This is where you live now, and no one will move you anywhere else. Me and Bernie think you're the best girl in the world so don't you worry over things like that.' He gives me a tighter squeeze. 'Promise? Promise?' He tickles me until I squeal.

Butter and eggs splash round the bowl. I have a big pinny tied round my chest. 'Let me do it.' The whisk kicks and whirrs, I must hold it with two hands. Bernie is teaching me to cook. I measure the flour and cut the cherries. 'Can I lick the bowl?' You need to learn to cook, she says, because you never know. I wonder what you never know, but don't ask because it doesn't sound like it's a good thing. I cut the biscuits with crinkly silver cutters. 'Pink icing's the best, Big-un likes yellow. What colour do you want, Bernie?' I think she likes green.

'Watch those sticky fingers, Nuala, and don't lick them till you've finished.' She's laughing and kisses the top of my head. 'I'll have a green one with a purple sweetie on the top please.' She's wearing a pinny too. We are real cooks.

On top of each biscuit I put a jelly sweet. I get to put sprinkles on my special pink biscuit.

'Shall I put three in a box to take to school? One each for Ella and her mum and one for the teacher. Come and help me choose.'

Mustn't fall over. I'm careful all the way to school. The biscuits are in a box with a clear plastic lid. I hold the box with both my hands.

I leave Mrs O'Neil's biscuit on her desk. She guesses who it's from. I think she saw me put it there.

'A delicious biscuit, Nuala. Did you bake them?'

I nod but say nothing. My toes are hot, so is my face. Keep staring at the stack of books in front of her. Mine is the top one. I can read my name from where I'm standing. She puts her arm round my shoulder. 'Thank you.' Her eyes are watery.

I often go to Ella's house and she comes to mine.

'I wish I lived in a wood,' Ella says. We're in our den sitting on the log we dragged in. Bernie has given us a bottle of juice to share and an apple each. Ella's my friend. She doesn't tell the other children at school I speak when I'm with her.

'Why haven't you got a mummy and daddy?' She takes a bite of her apple.

There's a funny fizzle in my tummy.

'I HAVE.' It's so loud, it's scary. 'You're stupid. Everyone's got a mummy and daddy.'

'Don't say stupid. Mrs O'Neil says it's not a kind word. Where are they then?'

'My daddy's poorly. He can't look after me. I've come to stay with Big-un till he's better. He'll come and get me soon in a big red car and bring me lots of presents – an X-box and a jigsaw and heaps and heaps of books.'

Ella says, 'Oh.' She squints through slanty eyes. Her lip is pink and soggy.

The fizzy feeling comes back.

'My mummy's … She's gone to … England. She was poorly as well. She lives in a big house, travels on planes and wears posh clothes.'

'Why? Why does she go on planes?'

I don't want to play with Ella any more. Don't want to be in the den.

'Anyway, your lip's horrible and it dribbles.'

I run all the way home, so she won't see my face.

'I don't want any dinner.' My knife and fork bounce when I thump the table.

'What's the matter, Nuala? Have you got a tummy ache?' Bernie touches my hand. I pull it away.

'NO, I HAVEN'T GOT TUMMY ACHE.'

Big-un's stopped buttering his bread.

Bernie pushes my plate closer. 'Then eat it, Nuala, and please don't shout. Macaroni cheese, it's one of your favourites.'

'NO, IT'S NOT. I HATE MACARONI CHEESE. I HATE THIS PLACE.

'Leave me alone.' I slam my bedroom door shut with both hands and pull the quilt over my head. Rabbit's fur is getting wet. He never tells on me when I cry.

'Go away.'

Someone is in the bedroom, sitting on the edge of the bed. An arm presses me like a hug.

'Go away. GO AWAY.'

Under the quilt it's dark and hot. A floorboard creaks and the door closes with a quiet click. Have they gone? I won't look. Not yet. I don't like it on my own. My throat hurts.

'Come back, come back.' Only Rabbit hears.

Joe

'I reckon you're turning into a right good farmer.' Jack's praise came after I'd handled the milking on my own, sent the cows on their way and seen to the milk lorry. I'd learnt the names of the cows and whistled as I milked. It calmed both them and me.

'There's few would have seen me doing this for a living. Me mam would be made-up if she knew.' I stopped, surprised. Would she? Did she ever think of me?

'Aye well, maybes as how you should be telling her.' Jack threw me my jacket. 'Sometimes you can leave it too late. Never get the chance …' I saw the old man's pained face as he turned away.

'Let's be at it. There's work needs doing,' Jack said over his shoulder. 'We need to see to yonder tree that's come down.'

The oak stunted from years of salt-laden winds had dropped its branches.

'Brown rot, I reckon.' Jack rested against the prone tree; his chest heaved in air after the walk across the field.

'Give me the saw. You can supervise. Make sure I don't injure myself.' I swept his protests aside.

I whooped at the raw noise of the petrol-driven saw, as I turned the unwieldy branches into logs. The pile grew and I wiped away sweat with the sleeve of my shirt.

'There, job done. Keep us going through the winter.' Jack shivered; I helped him up and held him while he steadied himself.

'Get off, I'm fine. Dizzy that's all. Think I've got a chill. Don't you be telling Mary 'cos she'll only make a fuss.'

I loaded the wheelbarrow, took logs home for the fire. In the cottage I'd repaired the table, found an old basket-weave chair in the shed and draped it with a rag rug Mary had given me. It all looked bright and cosy.

On one occasion I found a bunch of heather in a vase on the table. Today two scones in a tin with a little pat of butter. I arrived for supper to find Jack asleep, kissed Mary on the top of her head where her pink scalp showed through. 'You're not only the west of Ireland's prettiest girl, but also the best scone maker in the world. They were delicious, thanks.'

She bent her old neck back and squinted. 'Do you think I would be bothering to tramp over to yon cottage to take you a couple of scones?'

'But …'

'Look at this place.' Mary shuffled around in her slippers, chuckling. 'It's so clean, it scares me and Jack to breathe in it. We're going a take to eating our food off the floor it's that shiny. Do you think she suddenly loves cleaning?' Mary's bent finger jabbed me in the chest.

'Aoife?' My voice wavered.

'Men are such daft buggers and you be the daftest of them all, Joe m'lad.'

Aoife took to coming to find me wherever I was working on the farm. 'I've brought you a flask of hot tea and a hat. This wind is really going to blow. You're not familiar with the island's moods yet. You're a townie, Joe, I can tell.'

'No, I'm not. Country lad me. Man of the soil.' I gave her arm a punch.

'What's this then?' Aoife crouched beside a white flat-topped flower which stood proud of the grass. Two bumblebees crawled across its surface.

'Okay, smarty. You can be my teacher.' I pulled on the coarse wool hat and made a face as I modelled it. 'I used to have one like this as a kid; I hated it because it made my scalp itch.' I pulled it over my ears. 'I threw it in the canal.'

'You sound like my brothers. Wild, roamed the countryside getting up to no good. Both married now, five children between them. Settled down and serious.' Aoife sighed. 'Tell me about you, Joe.'

I stared into the mug of steaming tea she'd poured. 'Nothing to tell, nothing interesting anyhows. I guess I was wild too. A mum too busy to notice. Brought myself up you might say.'

'So what made you want to be a farmer?'

I pulled a blade of grass through my fingers. 'I never wanted to be a farmer, Aoife. I landed here because … because it was as far away as I could get … Only the Atlantic Ocean stopped me, or I'd have carried on running. Why all these nosy questions? One thing I've learnt is to look out for myself. Look out for number one as they say. Never get to needing anyone.'

'Will it always be so, Joe?'

'Yep, till something changes my mind. Safer that way.'

'Well, that's telling me.' She turned and ran back to the farm.

'Aoife.' I called after her. 'Thanks for the hat and the drink.' She didn't turn around, just gave a backward wave.

'Hi,' I greeted her next time she came. 'Aoife, I'm sorry if …'

'Leave it, Joe.'

I didn't know what else to say so I said nothing. I got to watching for her, disappointed if she didn't come.

When the tides allowed, I crossed to the bar on the mainland.

'Joe, how are ye? Is it a pint you're having? How's things?' Ronan called. He managed a wood yard overseeing the lorry drivers. Travelled all over he had – Donegal, Ulster, over to England and Wales. He had a wealth of stories to tell, had us all laughing.

'Sure and you're looking healthy these days, Joe. Old Mary's cooking is putting flesh on the bones. All the girls be after you.' They all laughed, I laughed with them. I saw the truth in the mirror. My skin had tanned, the beard suited me.

I left it late to get back, ran from the bar onto the sand. The sea raced in with incredible speed; the water swirled around my ankles by the time I neared the island's shore. It clawed at my legs, threatened with its undertow. I splashed through the waves breaking their crests into foaming spray, then collapsed laughing on the turf, the adrenalin pumping. A sensation I'd forgotten, same as when the syringe pierced the vein and the drug spread up my arm like a river in flood. It was like it was happening now, the memory catching me out. I stared at the water, a mass of heaving motion, knew if it had been possible, I'd have run from the island and found the guy on the street corner, the guy in the car – someone, anyone. I lay with my face in the damp grass and wept.

That night, Nuala laced my thoughts. I sensed her body curled against mine, imagined her sweet breath on my skin. I willed her to stay, needing to catch her murmurings, the dreams I couldn't share. In the morning she'd gone, replaced by an ache in my heart.

I opened my eyes to the remnants of the night, thrust my arms forward, to check, to be sure. No marks, no bruises, no tell-tale red lines, healed, brown and strong. The cows were waiting, I could hear their mournful moans. I pulled on a shirt, grabbed a coat and headed for the cowshed, the pink dawn soon swallowed by a clinging mist.

I'd been nearly twelve when I started to hang out with the older boys in Liverpool. It happened by accident. I went to the dentist and bunked off school for the rest of the day. Mam was at work, she wouldn't care. I'd get a belt round the ear if she found out. She didn't have much time for 'these posh folks an' all their learning'. Our Billy was working, dead proud of him, she was. 'A proper job on the building site'.

They called to me. 'Micky, come 'ere.' Three of them. Two of my next brother's friends, about sixteen, and another older lad. 'Here try this.' They smirked as they passed me a fag. It wasn't the first drag I'd taken. Used to a house filled with cigarette smoke I'd filched Mam's more than once. I took a long slow draw and let the smoke curl from my nostrils.

'Get him then, quite the big guy.' The boys mimicked me, made me one of them. I hung around all day listening to their talk of 'The Reds' and how it's bloody brilliant to stand on the Kop; a lot of talk about girls too. Didn't understand but laughed when they laughed and got by.

'Go nick some drink from the corner supermarket, Micky.'

'No probs.' They were setting me a challenge. I'd show them. I'd taken sweets before, so cool with it. The girl behind the counter was chatting to another customer, I was in, sidled around, took a tin of coke and two of shandy and scarpered. Impressed, they high-fived me, slapped my shoulders and passed the cans around. I was one of them now. After that I drifted over whenever I saw them hanging around, skipped school as a regular pastime, met others more daring in their exploits.

I smoked weed, everyone did, the practice passed on from older gang members to younger ones. Harmless, it made me feel good, big, gave me a sense of belonging. I tried sniffing glue but got sick. For mugs, never bothered with it again. By the time I reached sixteen I could break into a car in minutes, could drive a car, buzzed-up by headlights lighting the Southport shore road as I tried to reach ever faster speeds. I became the hero of the younger ones.

They respected me and I liked it. 'Joe's the one who knows about motorbikes and cars.' I liked the reputation.

'Learning a trade,' I used to joke with my brothers. It quenched my appetite for excitement, relieved the boredom. A rite of passage.

Now the wind swept across the dunes. The headland disappeared replaced by a screen of horizontal rain. The mornings were black. Winter had settled on the land, tearing at the sparse trees, bending the grass into hummocks and whipping sand into new shapes. Some mornings it was hard to drag myself out of bed. If I'd stacked the fire properly there would be embers to blow into life and I'd feel the warmth creeping back. The cows kept in the sheds had hay to munch each day but they were impatient, restless, moody. They produced so much excrement the smell stuck in my nostrils, clung to my clothes as I heaped the muck into great piles of steaming manure.

Mary would always have breakfast ready when we finished. Porridge and a plate of eggs. Often thick slices of ham or sausages. Soda bread cut straight from the loaf and spread thickly with butter and marmalade. Jack didn't always make it so early on these cold, wet mornings. 'You know what yer doin'. Get on with it,' Jack muttered. I watched the old man wince as he rose from his chair, his breath wheezing from congested lungs.

The sheds were falling apart. The wind ruthless, picking at the boards, loosening them, banging them against each other until they tore off and flew across the yard. I made repairs, first to the outhouses. I didn't ask if I should do it, caught Jack watching, saw the drop of his head and the slow stumbling gait as he turned away and retreated indoors.

Aoife didn't always make it if the storms were bad. I would struggle to the headland where the cairn of stones stood as a reminder of my early days on the island. I'd stare across the churning sea, hoping to see a little red car battling its way across the causeway. No sight of it and I'd pit my mood against the wind, let it tear my hood from my head. Sometimes Nuala would be there, a pause in the wind, an arrow of light shot from behind a cloud. She'd taunt me. 'It's how lonely feels.' I'd turn from her staring eyes, anger battering down my regret.

'I've brought us both a pasty.' More at ease with each other again, Aoife unwrapped them from a tea towel. I bit into the warm, meaty, potato mix. She'd found me across the fields sitting with my back to the tractor wheel, overlooking the ruined church.

'I love this place, it's like I'm part of its story.' I glanced sideward to see if she was laughing. She shivered in the cold wind, her arm tucked into mine.

'I know what you mean. Pilgrims came, centuries ago. A special place for them. Now it's our turn to be here. There's an atmosphere isn't there? Their ghosts are still present.'

'Do you believe in ghosts, Aoife?'

'I'm Irish, Joe. Of course I believe in ghosts and fairies and all the little people.' She laughed and took a bite of her pasty, chewing it slowly.

'No, but really.' Why pursue it? She would think me nuts.

'I'm not sure, Joe. It's never been important. Why, do you?'

I wound a piece of grass around my fingers. 'Oh, sometimes I could swear my little ...' I stopped. 'And in the cottage. When I open the door, it's like there's someone there. I asked Jack and Mary who ... '

Aoife put her finger across my lips. 'Leave it, Joe, let it be.' She threw a stone towards the ruins and we watched it bounce, coming to rest against an old wall.

'Joe, where did you come from?' Her question as lethal as gun-shot. The suddenness of it made me get to my feet. I lit a cigarette, offered her one but she shook her head. Aoife patted the grass beside her. 'Don't run away.' I stared across the sea, the mainland a hazy outline. Sat back down, half-turned away from her, legs hunched, arms clasped around my knees.

'What if I tell you it was a long and tortuous road. Passing through hell along the way. Is that enough?'

'It'll do.' Her eyes sad in her pale face. 'Joe, are you married?' she whispered.

'No, I'm not married.' My tongue dry, words jumbled in my throat.

'That's all right then. I can kiss you.' Her smile threw her cheeks into pleats. She leant across and pressed cold lips against my mouth. I unwrapped my arms and held her, my hand sneaking under her scarf to feel the warm skin of her neck.

'Will you believe in that then?' she asked, pulling my hat straight.

I shook my head. Part of me wanted to push her away, tell her to stop for her own sake, instead I pulled her close, aware of her slight form, and her breath warm on my face. 'Convince me. Can I persuade you to do it again?'

Nuala

Mrs O'Neil has been my teacher for two-and-a-half years. She's nice so I try hard for her. She tells me I'm clever. I write good stories too; she mounts them on coloured paper and sticks them on the wall.

My class has written a play but mostly it's me who wrote it. It's about animals who live in a wood and their adventures. I want to be Ruby, the girl who talks with them, who shares in their mischief. The teacher asks if anyone would like to play the part. Lots of girls put up their hands.

'Please can I, Mrs O'Neil?' My voice is a scratch.

It goes quiet, I mean really quiet. Only a blackbird sings in a tree. Mrs O'Neil is so surprised that I spoke she gives me the part.

Everyone makes a fuss. I have to see the headteacher. She comes from behind her desk, stands in front of me and beams. Her chunky necklace moves on her chest she's breathing so fast.

'A brave thing to do, Nuala. We're proud of you.' Her eyebrows arch like they're on strings. She wants me to say something, probably doesn't believe it. Look at my feet and shuffle so I'm standing in a square on the carpet not touching any of the lines.

'I've rung your foster parents and told them the wonderful news. I hope you will go on talking. So many things to tell us.'

I don't want to tell them anything.

When I get home from school Bernie's baked a chocolate cake for tea. She and Big-un give me a hug. Even Maisie kitten makes a fuss and rubs her head under my chin.

I carry on speaking in school after that. Ella says I should because I'm ten. She says everyone knows I can anyway.

I speak when I want to. It's not all the time. I choose.

We perform our play in front of the whole school. Mrs O'Neil says I've learned the lines well. Easy, I'd written them. Some nights when I go to bed, I creep from the covers and perform the whole play in the bedroom, whispering so no one will hear. I know all the parts.

The parents are invited to watch. We lay out lots and lots of chairs in rows. Big-un and Bernie come early and sit in the front row.

I'm wearing a yellow dress Ella and I made of paper, decorated with flowers. The fox, a boy called William, forgets his words and goes pink. I whisper them in his ear then kick him on the ankle to make him move.

At the end of our performance we take a bow like we've been practising for ages. All the teachers, the children, the parents, and Big-un and Bernie clap and clap. Such a lot of noise. Big-un stands and cheers, his hands above his head. He has the biggest smile. I don't want the clapping ever to stop.

Afterwards Mrs O'Neil puts both her hands on my shoulders, 'Wasn't Nuala wonderful? She remains quiet in class though.' Big-un says, 'She's shy.' He gives me a wink.

Ella and I don't play childish games any more. Next year we're going to the secondary school on a bus from the village. Bernie laughs and says, 'You'll have to get up earlier than you do already. How are you going to manage?'

If she would learn to drive, then I wouldn't have to walk to school. She says she can't drive because of 'fits' – whatever they are. At least she lets me go on my own. Only the younger kids have someone to take them.

Today I don't have to go to school. There's a meeting. Bernie and Big-un are sitting at breakfast wearing their best clothes. Bernie's in a dark blue skirt and a blue blouse. Big-un has a shirt with a striped tie, I can see the top button of his shirt.

'You both look funny. Why are you dressed up?'

'Nuala, put your new jeans on. Not those with the hole in the knee.' I pull a face because I like my jeans with the hole. Ella has some too and we made the holes bigger by tearing them with our fingers. Bernie's had her hair cut short and I'm not used to her. Big-un says she looks glamorous.

'And the top Sam gave you. It's nice.'

I like Sam, he's their son and he's funny. He came to stay a while ago, bought me a pink T-shirt. I love London on the front except the love is a heart-shaped Union Jack. He came for three nights, looked like Big-un but taller and a bit thinner. He laughed the same, said in London lots of the people come from different places in the world. Some from China and India and Africa and heaps of other places. He said one day I could visit him.

The meeting is at the Social Services Department. We go there every year. It's boring, same as always. Lots of people including Mrs O'Neil sit around a table talking.

'Are you happy, Nuala?' They always ask.

'Yes,' I murmur. I think they will tell me about my dad, but they never do.

I'm not saying any more because I remember what happened last year when I said, 'One day I want to live with my dad. He wants me too. He's told me.' They all looked at each other. Some coughed and moved in their seats. The lady in charge, the one writing things, said, 'How can he have told you, Nuala?' She had a freckly nose and shiny silver earrings. I could tell by her face she didn't want me to answer. They didn't believe me, so I decided not to tell them I speak to my dad. He hears me. I forget what his face is like sometimes. I don't tell them that either.

This year more people sit around the table. They all say their names and I have to say mine. I'm sitting between Big-un and Bernie; Big-un tickles me on the leg underneath the table and I try not to laugh. He passes me a sweet; the paper crinkles when I try to unwrap it.

Talk, talk, everyone wants to say something. I make up stories in my head and pretend I'm with Ella. Last time at her house we did each other's hair and tried her mum's eyeshadow and lipstick.

'We'll talk with Nuala. Explain what it all means.' It's Big-un's voice; he is nudging my arm. 'Well, young lady?'

I shrug and say yes. It seems to be the right thing to say because they all smile, gather their papers, push their chairs back and speak loudly to each other.

'Can we go?' I whisper. Bernie's cheeks are red, and she dabs at her eyes with a handkerchief. Big-un puts his arm around her shoulder and gives her a squeeze.

'Milkshake time.' I try to cheer them up. 'Can we go to our usual café?' I want to get away from all these smiling people.

*

'Nuala, we have something important to tell you.'

Bernie is standing by the door, Big-un is sitting on my bed. Bernie is scrunched up, her cardigan wrapped around her. I hunch my knees under the quilt. My book slides off the bed with a thud. Rabbit is on my pillow; I sit him on my knees and retie the blue bow round his neck.

'The thing is, you've been with us for a long time and we love you very much. Do you like living here, Nuala? With Bernie and me?' Big-un's eyes are bright, he keeps swallowing.

'Yeah.' I bury my face in Rabbit's fur and pull him closer. I don't like this talk. I wish they'd give me a kiss and leave me to read my book as they always do at bedtime.

'The meeting we went to, at social services – it was a special meeting. They have agreed we can adopt you. Do you understand, Nuala? It means you wouldn't be fostered any more.'

Cold tickly feelings wriggle inside me. The television is on in the lounge. They are waiting, still as statues.

'We want to adopt you, Nuala.' Big-un makes a noise like he's choking. 'We want that more than anything else in the world. It means you would be our daughter, like Sam and Chris are our sons. You would be ours – forever.'

'Would you like that?' It's Bernie who speaks. She has come over to the bed and is smoothing my hair. The tickly feeling claws up my throat trying to escape.

'Where's Maisie? I want Maisie.' I throw the covers back and push past them. The front door is stiff, but I pull it open. Cold air and darkness stop me.

'Maisie, Maisie,' I yell. 'Maisie.' She comes from behind the house and purrs around my legs. I pick her up, stroke her fur and shut my eyes so tightly they hurt. My head is a balloon full of air. Big-un brings me back indoors. They are crying, so am I.

'Let's have hot chocolate – with marshmallows.' Bernie boils milk in a saucepan, stirring with one hand and blowing her nose on some kitchen roll with the other.

Marshmallows. It's a special night.

I tell no one, not even Ella. It's my secret and I hug it like I hug Rabbit at night.

I want to live with Big-un and Bernie for ever with Ella as my best friend. 'You'll be our daughter,' Big-un said. Will I have to call them Mum and Dad?

I whisper my secret to real Dad, tell him what they've said. What will he think? He might not like it. Will he cry? He must be cross because he's not saying anything. He doesn't want to talk any more. I'm happy and sad. The thoughts buzz in my head. I think them in bed at night, I think them on the way to school. I think them when the teacher is giving out our books.

'Such a serious face.' Big-un tilts my chin with his finger.

'If I'm yours, does it mean Daddy won't be my dad? What if he's sad?' It comes in a rush. Big-un's going to be angry then they'll change their mind. They won't want me to be their daughter.

Big-un covers my hands with his. He's got a smudge of dirt on his cheek. 'Nuala, listen to me. Your dad will love you forever, always remember what a special girl you are. He can't look after you, so we get to instead. He wants you to grow up with us, your new family and have lots of friends and lots of fun.'

I try to pull my hands away but Big-un isn't letting go.

'He doesn't want me.' My scream is so loud it frightens me: Maisie runs under the table. 'He wouldn't say that. He wouldn't.'

'If you love someone, Nuala, you can talk to them. Always.'

'He doesn't love me. He doesn't. He doesn't talk to me any more.'

I bang my fists into Big-un's chest, butt his ribs with my head. He holds me until I can breathe again, and I cling to his shirt.

I tell Ella when my secret grows so big it's almost bursting from me.

'Wow,' she says. 'You're lucky. Can I tell my mum?' Her mum gives me the biggest squeeze ever, and says, to celebrate, she'll take us both to the cinema in town to see *Harry Potter and the Half-Blood Prince*. 'Yes, yes, yes. Harry Potter.' We jump around, holding onto each other until we're dizzy.

Ella tells Mrs O'Neil and all the children in our class we're going to see the film – and why. It's not just my secret now.

The very next day, Mrs Carey the headteacher comes into our classroom. She's talking to Mrs O'Neil. We are finding Egypt in our atlases, the River Nile, learning about the Pharaohs with their tombs full of gold and riches. About Tutankhamun. I want to be beautiful like Queen Nefertiti.

They're whispering about me. I know. My face goes cold, a pain stabs my tummy. I bite my cheek so hard it bleeds a sour, hot taste like at the dentist's.

'Nuala, go with Mrs Carey.' Mrs O'Neil puts her arm around my shoulder and pulls me gently from my chair. I can feel her shaking, see her shiny eyes.

The pain in my tummy gets bigger.

I follow the headteacher along the corridor. Her shoes tap on the tiles. She holds open the door of her room which smells of coffee. I've never seen the woman sitting by the desk before. She holds out her arm. I stop dead in the middle of the carpet.

'Sit down, Nuala. Have a little drink of water.' Mrs Carey is fussing, putting a glass of water in my hands, giving me a chair to sit on. A long way off the bell rings for the end of school.

'I have to go home,' I tell them.

'Nuala …' Mrs Carey starts to speak.

'Hello, Nuala.' The woman sitting by the desk interrupts. She's wearing long black boots over tight trousers. 'I'm a social worker. My name is Dawn. I'm here because your usual social worker Nicky is on holiday. You know Nicky, don't you?'

Of course, I know Nicky. She comes to see me. I like Nicky. This woman is asking silly questions. Her red lipstick is the same colour as her jumper. Why is she here? I pull the thread on my sleeve.

'The thing is, Nuala. I'm going to have to take you to somewhere different to sleep tonight – not sure where yet, but you'll be all right. I'll come with you.'

They are both looking at me. Wind the thread tighter, tighter round my finger so it hurts. Inside my head, a roaring noise.

'NO. I WANT TO GO TO BIG-UN AND BERNIE'S. DON'T WANT TO SLEEP SOMEWHERE ELSE.' I rush to the door, but Mrs Carey gets there first and stops me.

'Nuala. Listen to what Dawn has to say.' She steers me to the chair and stands behind me, her hand presses on my shoulder.

'There's been an accident. In the woods.' Dawn coughs and jangles the bracelets on her wrist. 'It means you can't go home tonight. We need to …'

Everything goes fuzzy. Daddy's here but he's hiding. They can't see him.

Don't let them take me away. He's flitting round the room. Daddy, please …

'Robert, your foster parent, is in hospital and Bernie is with him. There's no one at the house. That's why I've come for you.'

Daddy is going out the door. It slams shut with a bang like it did a long time ago. I'm all alone in a black room.

Mrs Carey strokes my hair. 'Nuala.'

'I'll go to Ella's. Ella's my friend. I can stay at her house till Big-un's better.' They look at each other, then back at me. 'I want to go to Ella's.'

They won't let me.

'It's not possible, Nuala. You see … It might be for a long time.'

'Ella's mum won't mind. I often stay there. She likes me. We're going to the cinema.' How can I make them listen? They look at each other again.

'I want to see him, to see Big-un.' I say it out loud and their faces go soft.

'You can't, Nuala, not for a while. Big-un, Robert, is having an operation.'

'I'm not going anywhere with you. I hate you. I HATE YOU.' I blink with tears. Snot tickles my lip and I lick at the sweet slime. I throw away the tissue Mrs Carey hands me and wipe my sleeve across my face.

Mrs O'Neil comes in with my school bag and my coat. I grab hold of her skirt. She crouches in front of me. 'You have to be brave. You're a big girl, Nuala. This is a horrible shock. Go with this lady and she'll take care of you until you can come back to school again.' She's got tears in her eyes, so it's not all right. My head is leaking like a balloon when the air escapes. I slide off my chair and sit on the floor.

Dawn puts me in the back of the car and tosses my school bag in beside me. She keeps looking at her watch and tutting like all this is my fault. We speed off, go past the start of the track through the woods and I see the chimney pot on the house. Nothing is different. They are telling lies, pretending there's been an accident. Big-un and Bernie have changed their mind. They don't want me any more. A sob choked with sick. I should have kept my bedroom tidy. Not complained when I wanted to finish my book and been made to dry the dishes. I would have done them later, I said I would. I bang my head against the window until Dawn tells me to stop.

We drive around for a while. She keeps stopping to answer her phone. Each time she jumps from the car and paces along the side of the road.

'I can't use the hands-free. She's in the car with me. Where do you want me to go? For God's sake there must be a bed somewhere. I'll bring her back to the office.'

I hear all this because I open the window. When she notices, she tries to turn her frown into a smile, but it's more like a snarl.

'Nuala, I'm sorry about this. We will find somewhere for you to stay tonight – an emergency foster placement or something. Fridays are always mad and … anyway it's our problem, all this.'

'I want to go to Ella's.' She doesn't reply.

Dawn is shouting into her phone again. 'I will be home when I can.' This time she hasn't stopped the car. 'Yes, I know we have to catch the train at eight.' She is turning the steering wheel with one hand as she tries to wedge the phone between her head and her shoulder. 'I don't know, do I?' She throws the phone onto the front seat and it slides off between the seat and the door. 'Oh Jesus.'

Inside me there's a massive scream, I bite at the tight skin on my bent knees until it hurts.

In the social services office, I stare at nothing. Someone brings me juice and a bun. It's someone's lunchbox. Underneath a piece of tissue there are dried crusts from a ham sandwich.

A man in a checked shirt ruffles my hair and stops beside me. 'Almost sorted, young lady. Have you safe and sound in no time at all.' He grins, ruffles my hair again and says, 'Expect it's been a long day.' He tucks his shirt into the top of his trousers and I see the black hairs around his tummy button. He wants to say something else, instead he thrusts his hands in his pockets and goes back to his desk.

Back in the car. A different social worker. Zach he says his name is keeps picking at a spot on his chin, but he has a kind face. I think of Matt on the lorries and the chocolate bar he always has for me.

'Ridiculous. Taking you thirty bloody, oops sorry, shouldn't be swearing. Thirty miles away. Tonight you'll stay in a children's home, Falcon House it's called. It's okay, I've been there before. Ignore the bullshitters, the stroppy teenagers. Right pains they are. Give us no end of grief. You'll be fine.'

The words are a fuzz blending with the hum of the engine. I am sweating from the car heater, but I can't stop shaking. I'm so scared I can feel it poking through my skin.

'You get ready for bed and I'll come back in a minute.' Martha, another name to remember, places a T-shirt on top of the quilt. 'Wear this tonight. We can take you shopping tomorrow. Get you a few things. Oh, and there's a toothbrush. Bathroom's next door.'

The room is small, only four strides and I can touch the other wall. Flakes of blue plaster lie on the floor and I bang my fist into the dent in the wall above them. I tear back the curtains to see the black sky, to hear the wind telling stories to the trees like Big-un says they do. There are only roofs, chimneys and car lights. Cold seeps into my hands from the windowsill. Someone has cut initials into the white paintwork. I dig loose a splinter of wood from the sill and scratch it across my wrist – again and again. The prick of a needle. The hurt swells. Red blood smears my skin.

All the next day I huddle in a chair in front of the TV. Waiting. Other kids make fun of me in my school uniform. A girl tells them to shut up. A boy lounges on the sofa, with his long legs dangling over the arm. They keep telling him he must go to his Saturday job if he wants to keep it. 'Bothered!' he shouts in their faces, flips over an empty plate lying on the floor, flicks my ear as he passes and bangs the door. A picture shakes on the wall.

'When can I go home? Is Big-un still in the hospital? Where is Bernie? Can I phone Ella?' No one has any answers. I keep asking.

'Shut that bleeding kid up before I thump her.' A girl with purple hair is skipping through the channels. 'Why are you bloody here anyway? What you done?'

'Nothing. I …'

'Yeah, right. None of us done bloody nothing. It's why we're bloody here. Run away, have you? Kicked out of school? Shoplifting? Arson? Or has your old man been having his way with you?'

I don't understand. I hug a cushion and stare at the flickering screen and wonder what I've done.

'New bra, pants to match. Sexy or what? Supermarkets are so dumb.' A girl older than me comes in swinging a red bra round on her fingers. When a member of staff opens the door, she stuffs it under the sofa.

'What, Debbie? Share the joke.' The other kids make rude gestures and one starts to slowly clap; they all copy.

'Come on, kid, join in,' the girl with the purple hair bellows across the room. They're all staring at me. I put my hands together, my thumbs meeting. 'She's praying. Too late, Dumbo. We are the damned.' She pulls an ugly face. They all laugh.

Debbie's coming over. I shrink further into my seat. She perches on the arm of my chair. Her perfume hurts my eyes. 'Don't mind them, they're all idiots. You stick with me. I'll see you all right.' I want her to stay sitting beside me and I try a little smile.

Martha's back on shift and she takes me to the shops to buy

clothes. All the way there she talks. I'm not listening. My arms sting.

'Do you like this pair or that pair, this colour or that colour? Do they fit?'

I don't know. Who cares?

She holds the items in front of her. The other people in the fitting room are staring. Whispering.

'Yes. They'll do.' It's hot, sweaty. I want to go. We buy jeans, two tops, a sweatshirt, new underwear, pyjamas, socks and a pair of trainers. Never have I had so many new clothes. 'Here, I expect you want to carry the bags.'

I don't.

'Let's go to the café. Get a drink.'

It's in a dark corner of the shop. The tables are heaped with dirty cups and plates. A trolley woman is trying to clear them away, but she can't do it fast enough. She swipes our table with a cloth. 'Such filthy habits.' She pulls wet wipes from inside a mug. I want to tell her it wasn't me, but I can't be bothered. I don't think she likes her job. I push the crumbs she's missed into a small pile.

Martha comes back with a coffee for herself, juice and a sandwich for me. The egg in the sandwich is yuk. Nibble it and gag. The bread tastes like dry cloth. I choke trying to swallow it.

Martha's stroking my fingers. 'You poor darling. This must be horrible for you.' Her finger pushes my sleeve back. She bites her lip and breathes in with a mew.

Her voice is soft, like Ella's mum. She's kind. Tears dribble down my cheeks and drip onto the sandwich.

'Can I go home? Maisie will miss me. I want Maisie.'

She takes my hand and bends her head; her face is level with mine. 'A few more days, Nuala. Two, three at the most. We are trying to find a foster placement for you. You shouldn't be in a children's home, but there are so few foster parents. We'll find somewhere soon, I promise.'

'I mean, can I go home to Big-un and Bernie?' It's quiet as a breath so I ask again.

'Is he your foster parent? He's had a bad accident. A pile of wood or logs or something fell on him. It's not good. They had to operate last night.'

Squash my ears with my hands, make the words go away.

Taste the blood, sour like foil paper on my tongue. 'Will he get better?'

'I don't know, Nuala.' She is fingering my hand, easing the sleeve of my school jumper past my wrist again.

She's going to say something. I stop breathing.

'Oh, what the heck. I'll tell you. Nuala. I'm sorry. His leg was so smashed the doctors couldn't save it. They had to take it off.'

'Let me go.' She's gripping both my hands. I fight her.

'He may lose the other one too. I probably shouldn't be giving you all this detail, but I remember … when my mother died. It's not what you know but what you don't know that's scary. Anyway, doctors are brilliant these days. I'm sure they're doing their best.'

At the next table a child goes rigid as his mother tries to put him in a highchair. She plonks him back in his pushchair and ignores his cries. The cleaner lady pushes her trolley through the swing doors and cutlery clatters to the floor.

The noise and chatter's gone. It's white. Big-un is laughing, holding out his hand. It's rough and warm, holding me safe. Tree scent is on his jacket.

Joe

A rich orange sunset turned the sand golden as I walked over to Rafferty's bar. I perched on my usual stool and was enjoying the camaraderie of the busy pub when the door swept open making the drinkers lift heads. Two gardai walked in – one a fresh-faced young man who fiddled with the buttons of his jacket and shuffled against the wall. The other officer, older, pumped up, squared his shoulders and stepped forward. His narrowed eyes drifted around the room. The men returned to supping their pints. Ronan's fingers tapped on the polished bar but otherwise no one spoke.

'Looking for a Michael Joseph McCurdy. Heard as there might be strangers round here.'

Seamus behind the bar stood motionless, his hand on a pump. A man coughed and waved his empty jar. 'Give the garda a whiskey, Seamus, and a lemonade for his little friend.' The drumming of men's feet on the stone floor accompanied their suppressed smirks.

Ronan twisted on his bar stool. 'Michael McCurdy you say. No one of that name round here, Garda Tierney. Seems like you've got it all wrong.' He looked along the bar at the shaking heads. 'Hey Paddy,' he called across to me where I sat at the far end. 'Ever heard of him?' I hunched over my Guinness, my name reverberating in my ears, heart thumping. I gave a barely discernible head shake.

'So, what's this Michael McCurdy supposed to have done then?' Ronan growled. 'Will we all be getting murdered in our beds?'

An outstretched arm prevented Garda Tierney, a whiskey in his hand, from moving towards the bar. 'Abandoned a kid. Up in the north. Left it on its own. A crime. Mother's dead, drug overdose.' He spoke loudly, to impress his silent audience. 'We'll find him.' A big breath puffed his chest. 'Kid's going for adoption. Best thing if you ask me, poor little blighter.'

Ronan sucked air through clenched teeth. 'There's many around here guilty of the same crime. Abandoning a kid.' He leapt from his bar stool. 'Isn't that so, Garda Tierney?' His words rang across the pub. The young officer by the door scuffed at the floor and inspected his shoes. 'Know of a little boy in the village. Nearly five. Best wee lad in Connemara but the mother, she won't ever say who the father is. Up and left her. Mind you I have my suspicions. Hey, Garda Tierney? Wouldn't take too much to find out. In fact, I've quite a mind to do it. Maybe you'd like to help me? I could pay a visit to your inspector – see what he thinks. Remind me, you a married man, Garda Tierney?' Ronan lifted his glass and took a long slurp.

'Now,' Ronan said, his tongue wiping the froth from his upper lip. 'You two as best be putting your hats on as you'll just be leaving us, and it's mighty cold the night. Tut, tut, drinking on duty. What kind of example is that to set, Garda Tierney?'

'Good night,' the chorus of farewells expelled the gardai into the night and the sound of their car receded.

Someone slapped Ronan on the back and bought him a drink. Guffaws of laughter echoed in the pub. I finished my pint and collected my coat.

'Ronan, I think I need to …'

'Joe. Hereabouts we take as we find, not as we'm told. We none of us perfect. Be off before them tides come in.' I touched Ronan's arm and made for the door. 'Joe. You owe me one.' Ronan and his mates lifted their glasses making me smile as I left the bar.

It scared me. What had happened tonight with the gardai. I'd been Joe, not Michael since fleeing to Ireland, an identity I'd grown into. Got used to Joe, the farmhand, to the limits of my world being defined by nature's forces. The scars on my arms and thighs were faded. I didn't see them any more; if cravings ever surfaced, I drowned them in punishing physical work that left me exhausted but content.

Adopted. The word, on the bedroom wall, on the back of my eyelids as I threw off my clothes. Adopted. My tongue curled around it, wouldn't allow me to swallow it. What had the garda said? 'Best thing for the poor little blighter.'

'Nuala.' I probed the darkness when sleep wouldn't come. 'He's right. It's for the best. You'll have someone to love you. I love you but I don't know how to love you. I don't know how to love anyone. They'll be a proper mummy and daddy. Nuala, tell me you're loved. Tell me you forgive me.'

The curtains moved with the draught. No warm hand, no childish giggle. Alone like I'd always been. 'Baby, don't leave me.' My wail escaped through the open window into the fields, received by no one.

'To be sure you be as glum as a thirsty man stuck in a bog.' Jack greeted me next day.

We'd milked the cows, but I'd been sullen, rough, pushing at the beasts when they wouldn't co-operate. 'Get in there.' I thumped the stall as a stream of green shit fountained onto the floor.

'It's not their fault your sun hasn't risen today. You needs to be sortin' yourself out, lad, afore you come over for breakfast.' Jack's wheeze became a paroxysm of coughing.

I didn't go to the house. I wanted to be by myself, at the same time hating my own company. I tackled the roof of the shed, banged the sheets of corrugated iron into place with unnecessary force and swore when the hammer slid off the roof making me scramble to the yard below to retrieve it. Mary brought a bacon sandwich, passed it to me with a slight squeeze of my hand. The chickens milled round my feet while I ate it. Back on the roof the wind howled. I could see across the bay. White horses topped the shoreward-rolling waves. A small fishing boat made slow progress on an ebb tide. Aoife wouldn't be across today. I told myself I didn't care. Better if she never came again.

She did come. I saw her car drive onto the sand as I sat astride the apex of the roof. I slid until I found the ladder, jumped the last few rungs and ran along the track, reaching the island road as she drove onto it. I bent double to catch my breath. Somewhere along the way I'd lost my hat and my hair raged wild in the wind.

'Well, look at you. Not a sight to greet a pretty girl. You best be getting in before you're blown away.' She opened the car door. 'Cow muck and sweat. An attractive combination!' Her nose wrinkled, a hint of lipstick on her lips, small hands gripped the steering wheel.

I laughed, dragged my hands down my face. 'You came just in time. One more minute and I might have thrown myself off the roof I was repairing.'

'Joe.' Her finger grazed my cheek. 'Don't joke about things like that. Promise me.' Furrows etched her eyes.

I pecked her on the cheek. 'Today I've been a miserable sod but now I think Jack would say my sun has risen.' She began to ask a question then abandoned it and laughed with me.

I didn't see her for long. She changed the beds for Mary. I heard her curse the sheets as she battled to keep them on the line. Long enough though for me to finish the job and have a mug of tea with her before she had to leave.

'You'm in a better mood then.' Mary wagged a bent finger. 'Sour as sheep rot earlier, Aoife. Reckon as you'm good for him.'

'I reckon as you're right, Mary.' I winked at Aoife and blew a kiss in Mary's direction. Jack snorted from his chair by the fire.

'Get its legs. Uncurl them. Easy, pull gently. Got it.' The lamb slipped feet first from the ewe's body in a mess of slime and blood. It lay lifeless on the straw. 'Wipe it and swing it.' I'm clumsy, afraid to be too rough.

'Gi' on with it. You only have a minute.'

I wiped the membrane from the lamb's face and swung it by the legs; the cold air made it gasp. The ewe struggled to her feet, licked at her lamb when I laid it beside her. It mewed like a kitten then lifted its head and surrendered to the rhythmic massage of its mother's tongue. I trembled. My nostrils were full of the warm scent of birth.

'Well done, Joe. You done well.' The old man's cough was raw as he hawked phlegm. 'I'm goin' back to bed. Them'll be fine.' Jack steadied himself against the big barn door. Without turning he raised a hand and shuffled home.

Left amongst the bleating lambs and tired ewes I needed to rest but I couldn't pull myself away from the pen. The lamb nuzzled its mother and fed noisily. It had a black head and spots on its legs like knee pads. I ran my hand across the soft damp wool as the mother bleated a protective warning.

'Seems an age since I arrived here – on the island, I mean,' I told the sheep. 'The first lambs were running on the heath then, as you'll be doing soon. Exploring the new territory, they were just like me.' Moonlight filtered through the cracks in the shed wall. A loose piece of wood creaked as the wind blew behind it. More repairs needed. A constant job, patching the old farm buildings, keeping the ancient tractor running and tending the animals. But I loved it.

Derry now a place I struggled to recall, the dark basements, life in the shadows. Even harder to remember was being a boy in Liverpool. The first time I'd gone on a bus to the docks, the sky had been immense, stretched across cranes and derelict warehouses. The Mersey ribboned in a muddy line to beyond where I could see. I remembered how all the space made me uneasy. Then I needed the pinched streets of terraced houses, dogs rummaging in the rubbish sacks, people who knew me and the boys I called mates.

I shovelled soiled straw into a heap, wondered about Mam and my brothers – what were they doing tonight? I tried to recall their faces.

Nuala

They've given me a night light and its faint glow makes all the corners of the room dark. Black like a cave. The quilt's heavy and the lumpy pillow is damp from my crying. I search for Rabbit. He isn't there. He'll be waiting at home, waiting for me to come back. And Maisie. I pretend she's lying on my legs, purring me to sleep. Rabbit, Maisie – I WANT THEM. My throat hurts from choked sobs.

'MAISIE.' I freeze. Someone will have heard. A floor creaks. No one comes. The first time I saw her – stuck in the drainpipe. If I hadn't found her, she would have died. What if no one finds me? Muffled tears leak into my pillow. They get louder, escaping from under the cover making my head throb.

'Hey, what's the matter?' It's Debbie, the girl with the red bra. She's sitting on the bed.

'I want Maisie. She always sleeps with me and ...' Something stops me telling her about Rabbit. 'Maisie's my cat.' Saying her name makes me cry more and I curl against the wall.

'I had a cat once.' Debbie is pulling back the quilt and climbing in beside me. 'It got run over.' Her breath on the back of my neck is like being tickled with a feather. She puts an arm over my shoulder. 'Shh, for Christ's sake. We don't want anyone to hear. You don't want me to go, do you?'

I try to hush. She is warm and real. I want her to stay. She snuggles against my back and I feel her soft breasts pressing against me.

'I used to cry myself to sleep. It's not worth it – only makes you feel worse. Makes no difference anyhow. After a while you stop.' I sense the shrug of her shoulders and wriggle onto my back to stare at the ceiling. Her hair wisps against my cheek.

'How long have you been in this place?' I whisper.

'It's okay here.' Her hand finds mine as we lie side by side. I grip it tight like I'm a dog on a lead. It's nice to hold her hand. 'Dunno how long, months anyway. When I'm eighteen I'm gonna get a place of my own. Next year probably.'

'Aren't you going to go home soon?' I suck in my breath and wait.

'Ugh.' Her body shivers. 'Like fucking never.' Somewhere a door bangs, Debbie stiffens, her leg across mine pins me down.

I want to tell her I'll go home as soon as Big-un is better. I'm going to be their daughter. But I don't let on. It's my secret, same as Rabbit.

She's squeezing my hand, our arms squashed and hot. My heart thumps. What if someone comes? Something's not right. We'll be in trouble. I fidget to be free of her, want her to leave me alone, to take the words fucking never and their meaning with her.

I want to go home.

She's whispering in my ear. 'Hey. We can be friends. Look out for each other like.' Her other hand creeps under my pyjama top and traces circles around my tummy button. She is drumming on my ribs, humming softly. I tug at the edge of the T-shirt, but she pushes my hand away. Her humming is louder. 'Mmm, shush now – it's nice.' Her fingers crawl upwards, rubbing over the bumps of my chest.

'Baby breasts,' she says.

A tickle starts deep inside me. Debbie's thigh is rubbing against mine, her hand sweeps across my skin, between my legs, playing with parts I have never dared to touch.

'You like it, don't you? We're mates, like sisters. You don't have to cry.'

I want her to stop, don't want her to stop, want her to hug me. A proper hug. She's soft and kind and I let her stroke me. My friend. But ...

'Leave off.' I squirm in fear, half-wanting not to have said it.

Her hand jerks to my breast and she squeezes hard, so it hurts. Really hurts. I squeal.

'Tell anyone and you're dead. Got that?' She's someone else. She draws her finger across her throat, tosses the duvet to the floor and stands over me.

'Dead.' It's a hiss in my face.

Cool air goose-pimples my skin and I curl into a ball, hair falling over my face. I shiver, squint from smarting eyes; she's gone. No sound of breathing, no white shape in the dark. Flop onto the floor, roll in the quilt. A cocoon. Bang my head to make the pain stop.

At breakfast I stir my Coco Pops round the bowl watching the milk turn chocolate brown. It makes me feel sick. Debbie is telling jokes, waving her spoon, grabbing attention. Everyone is laughing. She pushes an orange plastic plate towards me. 'Here, babe, have some toast.' I can't look at her.

A boy with a spotty face is ogling me. 'You anorexic or something?' He shouts to impress the others. 'Another of those fucking weirdos.'

Debbie swipes the back of his head. 'Leave off her. Got it? Remember when you first came you snivelled for days. Right little cry baby you were.' The boy grunts, eats his toast, pulls a face at Debbie. I catch her wink, feel the red creep up my spine to my ears.

Keeping out the way is hard. In my room I remember Debbie and think about things. There's no one in the lounge; I slouch on the purple sofa with its lime green cushions, prop my feet on a see-through plastic table in the middle of the floor. People on the television are talking to each other, hugging, squealing, jumping about when they win money. They're so pathetic.

I stick my fingers in my ears, hide my head in a cushion. Bernie is flicking at the mantle shelf above the fireplace with her duster; Maisie is mewing for her food. There is a rush of air as Big-un opens the door filling the room with his bulk and his laugh.

'You are a weirdo.' Spotty-face is standing in front of me sneering. He has his fingers in his ears and is waggling his head from side to side. 'What's on telly? Celebrity bloody Chase – It's a load of bollocks.' He kicks the remote control across the carpet out of reach, throws a cushion at me and leaves the room.

A magazine lies open on the floor, I grab it and head for the back door. No trees in this garden, just grass surrounded by brown fence, taller than me. I sit on the ground, in a patch of sunshine, my back against a small shed and tear the pages of the magazine into tiny pieces, let the breeze scatter them.

'Nuala, your social worker's here.' A voice outside my bedroom door.

'Nicky.' A face I recognise.

'Is he better? Can I go home?'

She pats my shoulder, her face scrunched like she's sad. She's not saying yes.

'Oh, poor you. I'm so sorry not to have been here when it happened. I was on holiday. How are you?' She glances round. 'A children's home isn't the right place for you. We may have found somewhere else – should know today.' Her breath smells of mints. She's wearing a silver necklace with her name on it and an engagement ring which she didn't have before. She sees me looking. 'Do you like it?' She lifts her hand to show me. I turn away.

'I want to go home!' Loud so she hears this time. It's the only thing that matters. To be with Big-un and Bernie. 'I hate this place. I want to see Big-un.'

She squeezes my hands and pulls me into a hug. I feel her shaking but it's not her it's me.

'Has no one told you anything?'

I stare at the picture of a horse above her head. She's talking, keeps looking at the door. I think she wants to run away like I do.

'In hospital – stabilised – infection – another foster home – keep you safe – you'll like them – nice people.'

Snatches, words, I can't breathe and suck hungry gulps of air. I'll die. I want to die.

'Put your head down, Nuala. Between your knees.' Someone, far away. Waves of swirling colour; swim into a tunnel. I'm lying on the floor, feet, lots of feet. I feel like I've been asleep and don't want to wake up.

'Have a sip of water. Can you sit?' Cold liquid wets my lips and tongue forcing me to swallow. Can't stop shaking. Nicky puts a blanket round my shoulders. The room is full of people.

'We've got to get this sorted today. She's only eleven. The kid's in shock. Why hasn't anyone told her?' It's Nicky being cross, her voice rising, her hands fighting her hair into a pony-tail.

I want her to hold me.

'Can I see Big-un in hospital?' My voice is a squeak.

The room goes quiet. They all turn towards me as though they've remembered I'm here.

'One day, Nuala.' Nicky crouches on the floor. I smell her perfume. 'At the moment it's only family. His sons, Chris and Sam, are there. You remember them, don't you?'

'But I'm family. Soon I'll be their daughter, their real daughter.' My squeak turns to a wail. They need to understand.

Nicky frowns, strokes my cheek. 'As soon as I can I will take you to see Big-un, but it won't be for a while. He's, he's … very ill. In the meantime, be brave.'

Brave! Why? Why do I always have to be brave?

Another foster home. I pack my new clothes into a bag and shut the bedroom door without looking back. The staff wave goodbye and wish me luck. Debbie runs up as I'm about to get into the car. 'Babe, I'll miss you,' she says, flinging her arms around me, pressing herself close. Her nails dig into my neck, scratch my skin. I get the message.

Nicky grips the steering wheel with both hands. 'Ready?' She turns, sees my face and gives me half a smile. She cares but I don't.

'Whatever.' It's what the other kids say.

Joe

'I'm thinking of going up to town.' Aoife tied and retied the lace of her trainer.

'What for? Shopping or a day's fun?' I ate the pork pie she'd brought as part of the picnic lunch. We did this on occasions in my lunch break; took food onto the cliff tops or, as today, found a sheltered spot on the beach. A glorious spring morning, the air fresh, the clouds high, a pale sun lending its warmth.

'What if I'd never found this island, Aoife? And never found you.'

'To Dublin, Joe.' She paused. 'Better job, more money. Why not?'

'DUBLIN.' Volume disguised my shock. 'Dublin. Why, Aoife? Why do you want to go there?'

'Why do you think?' She whispered her words into the sand. 'You know why, Joe.'

You know why. You know why. The words crashed into my head. Each thrash from my stepfather's belt carved those same words into weals on my back. Most times I hadn't known why. Just like now. I'd learned to keep quiet, not give my stepfather the satisfaction of seeing me cry. Now Aoife's words lashed.

'What's for me to stay for?' She pulled me round to face her, but I couldn't meet her eyes.

'The gardai were looking for you. A child. Talk to me, Joe.'

I brushed her off, fighting a desire to run.

'It's like you're afraid. Tell me about yourself. Tell me why I should stay. Give me a reason.'

I thrust her fingers off my chest, stood and faced the sea, back turned, hands in fists by my side.

'You always put up a barrier, shut me out like a feral cat. Why don't you trust me? Who are you?' she shouted, her demands a poking finger.

Hide, under the bed, in a cupboard. Not this time. I squeezed my eyes shut and hid in the blackness.

'Don't turn away from me whenever we touch on something important. Is there an us, Joe? Is there? You take but you give nothing. You appeared from nowhere. You've wheedled your way onto the farm so Jack and Mary can't do without you, but we don't know you, none of us do.'

I wheeled around. She sat on the grass, less than an arm's length away, meeting my eyes. 'I am who I am, Aoife, and if you can't accept me then maybe there isn't an us.' My retort not what I wanted to say.

You're a loser, Micky Joe, always a bloody loser. A stepfather's drunken words swarmed in my head leaving little room for Aoife's.

Shut up, I squeezed my head with my hands to strangle the memory.

'I work bloody hard on that farm. Leave me alone and mind your own bloody business.'

'Feck you, Joe Morgan, Joe McCurdy, whoever you are.' She ran to the water's edge and walked off along the damp sand heedless of waves soaking her feet.

Left amidst the debris of our picnic, a kind of anger I'd forgotten transfused my body, inch by inch rebuilding the defensive wall Aoife had breached. I threw the mug she had been drinking from against the rocks. It shattered into pieces.

I wanted to go after her but sank instead onto the sand. She ran, her profile shrinking into the shoreline. Cold gripped my chest. I didn't want to heed the voice telling me I was doing it again – hiding inside myself where no one could reach me.

Mary knew. She took the picnic basket from me and tossed the half-eaten food into the bin. Aoife had gone, her car missing from the yard. A small oil stain left on the ground claimed the space it had occupied.

I grabbed an axe from a hook on the wall and began chopping wood into logs. The battered block had years of cuts etched deep into its surface. I swung the axe in rhythmic strikes, the vibrations shooting up my arm as steel hit wood. I worked until I hurt. My shirt clung, damp and pungent.

Mary brought tea, set the steaming mug beside me and eased herself onto the growing log pile.

'There's a telephone in there. Go on, use it.'

'My old dad used to say, "Never let the sun set on an argument. 'Cos you may never see it rise again." Worked for Jack and me.'

I wiped the moisture from my brow. 'I can't believe you two ever rowed, not like you meant it anyhows.'

'Huh, well we did. Jack was cussed as an old crone when he was younger. Had all the answers. Wouldn't listen to no one. If things went wrong – well, it was never his fault – always the weather or the markets or bad advice. Bad advice, my foot. Pig-headed is what he was and many a time I've had to swallow my words and let him think he was right. That's what loving someone lets you do, Joe.'

'Loving someone – what does that mean?'

'It means folk say things they don't mean, the opposite of what they're trying to say. Sometimes, Joe, you have to trust.'

Trust. I'd learned not all kids had it like me. I used to watch them hug their mothers when they came out of school, wondered how it would feel. Tried it once. Let myself into the empty house as I always did and waited for Mum to come home from work. I ran to her and threw my arms round her waist – she biffed me across the head, told me she was screaming tired and to make myself scarce until bedtime. My stepdad never took me anywhere; other lads went to the football with their dads, holding hands. Soft in the head. The streets were my sanctuary where I knew the rules.

'Go on then. What you waiting for?' Mary tutted. 'The telephone, Joe.' She gave me a little shove. 'I'm agoin' to feed the chickens and when I get back, I want you out of my kitchen, out of my way and off home with a smile on ye face.'

I listened to the dialling tone repeating itself over and over until it switched to voice mail. 'Aoife … I don't know what to say. Don't go. I …' My resolve crumbled. I placed the phone back on its hook and stared out the window where Mary mithered. If you love, you lose. I must finish stacking the logs then give Jack a hand with the cows. Animals were simpler to understand.

I couldn't sleep, replayed the scene like a newsreel, Aoife yelling, walking away, the sea lapping at her ankles. Anger had gone leaving a hole like that of an uprooted tree. Nuala danced in circles round the bed. I rose, pulled on a sweater and sat beside the fire where red embers faded to grey ash, didn't move until fragments of light spread from the horizon.

How long ago? I didn't want to remember. Why did I let my

stepfather get to me that night? Nothing different from the many other nights, ritual abuse heaped on us all. Asleep when my step-dad came home, I was woken by the bawdy singing and the sound of furniture being overturned. Downstairs I found Mum, in her nightdress, holding a cloth to her face trying to stem the blood from a cut above her eye. My stepdad hurled obscenities at us both. Foul words he wouldn't remember using the next day.

'Black eye's what the bitch deserves.'

'Your bloody fault. Drive me to it, bloody loser,' he screamed at me.

I plucked him from where he slumped in a chair, lifted his feet from the ground and threw him across the room. The crack of skull against fender was louder than my mother's squeal.

I sat by his bedside in the hospital not touching the cold hand with its blackened fingernails. Willed my stepfather to die. When he did open his eyes, they were empty, drool seeped from his mouth and the stink of urine and faeces pervaded the hospital room.

It wasn't hard to convince the police it was a drunken accident. They knew my stepdad, had often been called to domestic incidents or picked him up from the streets, bloodied from brawling, the address notorious, the family considered to be troublemakers, the oldest boy already in prison for burglary.

Word on the streets was I was responsible. My stepdad owed money – to lots of people. Now they were coming after me. I fled. Took the night ferry from Liverpool and disappeared into the streets of Belfast.

All this I remembered as I sat in the cooling room of the cottage, borrowed furniture around me. Was my stepdad dead or still helpless as a baby? I searched in vain for a flicker of emotion, something to tell me I cared, to tell me I'd changed.

Nuala stopped dancing, she stood in front of me out of reach.

'Feck you.' Aoife never swore and her words wounded, sharp as a knife cutting off a chicken's head. I screamed, 'I'm protecting you. Protecting you from who I used to be.' Jack, Mary, Aoife, they fogged my brain, clutched with clawing fingers. I'd tried but I'd failed them.

My stepdad's voice. *You're a bloody loser.* The pounding in my head began. Nuala danced again.

Aoife didn't come and as the week ended the weekend stretched like a barren waste. I watched the road even when the tide covered the causeway and I knew she couldn't get across to the island.

'You'm like a cow with sore teats,' Jack taunted. 'Let me tell you, Joe m'lad, if you let that lass slip away, you're dafter than a brush. Loved Aoife since she was a little 'un. Her dad's my cousin a dozen times removed. Never cared much for him and too fond of the drink. Lost her mum real early so she did. But Aoife is a grand lass. Used to come and spend her holidays over here. She ... saved me.' His voice faded.

'Yeah and I'm as much use to her as a cow with sore teats, ain't I? What have I got? Do you know what I own? Do you, Jack? A bloody tin-opener. That's all.'

Jack's eyes accused.

So, you're nothing to me, none of you.

'I'll move your sheep. Put them in the high field. You can't do it, Jack. You could once but not now. Forgotten, have you?' I stomped off as the wind blew cold on my wet face.

Nuala

Nicky chatters while she drives, telling me about the place she's taking me to, who lives there and why I'll like it.

I won't.

'Nuala, you're quiet back there. Not too far. Cheer up. You must be pleased to be away from all those older kids at least.' Nicky temporarily blots out my face in the mirror as she cranes to see me. 'You can make this work.'

Or not. It's like the sudden flash of a torch. From here on in it's up to me. No one will ever mess me around, mess with my head. FUCK THE WORLD. I mouth the words and the girl in the mirror smirks back in approval.

It's a plain semi, half brick, half grey pebbledash. A sagging trampoline sits in the front garden, its netting torn and blowing in the wind like a flag. We wait at the green door next to the pots of dead geraniums. Nicky gives my shoulders a squeeze. She smells like flowers on a summer's day. Children's voices carry from inside and something hits the door with a thump. A woman appears, not disguising the frown which she reinvents as a smile.

'I was expecting you later – oh well, you're here, come in.' She turns to the two children gawping behind her in the hall. 'You two, get lost. Go in the garden or something.

'Give Nuala …. I've got the name right, haven't I?'

Who's she's talking to?

'Give Nuala some peace.'

They go as far as the stair and sit on a step. The boy pulls a face.

It's not like Big-un and Bernie's. These people are not them. I mumble no more than yes and no. It's easy, I'm well practised. I'm not sure they notice.

'Call me what you like,' she says, so I don't call her anything.

She's gross, a roll of fat wobbles around her middle. She puffs pushing a vacuum around. He's big too, a tattoo of a wolf on his arm ripples and snarls as he moves.

I won't eat at mealtimes. They cajole, make something they think I'll like, bribe me like a baby: 'If you eat your dinner you can have pudding, cake, cola.' They sometimes explode, and I've learned to perfect the look that fuels it. 'Well, go hungry then. You'll eat eventually.' I watch them getting angry with each other.

'Leave her. It's tough for her.'

'Fine for you to say, you don't have to cook, see it go in the bin. She wants control.'

'Perhaps she needs to feel in control.'

'Christ, she's still a child.'

A child. Not any more.

The other children, a brother and sister, are much younger than me. 'We are Mum and Dad's real children, you're not,' the little shit of a boy keeps telling me. I don't bother to remember their names. Mealtimes get to be fun.

'If Nuala doesn't have to eat her dinner, why do we?' The girl says it in a whiny voice and her mum bangs the table.

'Eat it.'

The girl pushes her plate away and knocks over her glass of juice. Sticky liquid spreads a dark stain and drips onto the carpet.

Smile, watch and wait.

I don't go hungry. I wait until there's no sound in the house, the television's off and they're all in bed. Quiet is good, I creep downstairs, open the curtains, stand at the French windows and watch the moon hide behind the passing clouds. I think about Big-un and Bernie, pretend I'm a little girl again playing in the woods, making fairy houses. It's the best time. You wouldn't like this garden, Maisie. It's so small, grass, no trees, no birds to chase. Do you miss me? Soon, soon I'll be back. I love you.

Tonight I open a tin of spaghetti hoops and eat them cold with some slices off a chicken from the fridge. I smear some sauce along the work surface and leave the empty tin in the sink, so they'll see I've been there. There's a packet of biscuits, and some cake in a plastic container. Back in my bedroom I hide them for another time. Don't be a baby. Don't let them see you cry. FUCK THE WORLD. It saves me. FUCK THE WORLD, FUCK THE WORLD. The words scream into the space.

I'm getting by. How I want to.

Nicky comes over most weeks. I don't talk to her either. It takes her two hours, she complains of the traffic, doesn't smile much, just looks sad and helpless. The adults huddle in the kitchen with cups of tea. Talking about me. I am causing them trouble. Good, I say.

Nicky's here again. She comes into my bedroom wrapping a big cardigan across her front. 'I think we've seen the last of summer. Can you smell autumn coming?' I stare at her like she's a fly in the jam; watch her stutter while she thinks of what to say next. She sits beside me on the bed, I press against the padded headboard so we're not too close.

'Nuala, I have some news for you.'

I wait. My blood's stopped flowing. Does she want me to get all excited or something?

She twists her ring on her finger, coughs to clear her throat.

'Would you like to see Big-un?'

'What!' I try hard not to look to see if she means it. I squash my pillow against my ribs and shrug like I don't care.

'He remains in hospital, getting better but it will take a long time. We, I,' she waves her hand in a circle, 'think it might help you.'

She dries up when I don't reply. I want to ask questions but I'm not giving in yet.

'Big-un and Bernie want to see you too. We won't be able to stay long because he's not very strong. Would you like to visit him?'

What does she mean? Big-un's not very strong. I've watched him cut down trees and heave great branches off the path, can feel his arms lifting me off the ground when I run to the yard to see him. In case she thinks I haven't heard her I nod. I want to see them, I do, I do, I do.

Look out the window to stop her seeing the smile I can't stop.

Tonight I eat dinner, roast beef. The adults smirk with satisfaction. Let them think it's because of what Nicky's said but I'm hungry and it's tempting.

The kids are bickering.

'When do we go back to school?'

'I want it to be the holidays.'

'I need a new jumper.'

'No, you don't. You can have mine. I need a new jumper.'

They're such babies.

It's raining, jagged streaks slash the window. Big-un and me, we used to stand in the rain and stick out our tongues to catch the drops. Sometimes we'd dance in circles shouting to the sky to make the sun appear again. 'There it is, Nuala. Sneaking from behind the cloud, playing hide and seek.' He'd throw me into the air so I could catch the sun.

Stupid kids, stupid table, stupid house. I'm not hungry.

I run upstairs and let the little squirm of happiness grow inside me.

'Let it work out. Please, please, please.' Anything to make it so.

Joe

Aoife came a week later. I felt her presence before I saw her. I was clearing briars that grew a foot each day, blocking a gateway. The thick new growth grabbed at my face and clothes, scratched my hands and wrists despite wearing gloves.

'Who's fighting who?' she breathed as I ripped a trailing bramble off my sleeve. Not waiting for the reply, she prised open my arms and stepped in clasping her fingers behind my back. I felt her trembling frame, her small breasts pressed against my shirt. I traced the parting of her hair where her head lay on my chest. My arms encircled her, like a precious ornament, something you saw in a shop but mustn't touch for fear of breaking it.

'You haven't gone?'

'No, Joe, I still might unless you kiss me here and now but first put those secateurs aside before you stab me.' Her lips were warm. Desire stirred as her tongue probed. The earthy smell of sweat met the lightness of her perfume. I wanted to crush her, blend her body into mine, each curve, each crevice.

'Ouch.' She pulled her hair from my fingers, her squeal vibrating against my cheek.

I let her go, in the way I'd drop a hot poker. She stumbled backwards. My arms rigid by my side, eyes strafing her startled face. 'Joe, what is it?'

She wasn't screaming. She wasn't yelling for me to hurt her more.

Had I slapped her?

'I hurt you. Don't let me hurt you.' Aoife wiped away my tear. Wind chilled my cheek.

'Joe, you tugged my hair, that's all. I'm not made of porcelain. I won't break.'

I picked up the secateurs and hacked at the attacking bramble.

She struck me between the shoulder blades. 'If you think you can turn away and leave it – well, you can't. You think you're the only one who has had something bad happen. That you've been singled out as the one most allowed to feel sorry for yourself. Look Joe, look around you. At Mary and Jack. At me. Shit happens. Get on with things. Don't let it grind you down. Smile, laugh and … love, even love, Joe.' Aoife gripped the gate, her breath a sob.

I stared at my feet while the surrounding air stilled. I stood in front of her and rolled up my shirtsleeves, each fold stripping time away. Held out my arms, palms showing, fingers quivering.

'What, Joe. What am I looking at?'

She was feigning naivety, mocking me, not seeing. My arms shook, dirt ingrained my fingers and the fissures of my hands. A trickle of blood had dried from a scratch; above my wrists, my skin, brown, paler on the inside but weathered, muscled. My limbs looked like they belonged to someone else. She stared, first at my face then at my arms, stroked a blue vein with her finger, letting it rest on faint scars.

'Why, Joe?'

'Why? The question is as crazy as the act.' I spat the words and saw her flinch as she kept her eyes fastened on me. 'What you're asking is why did I lie, steal, beg on the streets, scavenge food from bins, hurt people, all for a fix. Right, I'll tell you.

'So I could live in a cottonwool house where nothing hurts any more.' I pulled down my sleeves, threw my hand in an encompassing arc. 'That's what this is, Aoife. A cottonwool island where I can pretend the memory of the lovely warm feeling of shooting doesn't exist. Sometimes I think I'll shoot water just to experience it again.'

She turned her head; I noticed for the first time a small mole on her ear lobe. I wanted to touch it.

'And I'm in the way. Is that what you're saying? I've seen addiction, Joe, in my dad, with his benders. It's ugly and selfish. I used to plead with him not to drink. I'd bring him sweets or a cake, trying to bribe him, the bribes of a child. I tried so hard.'

She took my hand, lifted a sleeve and kissed the inside of my elbow.

I held her. We stood by the gate my head resting on hers. The discarded past around my feet.

'I don't think I have the energy to do it again, Joe.'

'Aoife … I'm clean now. For well over a year.' I fumbled to explain. 'If you're an addict you're either clean or dead.'

'And is it forever, Joe?' She held my face between her hands.

I couldn't give her an answer. I twisted free and stepped away. A distant rumble of thunder tremored out at sea and wind, heralding a front, played in the trees and grasses around us. Aoife zipped her jacket.

'You said Jack and Mary … Tell me.'

'They had a son, Joe, their only child. He died. An accident. No one talks about it.'

'The photo on the dresser, I've seen it.'

She nodded. 'It's the only one Jack lets Mary display. Tragic.'

I watched her go. My urge to follow, catch her up, ask her to give me a chance. She'd opened a window and through it I'd glimpsed a gentler self. I needed to hold her, to feel the beat of her heart. I wanted her. The more I struggled against it the more entwined I became like a sheep tangled in brambles. Fear kept me immobile, a fear I knew from before.

It happened not long after I was initiated into the local gang; I saw a pigeon hit by a car. It spun off the headlights and rolled into the gutter. I watched it flap, trying to fly, one wing useless, stretched to the side. I stroked the grey head, eyes black and open wide, its terror pulsing through my fingers. The boys scoffed when I took the bird over to where they sat smoking on the wasteland. I held it for a while feeling it calm then set it apart on top of some bricks. I don't remember who had the idea, but the lads used the pigeon for target practice, picking up stones and throwing them. I sat immobile. 'Jelly Joe,' one of them shouted. 'Jelly Joe's a big girl.' I can see them in a circle chanting. 'Jelly Joe, Jelly Joe.' I found half a brick and flung it at the bird. It fell sideward, its head lolled on the ground. It didn't flap any more. They cheered me, slapped me on the back and got on with smoking their cigarettes.

Who's cheering now? I saw only rush-spiked grassland and Aoife as she reached the rise, a silhouette against the sky. She waved, waited for a moment then descended out of sight.

Nuala

My jeans and a shirt – hoodie? What to wear? All my clothes are black. I like black, I won't wear anything else. Bernie used to call me pretty. Now people say, 'She's so thin,' like being thin is a crime or something. It's a long way, to the hospital, right into Belfast, Nicky says. Never been there before, never been to a hospital except when I fell out of a tree and Bernie suspected I'd broken my wrist.

I want Maisie to be there, but she won't be. Will they bring Rabbit?

I'm in the front seat of the car. Must be a special day.

'Nuala, we're all worried about you – you're unhappy.'

Yeah, so. Today I'm not. I keep my eyes on the lorry in front. The silly question *How did I do?* written in red letters on the tailgate, a telephone number beneath.

'Look, we're taking a chance on this. I said it would be the right thing to do. Others don't think so. I've had to stick my neck out on this one. Do you know what I'm saying? This is not just about you. It's about Big-un too. He had a serious accident, nearly died. Months of rehabilitation to go through. He wants to see you despite the doctors having told him to leave it a while. You must talk to him, Nuala. It will be hard enough.'

Course I'll talk to him. Why is she going on?

I push my hair back and sit straighter.

'This car smells funny.' Nicky beams because I've spoken.

She sniffs. 'Oh, it does. Sorry. I'm used to it. Wet dog.' She laughs. 'I walk her before I come to work. She was soaked this morning – push the towel over the back – I wiped her with it. I expect it whiffs. She's a spaniel, she's black-and-white, her name is …'

94

Stop listening, I want to concentrate on seeing Big-un and Bernie. Why will it be hard? Should I mention his missing leg? Will he know I know about it? Will the stump be disgusting? I don't want to see it. I want them to notice how grown-up I've become. First, I'll hug him then give him the chocolates I've saved up for. Won't tell him about where I live or about the children's home – or Debbie – not yet. I've told no one. I'll ask when I can come home but not blurt it out straight away even though it's the most important thing. Days, a few weeks perhaps – not months – don't let it be months. Please don't let it be months.

Nicky stops talking, puts on the radio so she doesn't have to try any more. It's Adele singing *Someone Like You*. I hate the song.

The hospital is huge. A big orange building towers to the sky. We drive around for ages trying to find a parking place, end up parking on a grass verge where it's not allowed. Nicky fiddles to find the right change for the pay and display machine.

Hurry up. Hurry up.

All the signs confuse Nicky. A man in pyjamas sits in a wheelchair by the main door like he's waiting for a bus or something. People are walking in all directions; a huddle of nurses crowd around a crying woman. We follow arrows along a long corridor. The place smells … clean. Nicky says it's disinfectant, to kill the germs. A man is mopping the floor, we step sideways to avoid the wet floor signs and squash against the wall to let a patient on a trolley pass, someone old and tiny with white wispy hair. I hold on to Nicky's sleeve until we reach the ward.

'Wait while I see if we can go in.' She disappears through swing doors. I want to go to the loo, but I can't see any toilets anywhere. Two women in blue uniforms stop talking to each other to ask me if I'm lost. I shake my head and lick my lips. They smile at me and head off through the same doors. My insides are full of bubbles waiting to escape. I push open one door, a thin crack. More doors and curtains, the sound of coughing. I close it again, lean against the wall and thrum with my fingers.

Big-un is in a side ward. Before we go in Nicky puts her hands on my shoulders. 'Are you all right?' Her hair isn't in a ponytail today, it's curling round her face, touching her shoulders. Her eyes are shiny wet. 'Oh, Nuala.' Her hug is crushing, my heart thumps against hers.

I wish I wasn't here.

The door squeaks when she opens it to let me go through.

'Hello.' A man holds out his arm, the one he can lift, with no tubes attached. But it's not Big-un. It's a man with a shrunken face and thin lips who's lying against a mountain of white pillows. White bedclothes rise in a mound below his waist. 'Come and give me a kiss, let me see you. So big now.'

I can't move, I clutch the box of chocolates. Nicky nudges me. I edge towards his welcoming arm afraid if I touch him, he'll break. He pulls me in and kisses me on the forehead, a smell of soap and old breath.

'Bring a chair over. Bernie's slipped off to buy me some juice. She'll be back soon. It's so good to see you. Better than any medicine.'

It's hard to tell what he's saying; a blue-red scar across his throat creases when he speaks. Where's Nicky? She's gone.

He pats my arm. 'It's a shock, I expect – seeing me in here.'

'Are you feeling better?' Try to remember what people in hospital programmes on television say. 'I've brought chocolates.' Can't look at his face or where his leg should be.

He guesses because he says, 'Do you want to see it or not? I call it Bertie the stump, got used to it now but at first, like you, it scared me to look. Shall we keep him under wraps for now? Wait till he's got trousers on, eh?' He laughs from the belly like he always used to. It is Big-un.

'What happened to you?' I bite my fingers. Shouldn't have asked, shouldn't have reminded him.

When he takes my hand, his is bruised and yellow around a plastic thing held in place with strapping.

'They always want more blood, won't be any left soon. Let's open these chocolates, shall we? You do it. Not much good am I with one hand and one leg? What happened, you ask. I'll tell you what I think happened. Do you remember those scratchy socks Bernie always knits for me? Well, I reckon as how Bertie and Billy here, my two legs, got fed up of wearing them. Don't tell Bernie, will you? I think they hatched a plan so as not to have to wear them any more. I reckon they made it so a whole pile of logs would come tumbling down. Bertie got well and truly squashed. Billy not so clever, he only got himself broken in lots of places. The doctors have pinned him back together and he doesn't know it yet, but he'll still have to wear those scratchy socks and there will be twice as many, 'cos Bertie's not here any more.'

A tear escapes as I giggle. I don't tell him I'm too old for stories.

'Which chocolate do you want? Not caramel – my favourite and as I'm the patient, I get to choose.' He's pulling faces, making me smile.

'I bought them for you.' I take one all the same. The soft strawberry cream is sweet and makes me want more. I select all those with caramel and place them in a line on his bed cover. He winks at me and we chew our way through lots and lots.

'When can you come home? When can I come home?'

His fingers let go of the chocolate he's holding. It rolls off the bed onto the floor. I put it in the bin as Bernie comes through the door.

'Nuala.' She gathers me into her purple cardigan. 'Let me see you,' she says, holding me away from her. She gives me another hug, but I've already seen her wet cheeks.

Bernie has shrunk too, her hair is thinner and grey, her chin's sunk like she's lost her teeth.

'Nuala, come and sit on the bed beside me.' Big-un pats at a space. Bernie stands between me and the chair. I feel squeezed in like a burger in a bun. I'm getting used to how they've changed.

'Nuala, we have something we must tell you.' Big-un wraps his good arm around me. He swallows whatever's stuck in his throat.

I want to run, to find Nicky.

'They won't let me do my job any more, not with one leg.' He hiccups and Bernie hurries round the bed to give him a sip of water.

'We've got to leave the cottage.' He struggles to form the words. 'Move to a bungalow in town somewhere.'

'But you live in the woods. You like trees – not factories and shops and things.' I'm shouting, reminding them because they've forgotten. 'You'll hate town.'

'We can't drive, Nuala. We need to reach the shops, doctors and hospitals.' Bernie is sniffling into her handkerchief.

'I'll be grown-up soon and then I can drive.'

Big-un pulls back my hair and strokes my face. Beyond the room someone is clattering cups and saucers. A head pops round the door. 'Tea? Milk and sugar?' No one answers; it swings shut again. His finger wipes the tears from my cheeks.

'We love you so much. You will come and visit us. You are the special girl we always wanted. We won't be able to look after you properly now. It's what they say. They want to see if we get over the trauma.' Big-un is crying so much I can't hear him; Bernie strokes his head. 'We've tried, Nuala. We really have. We wanted to tell you ourselves.'

My face in his chest. Great wracking sobs howl from a hole deeper than the deepest cave. Their arms hold me tight.

It's Nicky who prises me away, releasing Big-un from my grip. She stumbles with me to the door.

'You knew, didn't you. YOU KNEW.' Lash out, my nails scratching her cheek. I want to hurt.

A nurse is bending over Big-un. He's slipped sideways toward Bernie who's cradling his head.

They've forgotten me.

I won't sit beside Nicky on the way back. We don't talk. I see myself in the rear-view mirror, just snatches, a wavy parting, greasy hair, black smudged eyes. Horrible and ugly.

She draws me back, the girl in the mirror.

You're frightened.

My eyes sting, I pull a face at her.

I'm not. I'm not bothered.

Her eyes are narrow slits, screwed-up with the lie. Her head drops to hide her face.

You're on your bloody own.

She's speaking saying the things Debbie used to say; I can't see her behind my curtain of hair.

Who the fuck ever sticks around for us? Show the shitty world you don't care.

Yeah. Scrape my hair back, look her straight in the eye, stare each other out. It won't be me who blinks first.

You're right. Who the fuck cares about me? A mother – dead. A dad – ditched me like an unwanted pet? First lot of foster parents – can't remember them. Social workers – it's their job. Not the kids in the children's home or disgusting Debbie with her creeping fingers. Not Big … No, don't say their names. Maybe, just maybe … Then I remember, kids like me never get lucky.

At the house the adults huddle around. I shrug them off and they disappear into the kitchen as they always do. I flick through the channels on the television,

'IMBECILES,' I scream the word all the kids in the home used to use. 'FUCKING IMBECILES.'

'Why have you come back? We don't want you – no one does.' It's the boy, standing in front of the television, blocking my view. His sister's there too. 'We don't like you.' He turns, shakes his bottom in my face and farts.

'Get lost.' I throw the remote control at him making him double over as it hits his head.

'Go away. Go away.' He's prancing around chanting, his sister joins in like it's a song. They're giggling. 'Go away. Go away. Go away'. Gob shite lands on my arm.

Lunge. Knock him backwards and sit on him. Smaller than me. Fear bulges his eyes. Squeeze and squeeze, my hands around his neck. Harder. He's choking. Blubbery noises. I don't stop. I bang my forehead on his. Blood spurts.

He's floppy.

A thud. Hands drag me, push me. Onto the floor, face down, my nose jammed into the rug. Hands twisted behind my back, a knee on my thigh.

'GET OFF ME, FUCKING GET OFF ME.' Kick backwards. Keep kicking. Someone pins my legs.

They lift the boy off the floor, fuss over him. He whimpers, baby noises.

The carpet is burning my cheek. I can't move. Red, white and purple lights flash behind my eyes.

'I CAN'T BREATHE.'

I'm back. Nicky's brought me. Driven for ages, the dark hiding us from each other.

Falcon House, the name over the door. Months since I saw those lime green cushions and the purple sofas. They're stark in the empty lounge. It's late and staff I don't recognise take me up-stairs. Not to my old room. They take away my clothes, my belt, the pottery lamp. I know why. Anything I can use. They don't trust me. They give me some water and a tablet to 'settle me'. The pillow smells clean, it's cool to my burning face.

Nicky sits on the bed beside me. 'Nuala, we have to discuss what happened tonight. It was a serious incident. But not now. You need to sleep. I'll come back in the morning.' She's been blubbing; mas-cara's streaked on her cheek. She pulls the quilt around my shoul-ders, pats my head, won't kiss me, but I want her to, like Big-un and Bernie used to.

I'm on my own.

It's dark, monster dark. Blood thuds in my ears. Voices outside my room; the scrape of a chair. When I open the door a member of staff is there, a book across his knee, a beaker of coffee in his hand.

'Have to keep an eye on you tonight. In case … You know …'

Slam the door on him, pull a chair over, jam it under the handle. They'll panic when they can't get in. Let them.

Bite, pick, bite. Virgin skin. Raw. Tear it from round my nails. Blood crazed down yellow walls. Stare into darkness. Nothing.

Joe

'We'm going up to town. You'll manage things here?' Jack lit his pipe.

I looked from one to the other. Mary nodded in agreement, rattling the dishes as she cleared the supper plates.

'I'll take you. It's no problem, make sure the old jalopy gets you there.'

'No, we're going to Galway. We'll spend the night there, find a bed-and-breakfast. A break like. Someone will have to milk the cows.'

Jack never ventured beyond the market in the local town. Mary had never been off the island in all the time I'd been here. 'A dirty weekend away you mean. Good on you, Jack. Keep the lovely lady keen.'

Mary scoffed and pulled my hair. 'Less of your cheek, young 'un. We could teach you a thing or two. Seems like you need to learn an' all.'

She meant Aoife and a frisson of pain twisted in my gut. We chatted when she came over, but were tense with each other, awkward, drifting into the safety of small talk. I wished I hadn't told her, hadn't tried to be honest. Didn't want to lose her. I'd caught Mary glancing at us shaking her head.

'It's business we have to attend to. You make sure the cow shed's spotless by the time we'm back and that sheep, the one with the sore leg, needs more spray on it.'

'I know, I know, proper farmer me. Farmer Joe. Old Art from over yonder called me that the other day when he fetched back his escaped sheep. He asked me how I rated his herd. Dead made-up I was.' I tried to be frivolous to lighten Jack's pensive mood.

Mary flicked me with the tea towel. 'He'll be fine, Jack. Leave him be. Knows what he's about, good with animals at least.'

I filled the truck with fuel, checked the oil, put air in the tyres and even wiped the seats for them.

'Well, look at you.' I held Mary at arm's length. She wore a blue dress with a navy jacket. A small hat perched on her head; round her neck she'd tied a red paisley scarf. 'Men of Galway, watch out is all I can say.' Jack in a double-breasted suit which hung on his diminished frame. He'd fastened the jacket buttons to keep it together and ran a finger round his shirt collar where it chafed his skin.

I helped Mary into the vehicle, 'Aye and my knees are not so good these days.' She'd winced with pain as I lifted her up the high step.

'You take care. Have a good time.' They were small sitting together in the cab. I banged the truck door, so they wouldn't notice my concern, swallowed hard as it bounced off along the rutted track.

I'd almost finished the repairs on the sheds but ran short of sound pieces of wood. Art our neighbour had said he had spare if I wanted to come and collect it. I knew him quite well because of his straying sheep. I struggled to put an age to him but guessed he was younger than Jack. He'd farmed here all his life. 'Where else would I be wanting to go?' Art replied when I asked him if he'd ever yearned to see the world.

I walked over the headland to his farm on the northern side of the island. Art's animals wandered the shoreline picking their way amongst the rocks that would be covered in water by the incoming tide. Behind me I could see the posts of the causeway standing proud. The mainland coastline curved away in the distance as breaking waves foamed into surf.

Art wasn't around. The sheds were empty and only a sow with a dozen squealing piglets greeted me in the open barn. She rooted around in the straw but lay on her side when her young, either hungry or freaked, sought the comfort of her nipples. I leant over the pen and ruffled her ear. 'You've got your work cut out, old girl.' I mimicked her grunt and laughed.

Beyond the house stood a coppice of stunted trees and more sheds; corrugated iron sides had rusted to brown sienna, in harmony with the landscape's palette. I peered through the slats of a shed door feeling like an intruder. Saw a red tractor, its paintwork unscratched but dull. Cobwebs and strands of straw had draped themselves like washing over the bodywork and wheels. 'I'd like to get my hands on you, my beauty. Make my life easier for sure.' I rattled the huge padlock that secured the door, hoping to see more, but it wouldn't budge. In an open adjoining shed an old split-windscreen Morris Minor stood beside a Ford Anglia with its iconic reverse-raked rear window. 'You beauties.' A leather seat sat on the concrete floor beside the open car door.

'Discovered my secret passion, I see.' Art came from behind. 'Them's my ladies, so they are.' He stroked the roof of the green Anglia. 'I understand cars.'

'How are ye?' I pitched my greeting over the noise of the wind as it shook the fabric of the barns. 'You must be tough as old boots to live over this side.' Art was swarthy, his face leathered, and windbeaten. Black eyebrows met in the middle, an underscore to his forehead, one ear mangled and lumpy. Art used to box in his younger days. I could believe it; when I asked him, he'd only put up his fists and pranced around. I wouldn't want to cross him but today his welcome was warm enough.

'Aye, what do you think to this then? An old side-valve engine.' Art lifted the bonnet of the Morris Minor, like a proud dad showing off his offspring. 'Don't make them like that these days.' I was comfortable with engines and we fiddled for half an hour, adjusting the points, sharing the language of cars, lost in the joy of tinkering.

'What's with the tractor next door then? Looks a good 'un. I tell you old Jack could do with it. His ancient thing is always breaking down, should be in a museum. Dunno hows we keep it going.'

Art put aside his spanner, wiped his hands with an oily rag and pulled at each finger in turn making them crack. His hooded eyes were narrow slits, his brows knitted like an uncut hedge.

''Tis his an' all.'

'What!' I whipped round. 'Did you say it is Jack's tractor?'

'Don't go meddling in other folk's business.'

I recoiled at his tone of voice.

'What can I be doin' you for anyway?' Art folded his arms across his chest.

I floundered. 'Wood. You said you had wood ... for the sheds.'

Art inclined his head. 'Round the back of the house but you'll need a trailer. What was you going to do? Carry it?' He buried his head in the engine.

I bit back a retort, but my face burned with the harshness of the slight. 'Right, I'll come back then.' I left Art tinkering. Neither of us said goodbye.

The seasoned slats were perfect for the job, and I collected what was needed later in the day. I stared at the shed with its abandoned tractor, could only guess at a story no one shared. Art stayed out of sight and I didn't care to find him.

The farmyard felt empty without Jack and Mary. No light shone from the window. How were they enjoying Galway?

I collected logs on the way home after milking the cows, breathed in the air, tinged with the departure of winter, detecting a freshness not there before. The rhythm of the seasons, Jack's favourite saying.

Another winter. I watched night clouds humping into swathes and remembered what the garda said about adoption. Hated that Nuala was someone else's now. So wanted her to be happy.

A smell of roast dinner as I pushed at the half-open cottage, the room full of smoke made me cough.

'Joe Morgan, your oven is a disgrace. When did you last clean it?' Aoife wore one of my old shirts, the sleeves rolled to the elbow. The ripped edge where I'd torn it on barbed wire hung to her knees.

'I've never used it.' I couldn't think of a single other thing to say.

'I can't open the windows either. They're so stiff.' She stirred a pan with a red plastic spoon I'd never seen before.

I thumped the frames opening the windows as wide as they would go. Cold air raced in and the fire roared in the chimney. Aoife flapped at the smoke with a cushion like a beleaguered bullfighter. I grabbed her wrists and pushed her onto the sofa, collapsed beside her, kissed her forehead, eyes and nose before our giggles got in the way and we sat clasped together, shivering under a throw while the smoke dispersed.

'Best dinner ever,' I declared, eating the last of the blackberry crumble. I'd found an old tallow candle and set it on a saucer. The firelight provided the back glow and the shadows retreated to the recesses of the room. We'd picked off the charred skin of the chicken and ignored the smoky flavour of the roast vegetables. 'You can always bribe a man with a good meal.' Aoife turned her head, but I saw the quiver of her bottom lip in the candle's flicker.

'God, I'm such a clumsy sod. You told me about your dad – trying to bribe him an' all. I didn't mean ... Aoife, what I mean is ...

I'm glad you are here. This is the best night ever and …' I moved round to where she sat and smoothed her hair, pressing her head against my waist. I crouched, took her face between my hands and wiped away her tear with my finger.

'Please will you stay. I want you to stay.

'Shall we go for a walk?' I stacked the dishes in the sink. 'I often do at night. It's so beautiful in the dark.' She smiled and fetched her coat. The night cold and clear, I took her hand and rubbed her fingers to keep them warm. Stars papered the sky; a new moon carved a sliver of silver. We walked as far as the old church where the ruins formed ethereal sculptures.

'Aoife, I'm scared. Scared this, you, will disappear.' She squeezed my hand and lifted it to her lips.

'You asked me once if I believed in ghosts. I think I do, Joe. Here. Now.' Aoife whispered into the blackness as a single cloud shrouded the moonlight and shadows flitted between the tumbled walls.

I batted at the air, pushing Nuala from my vision, closing my mind to her.

'Not tonight. There are no ghosts tonight, Aoife. Just us.' We scrambled down into the nave of the church, the grass damp and slippery.

'What was it like to be a pilgrim? To have walked miles and to have reached here.' Aoife let go of my hand, lost in imagining.

I pulled up the hood of my jacket like a priest's habit, spread my arms wide. 'Venerable brothers, welcome to my humble island parish. Let us give thanks for your safe journey and may the love of …'

'Stop, Joe. You're giving me goosebumps.' Aoife stood on tiptoe to put her finger across my lips. I clutched her to me, we stood entwined. In the distance the sea boomed against the cliffs.

'Come on. I can't wait any longer.' I kissed Aoife's cold ear. 'Let's go back.'

We were shy with each other, like teenagers making love, cautious, hesitant. I buried my face in the pillow to blur the image of Bridget's distorted face as it danced before me, relived the pain of her nails tearing into my back.

'You won't hurt me, Joe. It's not the first time.' Aoife's voice, not Bridget's. She stroked the back of my head, curling her fingers into my hair. 'Now, Joe.' She snuggled her head into my shoulder and pulled me into her, moving like a warm breeze beneath me.

My hands skimmed across her pale skin, feeling the softness of a breast, the curve of a hip.

'Like music to a song. I didn't know love could be gentle.' I meant the words to be unspoken but Aoife heard them.

'Oh, Joe. I wish I knew where you've come from.'

I pressed my lips on hers, so she wouldn't say more, then pulled away to lie beside her in silence. I didn't want to muck this up. Panic a weight on my chest. What was I feeling? So close to something.

She stroked my arm, drew circles on my chest. We made love again, uncovering secrets, discovering each other.

In the morning, before the light, I woke and lay for a while, hands behind my head, bathing in the warmth of Aoife's sleeping breath. I eased myself from the soft mattress and tucked the quilt around her.

I didn't want tonight to end. I leant over the bed, my finger swept her hair from where it lay across her cheek. Better you never know who I was. I brushed her forehead with a kiss and pulled the door shut as I crept out to milk the cows.

Nuala

'Nuala, babe you're back.' Debbie rushes at me crushing her chest against my face as I sit at the breakfast table. 'I've missed you.'

The force I push her with takes her by surprise. She stumbles against the wall and falls over. The other kids all cheer, egging me on. I jump at her, kick her in the shin. 'If you come anywhere near me, I will tell – tell them what you do, what you did to me, tell them …. Got it?' I kick her again, this time in the ribs. 'Well, have you?'

'Go for it, kid. NUALA. NUALA.' It's a rising refrain.

'What's going on here?' Craig, the home manager, walks in with a plate of toast. He stops in the doorway. Debbie is a cat springing from the floor, her face flushed and blotchy, fingers bent like claws. She hisses in my ear and flounces out the door, knocking the toast from Craig's hand.

'Whoa there, Debbie!' He calls after her then glares, daring us to speak or move. No one does but the titters explode as he leaves the room.

'You told her, kid. Good on you.' The boy with spiky hair and big ears is the first to speak, his mouth full of cereal. I can't remember if he's Keiron or Ted. I pretend it's nothing but feel smug.

A few days later, Nicky arrives, announces she's here to take me to the police station. 'It's about what happened at the foster home. You almost strangled the child.' She doesn't want to be doing this, I can tell. Jams her lips tight, gives me wishy smiles. 'It's a warning, Nuala. You're lucky – this time. I won't always be there to fight for you.'

The room's bare, no pictures or anything, only a table and four chairs. A police officer comes in buttoning his jacket. He's tall, towers above me. Eyes bore into the top of my head; I'm hot, but my hands are cold. I sit on them.

'Hmm,' he says when he takes the seat opposite. He taps his pen three times on the table and tells me to sit up and listen to what he has to say. I shuffle in my seat. There's a bogey poking from his nose.

'… a vicious assault – could have killed the boy. Are you aware of the possible consequences?'

Think of something else. Think. Think of anything. Not Big-un – don't let them see you cry. Don't cry.

'… extenuating circumstances. Won't be pressing charges. Only thanks to your social worker …' He drones on. I watch a daddy-long-legs bashing against the window behind him. It falls exhausted onto the windowsill.

'… grave incident. If there is ever a repeat …' The daddy-long-legs attempts a last escape but its time is up, it crumples in a mess of torn wings beside two dead flies.

It's quiet. I drag my eyes back to the police officer, then to Nicky. She puts her hand over mine and squeezes it.

'Sorry.' I say in a whisper hoping it will shut him up and we can go. They both exhale at the same time. The officer collects his papers. A whiff of something unpleasant floats from his armpit when he stretches across the table and taps his pen again in front of me.

'Be warned, young lady. Be warned.'

I mooch around for a week. Work out Falcon House is the best place to be. It's not so bad, it's safe. There are rules and regular meals. Different staff, some better than others. I don't have to like them all. They don't have to like me.

'I want to stay here. No more fucking foster homes, no more fucking foster parents.' I say this to Nicky. 'I'd rather you bloody send me to Secure.' Her face distorts. She holds the back of her head.

They send me to school. Another school. Secondary school. A school up a long driveway, a jumbled collection of buildings, where all the kids know someone, and no one knows me. After each lesson we change classrooms. Most times I'm lost and late. Somehow that's funny. At break and lunchtimes I'm on my own. Some kids try to be friendly but stop bothering when I shrug and walk off.

There's a group of year 10 girls, three of them, sometimes four. They wear tight trousers, black bras show through white shirts, like they all have to be the same. They're noisy, always fooling, hurl comments at other pupils, usually boys, then huddle together like a pack of dogs. Kelly's the name I hear most. Hair piled on top of her head, she sucks the straggly ends and applies lipstick with a lip brush holding a pocket mirror in her other hand. I saunter close and listen. They're talking *EastEnders* and boy bands. After a while I butt in, 'Justin Bieber's sexy. I wouldn't mind a bit of that ...' I leave it hanging, like Lisa from Falcon House did when she said it. The group stare like I'm an alien or something. I lean against the wall, hands behind my back, breasts thrust forward. The bell goes. 'I'm not going to English. It's bloody rubbish.'

'Ooh, who's a little rebel then?' The one called Kelly says, 'OK, meet you in the shopping mall by Boots in half an hour. I dare you to be there.'

Down the school drive I keep close to the wall, praying no one asks me where I'm going. I know the shopping mall in town but not how to reach it. I hide in my hood and dump my school bag behind a wall on waste land where I can find it later. Each time a car passes, I expect it to stop and a teacher to haul me back to school. I head for the town centre and tag onto people who might be heading for the shops.

The sweet smell of frying doughnuts in the mall makes me hungry. I buy five mini ones in a paper bag and eat them on a bench next to Boots, licking the sugar off my fingers. A woman sits beside me squashing her bags between us. 'My feet are killing me,' she offers. 'Need to sit for a minute.' A security guard walks past and he's looking. 'Yeah, it's hot in here, isn't it?' It's something to say and I hope he thinks she's my mum or something.

'Get you then.' It's Kelly, wearing a scarlet top and high-heeled shoes. I guess her school uniform is in the knitted bag she carries. She kicks at my feet. 'Come on. Things to do.'

'Have a doughnut.' She doesn't want one, so I throw the rest on the ground and follow Kelly into a department store.

'Jesus, you look like a school kid.' We disappear into the toilets. 'Bit of lipstick, eye shadow – loads of it, mascara, liner.' She's so close I smell chewing gum on her breath. 'Yep, getting better. Now the hair.'

'Ouch,' I yelp as she pulls it tight back from my face and scrunches it into a bobble. She flings open the cubicle door. I don't recognise myself in a mirror.

'Wait there.' After a few minutes she comes back with a black jacket. 'Put it on, then walk fast out the shop.' I'm fizzy as a bottle of coke and want to run. 'Act normal,' she squeals at me. We burst from the shop and weave between the shoppers before collapsing in a sniggering heap in a doorway a few streets away. I am so jazzy I want to stay with Kelly forever. In the jacket pocket I find a tissue and a key. I balance them on my palm.

'People are so careless these days,' she says in a teacher kind of voice. 'Leave things lying around in communal fitting rooms where anyone can pick them up.'

'So careless.' I copy her voice. 'No respect for anything.' We dissolve into giggles and I toss the key into a drain.

School's bearable. Skipping afternoon lessons or whole days is easy. If I'm on my own, my favourite place is the top of the multi-storey car park. Few cars, no people. Space, air. The town stretched below and at its edge – trees. Trees make me remember. Sometimes I want to, most times I don't. Sod them I say, but I'm not sure who I mean. I hang out with Kelly and the gang. I filch ciggies from the home, then I'm in.

Nicky keeps asking me how school is going. I tell her what she wants to hear. They've decided to leave me in Falcon House, not find another foster placement.

Hard to place. I tell Kelly how my social worker describes me. A badge I've earned.

'Here we have Nuala, OUT OF CONTROL and HARD TO PLACE.' Kelly presents me to the others, the gang she hangs around with, like I'm a dog at a show or something.

'Why are you back so late, Nuala?' Craig is annoying me with all his questions.

'It's only bloody nine o'clock. What's your problem?'

He shakes his head. 'You're in with the wrong crowd.' He looks sad.

'And?' I challenge him.

'And,' he says, 'you had a visitor. She brought you something. It's on your bed. Waited for a while for you to come back from school but …' He walks into his office leaving me in the hallway to stare at the coat hooks and the picture of the Giant's Causeway hanging at a rakish angle on the wall.

An orange holdall is on the bed. I've not seen it before. I undo the zip inch by inch as if the bag might explode. On top is a card.

And Rabbit lying there in his red trousers staring at me from glass eyes. He is soft and scruffy and mine. Inside I dissolve like a jelly cube. I rub him against my cheek, breathe in gulps of him, sure I can smell Big-un, pine trees and Bernie's soap. I empty the bag, scattering items across the quilt and onto the floor. Books, I've read over and over again, *The Secret Garden*, three Harry Potters, an annual I got at Christmas and a baby book, *The Tiger Who Came to Tea*. I hear Big-un's laugh, big belly laughs that had me laughing when he read it. There are clothes, all too small for me, pyjamas, jeans and my favourite T-shirt with the 'I love London' heart. I open the card.

An address I don't recognise.

Darling Nuala. Come and see us when you're ready. We love you.

My precious belongings deliver their message.

YOU'RE NEVER GOING BACK TO THEM.

I hug Rabbit, pull my pillow round my head, hot and sweating, I thump the bed. I won't cry. I don't care. I don't care. I've moved on. I don't need a pathetic rabbit, fling him across the room, drag the mattress off the bed and upend the base. It crashes against the wardrobe. The castor wheels spin to a stop. I tear the pages from my books wedge by wedge.

Martha, my keyworker, opens the bedroom door.

'Nuala ...' Her eyes flit across the room.

'Hey,' she says, and slides onto the floor beside me.

Joe

All morning I waited for Jack and Mary to return, kept scanning the road, listening for the sound of an engine. 'They should be back. What if it's the truck? How are they going to manage?' I talked to the cows, stroking their coarse flanks. My mind flits between Jack and Mary and my night with Aoife.

She had gone, leaving me in a hurry, worried she would be late for her shift at the tourist office. 'Keep the bed warm,' she'd shouted, car tyres scattering the gravel and panicking the sheep.

I heard the truck before I saw it – the throaty roar of an exhaust with a hole in it – I determined to do a temporary repair this afternoon with some muffler tape.

'Hello, have you had a good time?' I opened the door on the passenger side where Mary sat, wearing the same clothes as yesterday.

'Them big cities. They're fine for a night but I'm pleased as punch to be home. Stop mithering and help me down. Me backside's gone right to sleep; I need a cup of my own tea.' Mary grabbed at me and I helped her inside. She sank into her chair with a long sigh. 'Put the kettle on, lad.'

Jack followed us in. He'd shed his stiff collared shirt, more familiar in his striped pullover. 'How's them cows? Did you get the milk off and remember the sheep? Fed old Meg?'

'Yes, yes. All's good. Haven't burned the place down. Dead easy being a farmer I reckon.'

Jack snorted. 'You'ms in a good mood anyhows. What's brought that about then?'

Could they know about me and Aoife?

'Jack, he's a grown man. Leave him alone.' Mary grinned; I saw her wink.

'We got you sommat, anyway. In the back of the truck. If you're goin' to call yousell a farmer, you need to look like one.' Jack tapped a dottle from his pipe. 'Fetch it in.'

A tarpaulin covered a square shape wedged against the cab. I lifted it curious as to what they'd brought me. Inside a wire cage stood a puppy, its little tail wagging. It stretched on hind legs; a pink tummy visible through the thin black-and-white coat. I grasped the end of the tarpaulin and stared. The little collie tried a practice bark. I put my finger through the mesh, the puppy licked it and whimpered.

'Hello, little lady.' I lifted the dog with one hand. A stream of yellow urine trickled down my arm as it scrabbled against my chest and nuzzled my chin and face.

I carried the small dog into the kitchen, couldn't speak. Words sat lumpen in my throat, my chest tight, pulse racing. I fumbled for a chair. The puppy curled itself into my lap.

'I've never, no one's ever ...' The stuttered words wouldn't form.

'Yeah. Guessed you'd never had a dog before. Treat 'em fairly and them'll be loyal for the rest of thems life. She's yours, lad. Better get training her so you had.'

I swiped at stinging eyes. The harder I tried to quell the tears the faster they came. The tears turned to sobs, erupting from the darkest reaches of my body. Loud, wrenching gulps knotted my shoulders and forced my head into my hands. Jack hovered behind me; the door shut as the old man retreated.

Mary put an arm around my shoulder, pulled me against her and ran her fingers through my hair. 'Them tears have been a long time coming, Joe. Spilt for many a reason I'm guessing. Stored up through the years.'

Her words so softly spoken only made me cry more. 'I'm sorry.'

'Don't be an' all. I'm not one of those who think a man can't cry. You let it come.' She passed me a handkerchief. 'Here, use this, better than your shirt.' She lifted the puppy off my knee and put her down on the rug.

'If Jack 'ad cried things might have been different all these years. I cried enough for the both of us, but I couldn't do his crying for him.'

'Your son?' I remembered what Aoife had said. I pulled a

113

kitchen chair closer for Mary. Her fingers were cold as death as she stroked my hand.

'Aye, Daniel, our son. We lost him – an accident. A long time ago now, Joe.'

'Mary.' My lip trembled, making it difficult to speak. 'I want to tell you something. I had … I had a daughter. I have a daughter – I don't know where she is. Her name is Nuala. Her mother died – from drugs.'

A loud silence. Mary caught her breath and nodded. 'Losing a child, Joe, is to fall into a chasm so deep it has no bottom. You climb up again, eventually, enough so as you see some light, but you never climb clear. It's the worst thing can ever happen. The child will always be your child.'

'That's it though. I didn't lose her.' I spat the words. 'I left her, abandoned her. Five, only five years old, for Christ's sake. I walked out, left her on her own. Callous, selfish, the lowest kind of scum, I deserve all those names. I loathe who I am. She'll not forgive me, and I'll never forgive myself.'

Mary nodded. 'You did wrong, for sure. Poor little mite deserved more, but perhaps it's all you could do at the time. It's easy afterwards, when times be better to know how you could've done things differently. Is it too late to make amends?'

Tears slipped off my chin. 'It is. The garda, he said she would go for adoption. I tried to ring. To tell the social workers where I lived, but I mucked up. I put the phone down when they answered. Couldn't even do that for her.'

'And you're here with us. Like it was meant.' Mary's finger tapped on the back of his hand. 'Me and Jack … You mean a lot to us.'

The puppy lay against my leg, its head resting on my shoe.

'What are you going to call her then? You must give her a name. I'm thinking this dog is already attached to you. You wash your face an all and I'm a goin' to fetch us a drink.' Mary patted me and pushed herself up. From the cupboard she brought two thimble glasses and a half-bottle of brandy.

'Mary, it's not lunchtime yet.'

'So, it's medicinal. Only for emergencies.'

The strong liquid burned my throat but brought life back to my limbs. 'You're the only person I've been able to tell.'

'Aye and it's safe with me.'

'All this because of a dog.' I tickled its ear.

'Aye, well, maybe things sometimes come right. Your life can change in the space of twenty-four hours, in good ways and bad. Maybe it's how it is for you, Joe.' She nudged my shoulder. 'Don't fight it. You can get tired from fighting things all the time. Away and find Jack for me. Send him in. He's got a cough on him like a cow with TB. Leave the pup here.'

Jack wasn't in the yard; I could see him leaning on the gate looking at the sheep.

'Reckon as how that 'un's near her time. We'll have a lamb soon. Better take her inside. She's a first-time ewe. Sometimes they need a bit of help.' Jack acknowledged me without comment.

'Thanks for the dog. I can't believe you travelled all the way to Galway to fetch me a dog.'

'What you say? We didn't go up town for that. Had business to attend to. Dog came from farm near Clifden. Bit of a runt. One ear flops. Have you noticed? No good for showing. Nobody wanted it like. Don't be thinking I'd go spending lots of money on you.' He grunted, his gruffness a disguise. 'I knows well we've not been able to give you much extra since you've been 'ere. Anyways it's yours now.'

'You're all heart, Jack. Soft as toffee. Mary says you're to get yourself inside. You'd better do it too or she'll be after me for not telling you.'

'Bloody woman.' Jack coughed, fighting for breath as he faltered on his way back to the house.

I set the dog a box near the hearth, watched her sleeping, twitching as she dreamed. With the lamp off, I stared into the fire's flames as they rose and fell in orange, red patterns. Guilt, a tumour, clawing from inside. It would never leave. Glad to have told Mary about Nuala, tonight I found a new quiet.

'Millie, Floss, Blue.' I tried a few names. 'Clemmie,' the puppy pricked her ears. 'Okay. Clemmie it is then, Clems for short. Jack says you should be in the kennel with old Meg, but I told him you're too young. Don't you go letting me down and widdle all over the floor.' The dog cocked her head.

She whimpered and whined. Lying listening from the bedroom I tried to ignore her cries, but they only became louder. In the end I gave in and went through; she licked me an enthusiastic welcome. I stroked her soft coat. 'Come on then, don't think you're sleeping with me every night. I guess you're missing your mum, aren't you?' The words knifed me with pain. I saw Nuala shaking Bridget, trying to waken her dead mother.

Clemmie's ear did flop. 'I like it better you're not perfect. Two of a kind we are.' She followed me wherever she could. Quick to learn, she heeded my commands unless a rabbit or a squirrel proved too much of a temptation. Then she would return from the chase, collapse at my feet panting, her tongue pink and wet. Sometimes I made her stay with Mary so she would rest her young legs. She'd lie like a curl beside the fire, her black head with its white line running from forehead to nose resting on her paws. When I returned, she ran to me, worrying around my legs until I lifted her.

'You'm too soft with that dog,' Jack said, but I caught him more than once with Clemmie sleeping on his knee.

Aoife made a fuss of her too. 'Collies are the most intelligent dogs there are,' she said with conviction. 'I think I'm jealous she wins so much of your attention.'

'I'll tickle you behind the ear if you want.' We were lying on the sofa. Mary had given us a cottage pie to eat for supper. 'You can be having it over in your place. Give us some quiet.' She'd never made it obvious she knew Aoife sometimes stayed the night. I knew she'd guessed – and approved.

'Joe, will you come with me to a ceilidh?' Aoife's head lay on my chest. 'I want to show you off, show them what a handsome fella I've bagged.' She tried to make light of it, but underneath her banter I detected an importance.

Her words were like a punch. 'Not really my thing. Never could dance. Besides I couldn't get over and back in time to see to the animals.'

'You could, Joe. I've checked and Jack says a night off would do you good.'

'This sounds like a conspiracy. Do I have a choice?' The idea terrified me. 'All those people, Aoife, and the noise. I have nothing, only work clothes.'

I stroked her hair. 'Okay, I'll come this once.' I couldn't believe I'd agreed.

She held my hand and whispered, 'Thanks, Joe.'

Alone with the sheep that night, tiredness and cold wrapped around me. A ewe struggled to give birth. Through the night she'd weakened and by the time I pulled her large lamb from her she no longer had the strength to attend to it. She attempted to rise and lick it but collapsed into the straw. I held the lamb close to keep it warm, its plaintiff bleats hushed in my coat. I stayed in the pen until the ewe

116

died, not wanting it to be alone. Jack had told me before: *A commodity. How you have to think of them. Can't afford to be sentimental about the animals.*

I'd laughed at him. 'I suppose it's why you call all the cows by name, is it?'

I doused the lamb with the birth fluids from an older ewe who'd lost one of her own. At first, she showed no interest until the lamb nuzzled close seeking sustenance and security. My spirits lifted when as dawn came, I found the two lying close, the black nose of the lamb tucked into the ewe's soft belly.

I walked home across fields wet after the stinging rain. The island's peaty breath clung to my clothes and formed droplets of moisture in my hair. The lambing nearly over for another year, only a handful of ewes left to deliver. Clemmie waited for me, barked a greeting as I opened the door. She was growing fast, hated being left behind. I ran a hand across her soft coat and surrendered to wild licks.

'Not a good night, Clemmie. Can I ever make a fist of this? What should I have done to save her?' Clemmie curled in a ball at my feet and listened.

'Aye, it's the way it goes sometimes, lad.' Jack and I were scrutinising the flock the next morning. 'Sheep have one ambition in life and that's to die. Don't always seem there's a reason. You did well with the lamb, Joe. The old ewe was a dab hand at being a mum. Reckon this was the last chance she had.'

I'd coped with the lambing almost single handed. Jack wanted to be there but the pain in his joints made him slow to rise from his bed and his rasping breath turned his lips blue with effort.

'He's not so good today.' Mary would say and I saw her anxiety as she hovered over him.

'You take care of yourself too. This winter will soon be over, we'll feel better with the spring weather.' I tried to raise their spirits, Mary shrivelling into herself, her back ever more bent. She rubbed her hip; I filled a hot water bottle and tucked it in where she sat beside the stove.

'Okay, no excuses. Look what I've bought you.' Aoife passed me a bag. A new shirt. Plain black and fitted. 'Wow, how handsome are you?' she said as I tried it on. 'Will you be letting me trim your hair and then you'll be ready to take the mainland by storm? I'll have to hang onto you.'

She hadn't though. I sat at a table watching Aoife swirling round the floor. She didn't want to miss a dance. 'I'm sitting this one out,' I begged, hot and awkward. She introduced me to her friends – she knew everyone. The names and faces blurred into one another. A cloying smell of bodies mingled with beer as the evening progressed. The music loud, made louder by people clapping and stomping their feet. The laughter, the jokes parried back and forth.

'I need fresh air. I'm going outside,' I shouted into her ear as she waved, so pretty in her short dress, her hair loose on her shoulders. I smelt the cannabis. It enveloped me with its sweet smell. I moved away from the crowd by the door, crossed the road, sat on a bench and rolled a cigarette, inhaled the tobacco smell, concentrated on each pull, letting the smoke curl from my nostrils.

'Here you are. What's wrong?' Aoife took my hand.

'Did you smell it?'

'What, smell what?'

'Weed, grass, ganga, whatever you call it here.'

Aoife stared into the distance. 'They're idiots, Joe. It's around. You don't have to join in.'

She snuggled close to me, the warmth of the dance on her hair.

'You go in, Aoife. I'll stay here for a while. Guess I'm not used to crowds any more. I'll come back in soon.'

She planted a kiss on my nose and for a moment was lit by the light of the hall as she pushed open the door.

I sat in the cold, my breathing returned to normal, the briny scent of the sea taking the place of fear. This is what she wants, what she deserves. Fun, company, a life. Not something I can offer her.

The island was blocked from view by a hill, but I wanted to be there amongst the restless cows, the earthy smell of warm straw. I took a deep breath and went back inside to Aoife and her friends.

Nuala

A hand bangs into my back as I loiter in the school corridor between lessons.

'Saw you slinking out of school the other day. Been doing it for months, haven't you?'

It's Ted from Falcon fucking House. His spots aren't as angry today and there are no white volcanoes erupting on his nose.

'Spotty! Do you come to this school? Since when?' I pretend I don't know. Ted is a pussy cat. Calling him Spotty makes his face burn. Big Ears is his other name.

He's plucking at his face. 'Where do you go?'

'What's it to you? Mind your own business anyway.'

'I won't tell. Wondered if … if I can come with you sometime.'

'You.' I look him up and down. He's not much taller than me and skinny. His shirt is out of his trousers, his tie askew, hands in pockets.

'I don't think so. The others wouldn't want *you* hanging around.' I sniff, hoping he'll get lost. Not cool to be seen talking to him.

'Just the two of us then. Catch a train, go to the coast.' His face is turning red and damp hair curls over his ear.

'You're joking, right.' I head off to the recreation area.

Go to the coast. All the next lesson it buzzes in my head. Bloody Ted has done my head in. I'm off.

The High Street is crawling with the unemployed, old women pulling trolleys or winos hogging all the seats in the mall. I lift a black lipstick and nail varnish, hoop earrings and a gift pack of thongs – under special offer — from shops so easy to steal from it's almost our duty to do it.

'You're bloody good at it,' Kelly says. I find them loitering behind the cinema and I show them my haul of goodies.

'Hey, Paddy.' I'm on a guy's knee, my arm draped round his neck. We call him Paddy even though he's English not Irish. 'Swop you these cans of beer for some weed.'

'And what else will you give me, darling?' I flick his fingers from where they're hooking themselves under my bra strap.

'Whatever you want, Paddy,' He gives me a love bite on my neck, strokes my breast like I'm a cat. When I've had enough of his smelly breath, I squeeze him between the legs.

'Weed, Paddy. Payment time.' I toss him some cans of beer and he gives me a foil twist from his jacket pocket. His hand slinks up my thigh. 'Yeah. Yeah. Later possibly. If you play your cards right.'

I roll up, like Kelly taught me, take a long drag and curl away with the smoke.

'I love you lot.' I beam at all of them lounged against the wall. 'Family. You're my family.'

'Huh, we're more than that.' Paddy works on a building site; he's always throwing dosh around. 'You can rely on us. Families stink.' I link my arm through his.

'Weed's good.' I breathe.

'You need to lose your virginity, Nuala. Let 'em have it,' Kelly said straightening her skirt. Robbo, draped all over her, pants like a hungry puppy.

'Don't you think I already have?' She's got to buy it. 'Think you're the only one they fancy? Give us another can.'

I want to do it. I'm scared as hell. I want to be like them.

Sometimes I'm not, like them I mean. A while ago I found a bag of books dumped with some clothes in the doorway of a charity shop. I grabbed them, took them to where the gang meet. *I'll Give You the Sun* by Jandy Nelson, the first book I pulled out. Jandy, nice name. Jazzy cover. I read. Nothing else to do. No one around. I used to love reading. A pain below my ribs, Big-un coming back from town, always with a new book for me, popped into a paper bag with handles.

'You swot. What you doin'?' Donnah and her sister, from the gang, stare at me.

'Something you've never learned to do.' I'd slammed the book shut and walked off, their jeers behind me. Next day I found they'd used the books to light a fire. I kicked the pile of white ash into the air.

*

'You ever been to the coast, Debs? The coast round here I mean. God, where is everyone today?'

Debbie shapes her fingers into quotation marks. 'Doing paperwork, so please don't disturb us.'

Since we had the fight, we're almost friends, Debbie and me.

'You're okay,' she told me once.

'Thanks,' I'd said, but in a couldn't-care-less way. I watch her in case she starts anything.

'I've run away a few times but not to the friggin' coast.'

Debbie's listening to music, her phone cupped in her hand, she's gyrating in front of the fireplace. 'Run away dozens of times. It's good. Six days in Belfast I had once. They bring you back. The cops. Give you a lecture. It's worth it though. You can get anything in Belfast, anything you want.' She's pretending to smoke. 'Know what I mean?'

'Yeah, course I know. About weed and that but what about other things?'

She smirks and takes the earpiece from her ear.

'What a dumb question. Ask your mate Kelly. She thinks she's so big. How old are you? Fifteen. You think you're smart. Well you're not. You're an innocent. Anyway, I'm off soon, got a flat.'

'Yeah. Yeah. Yeah. You're always saying it.'

'Well, this time it's true.'

'What's different this time?'

I sing the words of the song coming from her phone.

She grins. 'This is what's different this time.' She lifts her shirt, pushes down the waist band of her trousers and rubs her skin.

There's a just visible swell of her abdomen.

'See what I mean. Fifteen but an innocent.' She taps the side of her nose. 'Play the system, babe. Learn from me.'

'But aren't you a lezbo.'

'Oh, grow up.' Debbie flops on the couch and turns the telly on.

In bed my hand circles my abdomen. I feel the ache between my legs. What's it like, fucking, making a baby, having it in there – growing?

'I'd never give my baby away.' I want to be Debbie.

'You said you wanted to go to the coast.' I catch Ted on the way home from school. 'Well, I'm game if you are, before you leave school and all. This weekend? What do you say? Up for it?'

He's looking at me like he's never seen me before.

'You've forgotten, haven't you? Forgotten you said it. It's not that long ago. Sorry I spoke. Creep.' I march ahead. I don't want him to see my flaming face.

'I'm up for it, Nuala.' He runs after me, grabs my arm. 'You took me by surprise, that's all.'

He's way bigger than me now. 'When did you get so tall?'

'In all the time you've been ignoring me,' he says. 'I've grown into my ears too.' I'm mortified he remembers my cruel jibes. But he's laughing. He pushes me in the shoulder, I push him back.

'Let's not tell anyone. Let's just go. It'll be more fun.'

He cocks his head. 'If it's what you want. Our secret.' He high-fives me and I redden again.

The sun is a line on my wall when I wake. I bend my pillow over my head and turn over – then I remember. Ted and me. It's today. I run my hands down my body feeling the contours, the curves and the shiver between my thighs. What will it feel like if it's Ted's hands? I jump into the shower and let the water stream over me washing away the wetness.

We catch a train to Carrickfergus. Ted's cool. He's had his hair cut, wearing clean jeans and a grey T-shirt with a black sweatshirt slung over his back. I giggle. 'Look at you. Anyone would think you're on a date or something.' I toss him a piece of chewing gum from a half-empty packet in my pocket. He catches it and turns it over in his hand like he wants to say something.

'I bought this,' he's fingering the sweatshirt, 'in a charity shop this week.'

'What! You were done. Did they pay you to take it away?' His head drops, and I wish I hadn't said it. 'Sorry, a joke. It's nice. I feel funny, us doing this like.'

'Yeah. Me too.' He grins, and I see his front tooth crosses over the other one. I grin back.

We reach the coast. I grab Ted's hand and we run to the prom-enade and onto the beach. There's the sea, shades of navy blue, white-tipped waves frothing up the sand.

'The sea. Freedom.' My arms spread wide; my words dissolve in the wind.

'Did you used to live by the sea – you know – before you came into care?' Ted says, kicking at stones on the beach. I pull a face at him.

He spreads his sweatshirt on the sand, and we sit on it. My thigh against his.

'You're not like the others, are you?' I say.

'What do you mean?'

A seagull struts close making patterns with its feet.

'Sometimes I dream I'm a bird. I can fly, fly to England or Africa or wherever birds go. Somewhere ... where I can start again. Be a different me. Know what I mean.' I squint to see if he's laughing.

He twirls a piece of my hair in his fingers and scares the gull away, but it comes back. 'They attack people sometimes, steal food. Aggressive.'

'That's it. That's what I mean. You're different, not aggressive like the other guys, and the girls at Falcon House. They all have bloody chips the size of houses on their shoulders. Like they're owed something because they're in fucking care.'

'Why do you speak like that?'

'Oh, for Christ's sake.'

He throws a pebble towards the sea. It rolls onto the wet sand. 'You sound like Debbie. She's a moron.'

'Not just a moron but a ...' I stop, pregnant moron fading, before I say it. 'Let's bin her today, shall we?' I swallow the lump in my throat.

'I've only been to the sea once. At least only once I can remember. The best day of my life.' I didn't mean to say it, feels like I've been sick, spewed up over the beach. Ted says nothing, he scoops sand and lets it run through his fingers.

'My dad took me. He's a shit. Sorry, shouldn't use those words in front of Mr Goody-Goody, should I?' Why am I being such a prat? Shut it.

'Is that why you're in care, 'cos he's a shit?'

'I suppose so. Okay, you asked. My mum and dad were druggies. I don't remember them. My mum overdosed and died. My dad freaked out and abandoned me. Foster homes didn't ... didn't work. I tried to strangle a kid and I ended up in a children's home. Right, got it. Anything else you want to know?' Try to hit him but he throws his arm.

'I'm off.' Grab my shoes and walk towards the town, kicking the sand, wanting to cry when I stub my toe on a buried rock. At the sea wall I brush the sand off my feet. Ted is where I left him, his head on his knees. Cloud shadows streak towards the horizon. On the water a sailing boat wheels round and the sail goes limp.

Ted is behind me, I can feel him, not see him. 'My mother was a psycho. My gran brought me up. She died when I was a wee boy of nine – given up for adoption, but no one wanted me. Ugly, weedy and I wet the bed! After a while I didn't want to go anywhere else, so I stayed in the kid's home. It's a bloody shitty world, isn't it?' I twist round to look. His face is mottled, he lifts his eyebrows like he's waiting for an answer and the dimple in his cheek twitches.

'Ugh, grim. Parents seem in short supply – at least round here.' I laugh first or is it him who starts it? We can't stop.

A boy on a red bike halts to stare at us, his stabilisers making him wobble to one side. 'Look, Mummy.' His mum smiles at us. 'Yes, they're having fun.' She gives him a push in the back, and they go on.

'I want an ice cream. No, I need an ice cream,' Ted declares, his tongue as long as a thirsty dog's. It starts me laughing all over again.

We've only got enough money for one ice cream, so we lick it in turns and wander towards the castle. It's greyed over, drizzling. We huddle in the shelter of the old stone wall, stare at the sea and track a ship on the horizon.

Ted asks, 'What do you want to do when you leave school?'

'I don't know. Never thought about it. Nothing I suppose.'

'What do you mean nothing? You can't do nothing.' His face is so close I can see myself reflected in his eyes.

'So, what are you going to do?' I want him to stop looking at me.

'Join the navy.'

'You're only saying it because we're watching a ship.'

'No, I'm not. I decided ages ago. Been down the recruitment place and everything. It's why I don't mess in school.'

I want to say something, but his words have jammed in my throat. I don't want him to go away.

Ted puts his hand on top of mine. It's warm, mine's cold. 'Five years from now, where will you be? I might need to find you.'

'In a flat with a kid.' It sounds hollow.

He lets go my hand and clasps his knees. 'You're kidding me!' He pulls a blade of grass between his fingers. 'That's kind of sad. Not what I supposed you'd come up with.'

Anger is a bubble inside me, I swallow hard to keep it in. 'Yeah, well, now you know I'm useless. Cheers for the lecture.' Tears threaten to surface; I want to run. Instead I shove a fist into his chest, push him backwards onto the grass, stick my hand down the front of his trousers and squeeze. I feel him go hard. I wriggle on top of him. He's lying there with his eyes wide open, like he's in shock. Shit, what to do next. I pull my shirt over my head and unclip my bra. The air is cold on my skin and I lean onto him to hide my breasts. My mouth is on his, I kiss him, crushing his lips against his teeth.

'You don't have to do this.' He splutters and holds me away from him.

'I do, I want to. And you do.' I kiss him hard again.

His hesitant, wandering hand is so good; I put my nipple to his mouth. We fumble with clothes in gasps and pauses. He pushes, pushes. My fingers dig into his back, my scream stifled against his shoulder. The pain slices me in two. He doesn't stop until he's spent, his head in my neck, his back arching in what sounds like sobs.

We don't speak until we're dressed again. I'm shivering, though I'm not cold, I can't stop, like a rag doll being shaken.

'You should have told me,' he says. 'You should have said you were a …' He runs his fingers through his hair.

I'm sore, mad with disappointment. 'Someone had to do it. I chose you. Don't make a big deal of it. Wrong. You are like all the other guys. Gagging for it, weren't you? Weren't you?' I hate my sneer, I feel cheap. I want him to answer, to hit me, to walk away. Anything so I can't see the hurt.

In the gloomy station a man with a black dog squats on a dirty blanket and asks for change. We ignore him. Our hands brush as we walk along the platform, spring apart like we've been shot. I stare at the shiny rails and wonder what it must be like to jump.

We're in the carriage. I stare out the window, the trees, the fields are a blur.

'Nuala, I don't think you're useless. I like you.' He says it so softly I think it's only in my head.

'Lucky for you then no one likes me for long. You'll get over it.' I drum my fingers on the table like I don't care – except I do. 'I only asked you to come today because I wanted to … and we did, didn't we – and you're going to tell me, and the whole world, it was crap.'

'Nuala, shut up being such an arsehole. I'm not going to tell anyone. Remember – "our secret". What you said.'

When we get back, it's dark.

'Wondering where you two were.' A member of staff smirks in the corridor, his hands in his pocket. 'There's supper in the kitchen unless of course you're not hungry.' I run up the stairs. Ted touches my arm as I reach my room.

125

'It wasn't crap. Neither are you.' He makes off before I can shoot another arrow.

Behind my door I slide to the floor. I want to cry but I smile instead and hug my knees like they're Ted.

Joe

'I can't fix the bloody thing.' I burst into the warm kitchen letting in blasts of icy air. 'It's fucked.' I rubbed my fingers and stuck them under my armpits to try and get some feeling back. 'All day I've been out there and there's nothing, not a bloody spark. The tractor's knackered, Jack. Completely and utterly knackered.' I thumped the table, the dishes rattled. 'Knackered, Jack. I can't fix it and the cows need the hay – not tomorrow or next week. Today.'

'Joe.' Mary's voice held a warning.

'No, don't shut me up. I can't do it any more. I waste hours coaxing the bloody thing into life – well, no more. It's dead, Jack, finally dead.'

Mary handed me a mug of tea and I warmed my fingers, clenching and unclenching my fists as the blood returned.

Jack coughed, a loose wracking cough, hawked phlegm into his handkerchief and struggled to relight his pipe, the flaming match wavering in his shaking hand.

'You're not listening, are you? Look, I don't know what it's all about because no one will bloody tell me anything but there's a tractor over at Art's, locked in a shed. He says it's yours, Jack. If it's true, then let's fucking well fetch it and use it. Makes no sense …'

'Shut your mouth. Don't you ever mention that again. Do you hear me? Not ever.' Jack clutched at his shirt as he fought for breath. He pushed his chair back, so it toppled against the dresser, fumbled as he opened the outside door, kicking at its base. He disappeared into the late afternoon dark.

'Jack, you can't … Joe, stop him,' Mary pleaded.

I gripped the edge of the table, shaking my head. 'Stupid bugger.

What's with the bloody man?'

Mary's hands covered her face.

'Give him a minute, Mary. I'll find him. Give us both a chance to calm down.' I wrapped an arm round her and eased her into a chair.

'He can't ever …' Her crying became a wail and she rocked backwards and forwards. 'Go and find him. He'll catch his death.'

I headed for the barn. The increasing wind drove banks of cloud across the sky.

'Get out of my sight,' Jack shouted when I approached him.

'You are a stubborn bastard, Jack O'Shea. Bloody well freeze to death if that's what you want.'

I left him on his own. I'd see if I could borrow Art's machine for tonight. I walked the couple of kilometres along the track, shoulders tense, hands thrust into pockets, my breath a white cloud in front of my face. I didn't want to dwell on what had happened back there – the angry words and accusations.

In a moonless dark I reached the north shore and saw the shape of Art's buildings. 'Art, can I borrow your tractor? I need to shift bales of hay to feed the cows. Can't get ours started this time. It's a goner for sure.'

'Ugh, reckon so. Shan't be needing it till tomorrow. It's in the yard.' Art taciturn to the point of rudeness, but I knew him well enough.

'Was Jack always such a stubborn bugger?' I waved his arm to where Jack's other tractor remained locked away. 'I told him we need to fetch it, get it going. He went mental. He's got a right paddy on him which is fine, but the animals still need feeding.' My short laugh withered under Art's scowl. 'I'll bring yours back first thing. Thanks.'

I drove Art's tractor back along the tracks. The throaty throb of the engine and the rhythmic riding of the ruts allowed time and familiarity to soothe my temper. From the cab the rolling topography of the island thrust upwards into the high cliffs at its point. The sea lay like a scarf, a darker shade of black than the sky.

Oh, Jack. What are we going to do? We must do something. I'll try again tomorrow, give the old tractor another try.

Late before I shifted the hay, the physical effort of forking it into the troughs tightened muscles but didn't stop my mind whirling. I'd crossed a line. The knowledge niggled away, accused like a dirty, wagging finger. 'But what line? No one talks about it. Talks about what?' I shouted to the roof rafters. 'Jack, Mary, Aoife, Art, you're all the same. You shut me out. Buggered if I care.'

I'll leave Jack and Mary alone tonight. They won't want to see me, and I don't much want Jack's company either. 'We'll sort it tomorrow.' I threw the words across the yard to where a strip of dim light showed between their closed curtains and whistled to Clemmie. The temperature had dropped further; there would be snow on the mainland hills.

After a bite to eat I dozed off in the warm room. Clemmie's bark roused me.

'Joe, Joe.' I wasn't sure if I'd imagined the voice or the knocking.

'Joe, open the door.' Out of my chair, I grappled for the door handle.

'Mary, for God's sake what are you doing here on a night like this?'

I lifted her into the cottage and pulled a chair nearer the fire.

'It's Jack.' Mary's voice a squeak. She shivered; moisture glistened on her hat-less head. 'He's not come back.'

'Jack. Not come back. Where's he gone? Here, let's wrap this blanket round you. Where's he gone, Mary?' I took Mary's hands and warmed them between my own.

'At supper, he never spoke, kept watching the door. Ate nothing. Afterwards he said, "I'm going out."'

'I begged him not to.'

'Christ, it's freezing.' I threw back the curtains, peering through the window into the darkness. Dread, like an icy finger contracted my stomach, nausea gagged in my throat.

'He'll be with the cows, Mary. I'll find him, silly old fool. Gone to sleep, I warrant. Soon have him back in the warm.' The words belied my panic.

'You upset him, Joe. He is a stubborn old fool, but you shouldn't have said the things you did.'

I donned a coat. 'Mary, I'll find him, he won't have gone far. I'll put it right with him.' I kissed her on the forehead, trying to reassure. 'You stay here by the fire.' Wind fanned the flames when cold air swept through the opened door.

Mary struggled to her feet. 'I need to wait at home. Be there for him.'

I wanted to run ahead but didn't dare leave Mary to make her own way back. She stumbled, would have fallen several times if I hadn't held her arm. 'How did you ever make it over here?' The

129

question more to myself than to her.

'Because I had to.' Mary stopped to catch her breath. 'I couldn't find him.'

The emptiness of the farmhouse kitchen, bright after the dark of the night but devoid of its usual occupants leered at me.

'Go, Joe. Be quick.' Mary shooed me off and sank into her chair.

Jack wasn't with the animals. The sheep bedded down, the lambs bleating. The cows stomped around, the heat from their bodies filling the shed with a comforting odour.

'Jack, Jack.' The hens flew off their roosting spars as I threw open doors shouting ever more loudly. 'Answer me, you stubborn bugger.' He'd be by the hay.

You'd better not be trying to shift it. But Art's tractor stood silent and cold.

I ran to the gate where Jack loved to stand musing over the fields. 'JACK.' Nothing. He's fallen, ricked his ankle or something, but I couldn't dispel pictures of Jack struggling for breath, his lips blue, his shoulders heaving.

He wasn't in any of the obvious places.

Mary had opened the curtains and dragged a chair over to the window. I burst indoors. 'We need help. I can't find him either. I'll phone around.'

'Wait, Joe. There's a place we haven't looked.' Tears streaked Mary's face; she didn't try to halt them. 'With the tractor, the one locked away in Art's shed. He hasn't gone there for years but he used to – at first – after it happened.'

'Why, why there?' Mary's face told me it was not the time for answers. 'I'll ring Art.'

'No. You go. He'd rather it be you.' Mary put an old coat and a plaid scarf over my arm. 'Take him these. He's not much good at emotion, Joe, but underneath all his grumpiness he's come to think the world of you.'

I couldn't reply, gave Mary a quick hug and ran out the door. For the second time I ran over to Art's, this time taking the shortest route across the fields. I tripped over clods of earth, paid no heed as water squelched into my boots where the low ground had turned into winter bog. The coat I carried was a hindrance, but I clung on to it. Instead of running upstream and crossing by the plank bridge, I leapt the ditch, my lungs begged for me to stop. The pain in my side doubled me over. I closed my eyes against the dizziness, saw only the image of Jack earlier in the evening, trying to light his pipe.

I heard the thunder of the waves as they hit the rocks on the far beach.

'Hang on, Jack. I'm coming.'

The shed door was closed but the padlock gone.

'Jack, Jack,' I called into the pitch black. The tractor stood large and forbidding. I eased my way around it as I struggled to see in the gloom. My legs bumped against piles of wood and bits of machinery. I should have brought a torch.

Jack wasn't there.

'JACK.' My cry a sob and a shriek. I leant against the cold metal of the tractor guard. Where else? Not the sea. Jack wouldn't go near the sea. He knew the tides. Bog pools, the old church? But why? Jack never strayed from the farm.

The cemetery – of course. Hadn't Aoife said they had lost their little boy, their son. I knew of its location, had only been the once, a hillside above the causeway. Aoife and I joked it had the best view in the world, if you were dead you couldn't be dead in a better place. We'd laughed because then it didn't matter.

The wind opened the barn door a fraction letting in a slatted streak of patterned moonlight. I mounted the tractor steps wanting a quick peek inside the cab. This is a decent tractor. Between us we'd get it going.

Jack sat in the cab slumped sideways on the seat, his head, thrown back, rested on the far door. 'Jack. What are you doing, man?'

I knew he was dead.

Freeze to death if you want. The memory of my own fiercely spoken words rebounded.

I'd done this. I'd killed him.

Moonlight like striped wallpaper played on Jack's face putting a brightness in his eyes. He stared at the roof of the cab. I yanked open the door and leant in. Jack's body shifted into the space. A loose rope tied in a crude noose fell from his hand.

'No, Jack, no. What were you going to do?'

I leaned across letting my head rest on Jack's hip, smelling the farm, the animals, tobacco, Jack. I wanted to stay here, like this, forever. To leave Mary in the time between, the time of not knowing.

She didn't need to learn about the rope, no one needed to. I pulled it from where it lay on the floor of the cab.

'Our secret,' I whispered, pulling Jack upright in the seat, straightening his clothes and wiping his mouth. I placed his cold hands on the steering wheel and closed the old man's eyes.

The rope I coiled in the far corner of the shed and ran.

'Art.' My yell spliced through the darkness.

Nuala

'What's it like being pregnant? How can you tell for sure?' Debbie's in a good mood, she usually sighs like I'm not worth talking to. I want to ask loads. She's mooning around in tight leggings and a crop top, so everyone can see her belly. 'Who's the dad? What did he say?' Sometimes she's plain scared.

I'm obsessed. A week ago, I woke in a frenzy of dreaming. The streetlight had turned my room orange, I blinked myself awake feeling warm and special. Why? Something nice. Ted and me. Then brighter than a flash. We'd made a baby. I'd jumped up and pushed back the curtains searching the sky like it might be written in capital letters. I hoped, pleaded, even prayed more than anyone else in the whole wide world for it to be true.

It is true. It's sinking in, occupying every fold, every inch of my body. In bed at night I stroke my abdomen, singing songs beneath the sheets, rubbing between my legs until I come. Should I do that now? Who can I ask? Think about it constantly, glow inside, there's somebody in there who's all mine, growing bigger all the time.

Four days late. Debbie says your breasts get big and sore. Prod mine each morning. They're sore for sure. In the mirror they look bigger.

Shall I tell her, or should I tell Kelly first?

Ted's exams are over, and he's left school. We're shy together. He winks at me across the lounge in the home if we're watching telly; he's thinking about it too.

'Ted, guess what?' We're the last ones to go to bed tonight.

'What?'

I grin at him and kiss him quickly. 'Nothing. Nothing, it doesn't matter. Tell you soon.'

Five days late, then six. My breasts *are* sore.

Rain on the window wakens me. Thunder grumbles like a train. No. No, NO. The familiar cramp. Hug your knees, stop it being true. Worse cramps crease me in two. I'm wet. There are spots of blood, bright red fucking blood on the sheets. Blobs of nothing.

I don't get up in the morning and Martha who's on duty comes in to check on me. 'Poor you. Period pains are rotten, aren't they? I'll sort you a hot water bottle.' She brings it wrapped in a teddy bear cover and hands me two paracetamol and a glass of water. 'Hey, what's the matter?' A tissue brushes across my wet cheek. 'You'll feel better soon. Stay in bed until the pain goes off.' I sob into my pillow, squeezing the sheet into my fist, a hole as wide as an ocean inside me.

Everybody's fucking pregnant. Women in the street, in shops, in cafés. Holding hands with their partners like they fucking deserve a medal; or pushing a toddler in a pushchair to prove it's not a fluke. They clutch their abdomens – do they think it'll drop out? I want to punch them, right in the guts, see them keel over, watch their faces as blood drips onto the pavement.

'Would you like to go the cinema?' Ted's asking. 'Or for an ice cream, just talk if you want?'

'Nah. No thanks. Too busy.' He knows I'm not. He asked me to go for a walk one time before. We walked beside a stream, through the woods. I couldn't hack it. Felt awkward. I don't want to do it again.

'I have something to tell you. I've been accepted into the navy.' His voice rises as he tells me; he's waiting for me to be pleased, to tell him how fantastic it is. 'I have to go to England, Cornwall. Ten-weeks initial training.'

A hammer is pounding at my head. 'So am I bothered?' I choke, hide behind a cough.

'Nuala, will you text me or something. Be my girlfriend like – there isn't anyone else.'

'Huh. Looks like you wish different. You're sad, you know that.' I want to hug him, tell him of course I will but say instead, 'See you,' and walk off.

On the day he leaves we have a celebratory cake. Craig, the manager, makes a speech, uses words like achievement, ambition, proud. There are lots of navy jokes. The kids, the staff, all trying to give him a send-off.

He finds me round the back. I'm bored with the tinsel enthusiasm. 'Hey, Nuala.' He holds his arms across his chest like he doesn't trust them. 'You're the only one I'll miss. I'll text. I want to.'

'Do what you like. It's a free world.'

He tries to kiss my cheek; our noses bump and we both turn away.

'I'd like you to,' I call after him, too late. The blaring music wins.

I stop going anywhere; use a cigarette to burn holes in my arm. First one burn, then another. Sometimes I hide them, other times not. My badges of courage I call them. Now there are three. Red and puckered, blistered round the edges. Pain replaces missing Ted.

'Cream cake!' Nicky pushes it towards me as a peace offering. 'Nuala, I'm getting married, moving to the west of Ireland, to Donegal. I'm sorry, it means I won't be your social worker any more.' She is waiting for me to speak but I don't. She chatters on like a buzzing fly. 'I'll miss you. It's been a long time.'

I dip my finger into the cream, it sits like a lollipop on my finger.

'Goodbye. What do you expect me to do, burst into tears?' I flip the plate; the cake rolls across the table in a smear of jam and cream. I leave her looking like she's going to cry.

There's a new guy hanging around with the gang. I don't know him. Tonight I let him touch me, crawl over my skin with his calloused hands. His thing is in my mouth. I bite him. 'Yeah, baby. Yeah, yeah, yeah.' He's going wild, begs for it again.

I'm sick in the gutter on the way home It's in my hair and on my clothes. I'm dizzy, lean on a wall until the street stops spinning. Footsteps slap on the pavement behind me. The guy, the one I'd been with, is running up the empty street. I retch. He grabs my hand, twists me round, pins me against the brick.

'Here, take this. Hide it.'

'What, what is it? Gear?' He's put a cloth-wrapped package in my hand. I stick it under my coat. It's not soft. It's hard. Metal-hard. I've never held one before. I know what it is.

Sirens coming closer waken the street, curtains twitch, a door opens. A police car races in a frenzy of flashing lights towards the town centre.

He disappears across some wasteland, swallowed by the dark.

*

Falcon House is in semi-darkness. I go straight to my room sure that guilt waves like a flag above my head. Cold floods from my abdomen into my chest. I throw the grubby cloth and its lethal secret under the bed where I can't see it and pull the duvet over my stinking self. I'll get rid of it tomorrow, throw it away. Find the fucking bloke who's landed me with it. Give it to someone else in the gang. Turn it in.

Bile burns my throat. My head whirrs. I retrieve the package, unwind its wrapping. The exposed gun is heavy, cold and lethal.

Sleep is a mess of technicolour dreams. I'm being raped, a gun to my head. a policeman standing over me singing nee-naw, nee-naw, like a siren.

The duvet is on the floor, my sweat mixes with the smell of semen. I open the window and light a cigarette. My inner arm is pale and thin in the unlit room. Singeing skin stinks worst of all.

Joe

People came from all over Connemara to say goodbye to Jack. Distant relatives I had never seen before, farmers, auctioneers, contractors. I watched Aoife arrive with an older man. They walked in together, she with a handkerchief to her face but with no comforting touch from the man I presumed to be her father. They all piled into the church in the village on the mainland, followed the coffin topped with a simple woven basket. Mary had got me to cut pieces of ivy from the wall in front of the farmhouse and she'd picked some early spring flowers from the wayside to add to it. 'Never one for flowers, Jack,' she said. 'Didn't see the point.' I hovered outside, my mouth dry, shoulders heavy. I'd not been inside a church since childhood. I slipped in as the singing started.

Jack wasn't there amongst the formality and the ritual and the prayers. I could only picture him leaning over the gate, the two of us, watching the sheep. *It's the nature of the seasons, Joe.*

I fled the suffocating church and sat on the wall.

After the service a long cortège drove slowly back across the causeway to the island, a thin black snake almost connecting it to the mainland. Today the land and water merged in shades of grey and green. Rain fell at sea, a curtain against the horizon. I stood away from the mourners gathered round the graveside. In the cemetery a brief wash of sun touched the old headstones and rested on the figures standing in a circle round the grave.

Aoife clung to Mary. She hadn't been near me since Jack died. A heart attack was what they said. He wouldn't have suffered. I longed to talk, to explain, tell her what had happened that night. I wanted someone to hold me. Instead I only had images in my head; of Jack in the cab, the noose, the feel of the rope in my hand, a horror of what I would have found if Jack had done what he intended. I would never tell Mary.

They were moving off, down the path, climbing into cars. I turned away, stared out to sea. A boat sailed far from shore dwarfed and vulnerable, all around it a rolling expanse of water like billowing silk.

Goodbye, Jack; I could not give voice to the words. The rain had reached land. Alone, I placed a stone from the beach on the pile of freshly dug soil. A piece of me had been torn away and buried in the cold earth. 'You trusted me from the start, never asked questions, accepted me for who I was.' I knelt on the trodden grass and moulded soil into a ball. 'You gave me a chance, Jack. I should have told you. I should have said thanks.' A silent wail choked me. 'I'll ... I'll miss you.'

'You couldn't leave it alone, could you? You had to keep poking away. Picking at his grief.' Aoife stood sobbing above me, unfamiliar in her black clothes. 'I loved him. More of a father than my own father. Now he's dead ... all because of a tractor ... all because of you.'

I hadn't heard her footfall, hadn't seen her come back to the grave. Had no words for her.

'An old man, a sick man. You should have let him be. This, Joe.' She pointed at another headstone. 'This is what he lived with, what he never forgave himself for. He never talked about what happened – wouldn't let us either. His way of dealing with it, the only way he could. We respected that.' She pummelled my shoulders with clenched fists. 'Why did you ever come here? But for you he would be alive.' She turned and ran through the cemetery gate, her scarf blowing from around her neck.

'Jack.' The wind smashed her scream into my face.

I let her go. She was right. Other folk thought it too What I already knew. My fault. I retrieved her lace scarf and scrunched it, smelled her fragrance, then sank onto the wet grass, legs bunched, head buried in my knees. A little boy again, I felt the pain of my stepfather's belt. Here I had no bed to crawl under, only a grave to lie beside.

You're a good lad. We take as we find. You done well. Jack speaking to me, snatches of conversation coming from below the ground.

Someone is beside me.

'Nuala?'

I opened my hand expecting to see hers. 'You always come when I need you most.' Her body warmed me. Her arms gently turned me to look at the headstone next to Jack's.

Daniel O'Shea
Beloved only son of Jack and Mary
Born 20th April 1950 Died 29th June 1978

I read it again then wiped the rain from the marble headstone. Beloved only son.

Daniel. He was not a little boy, but a grown man. Twenty-eight. He died at twenty-eight. The same age as I am. Pieces of the jigsaw slotted into place. I remembered the half-painted wall, the tools in the bedroom.

'It's over thirty years ago. Why did no one tell me? Why couldn't you talk about him. Why, Jack?' I kicked at the pile of earth.

How strong is a love that silenced Jack and those around him for thirty years? I tried to imagine. I couldn't. I'd wanted my stepdad to die, left Liverpool, Mum, my brothers, without a tear – Bridget – drugs and despair stole emotion then. Nuala … a jagged chasm of despair. I touched the smooth marble. Like me it was as cold as stone.

I kept away from the house until the last person had left. I fed the animals and milked the cows, simple actions I understood. I hoped Aoife would stay with Mary tonight, but I couldn't see her car.

'Mary.' I didn't want to waken her, exhausted as she must be. I pushed on the door, the room was warm, the stove door open. On the hotplate the kettle sang just off the boil. Mary sat in Jack's chair holding his pipe, turning it in her fingers.

'Are you alone?'

'Course I am. Lots of folk wanted to stay but I said no. Can't be doing with fuss.'

'Aoife?'

'She's gone too, Joe. Adored Jack. Angry, hurting, grieving for all he was to her. I wanted quiet. Can't talk to Jack otherwise, can I?'

I looked around the kitchen expecting him to come through the door, to see the puff of smoke and smell his tobacco.

'He would be real grumpy.' Mary chuckled. 'All these people tramping around, getting in the way. I can hear him, can't you? He would have disappeared to the sheds, probably has.'

She sighed. 'Aye, well I guess he's got all the peace he wants now.'

'Mary, this isn't the time, but for sure I'll keep things going until you … well, until you decide what you'll do.' Large and clumsy I fumbled in the suffocating space. 'Jack and you. You've been the … I didn't appreciate what kindness was until I met you.' I tripped on the words; blood drained from my head.

'Joe.' Mary waved a hand in my direction.

'Mary, don't stop me. I need to tell you. I never told Jack and now I can't. You gave me a chance. Without it I would be dead. I want to say thank you … and I want to say sorry.' I sat at the table, my legs too weak to hold me.

'I saw your son's grave today. Daniel's. Next to Jack's. I didn't know.'

'Aye, they're together now. Jack'll like that. Another day. I'll tell you another day.' She struggled to her feet and opened the side cupboard of the dresser, removed a tin box, carried it to the table and prised open the lid. 'Here, Joe. This has not been opened in near thirty years.'

'What's …?' I looked at the key she'd placed in my palm then back at her.

'You'll be needing it. For the tractor, Joe. Fetch it from Art's shed. It's the right thing. Bring it over here.' Mary had sunk into her own chair. 'I'll tell you the story … another day.' She waved a hand at me.

I curled a fist around the key, tucked a rug over Mary's knees. The lock clicked as I shut the farmhouse door behind me.

Clemmie ran around in circles chasing her tail when I returned to the cottage. I buried my face in her coat letting her lick me. 'What we going to do, Clems?' She cocked her head, laid it on my knee and watched with soulful eyes.

Nuala

'What's going on?' They're jittery as bugs when I turn up.

'The dickhead's been nabbed. The police have got him. They've been crawling around the area all morning. They're searching for something.

'Hardware. Jax had hardware,' Kelly says looking at me.

'Jesus Christ!' My legs are made of glass, a kick will shatter them. A police car cruises by and slows.

'Beat it,' someone yells. We run, scatter in different directions. It's me they're looking for, I know it.

The summer holidays are over. The gang's running scared, noone's showing up. We occasionally drift together but never hang around, I pretend I don't have the gun, that it isn't at the bottom of my drawer rolled in a jumper I never wear. Most times I can kid myself.

I think I might cut school for good. I'm bored. Who will care a fuck if I'm in school or not? It'll be my last year. I remember Ted saying he didn't mess around because he wanted to get somewhere. I have nowhere to get to. He's been gone a few weeks. Another kid's in his room. Cretin.

Nicky's gone too. 'All change,' I said it to her face on the day she left. She looked like I'd punched her; wish I hadn't said it, she'd been okay.

'Nuala, isn't it?' Bloody hell, I hold the stolen school library book behind my back. There's a stash in my wardrobe.

It's the new English teacher. 'What are you reading?' Should I tell her I'm a waste of space?

'Ah, Edna O'Brien, *Girl with Green Eyes*. An Irish classic. You'll love it. I did. Read it and tell me what you think.' She's smiling.

'Yeah.' I nod like an idiot. Her red hair frizzes in curls to her shoulders. Her skin is the colour of butterscotch, same as her eyes. I stare, then turn away embarrassed.

We walk down the stairs. I'm bunking off, but she doesn't know. 'Do you read much?'

Nosy B. 'It's what I enjoy doing most.' I sound pathetic, like I'm a geek. 'After drugs and sex and self-harming.'

She's laughing. 'Well, of course, after all of those things. See you in the lesson after lunch.'

I stay in school. The first full day I've done in months.

When I get back to the house Martha waves a postcard at me. 'For you, Nuala, from Ted.' She nudges me on the arm.

'And I suppose you've all bloody read it.' She looks sheepish. I flick it from her hand and drop it in the wastepaper bin. After she's gone off duty, I retrieve it.

Hi, Nuala,
I'm knackered. Training is hard. I think they're pushing us to see who breaks first. It won't be me.
Hope things are good with you.
Ted xx

It's the second postcard. 'Ms Nuala McCurdy' My name sounds funny read out loud and I imagine him writing it. I tuck it in my drawer with the other one, under the shoebox where I keep my underwear.

Debbie's gone too. We had a special tea for her like we did for Ted, and gave her some presents for the baby. She unwrapped them slowly like she didn't want the afternoon to end. She held each piece in turn – a pack of Babygros, some vests and a white blanket. I got a teary-eyed hug when I gave her some bootees I'd nicked from Mothercare. She'd grown big, clumsy and ugly but she'd got her flat. She pushed a piece of paper with her address on it under my door. I didn't wave her off but I watched her from the bedroom window. She looked back at the place like it was home or something. She must have had the kid by now. How come she got to be a mother? I won't go and see her.

*

'Nuala, have you got a minute? I have something for you.' Mrs Leafe, the English teacher, is talking. Hers is the only lesson I go to.

The other kids stream from the classroom. 'Teacher's pet,' a girl sniggers. I lift a finger to her. Mrs Leafe sees me do it and struggles not to laugh. She hands me a bag; I can tell it's a book.

'Open it then. I think you'll like it.' She's watching me. I can't speak, clasp the bag and pull my sleeve over my wrist, so she won't see anything.

'It's not a present. I want it back!' She takes it from me and removes the wrapping. 'Here, let me show you. Have you read John Boyne? About people who were, still are, forced to live beyond the margins. Most of the class wouldn't comprehend it. I think you will.'

The Heart's Invisible Furies. What crap. Are you taking the piss? Her honey eyes freeze me. 'No hurry to read it but give it back – remember!'

'Thanks. Big-un used to buy me books.'

'Big-un?'

I shake my head. She lets it go

'Your name, Mrs Leafe, it's …'

'Unusual, I think the best you can say. Always ask a man his surname before you fall for him, Nuala.'

'The kids call you names.'

'Yes. Lettuce Leaf is one. Not so bad. I reckon if they invent names for you, they think you're worth something.'

'They call me names too.'

'Yes, I've heard them, Nuala.' Her voice is soft, her forehead creases in a frown, her freckles merge. 'Deb. Debbie Downer. I don't understand what it means, I'm guessing it's not nice.'

It sounds different when she says it, like it doesn't mean anything at all.

'Do you want to tell me?'

School buses rumble up the drive.

'You don't have to.'

I hitch myself onto the table and swing my legs. 'It's a social media thing. It means depressive – loser in other words.'

'And are you?'

'WHAT? A loser. I'M NOT.'

She jerks back her shoulders and grins. 'You're not, Nuala. I'm glad you realise it. See, I'm already out of date with the street slang.'

'Why are you bothering with me? I'm not clever.' It sounds ac-

143

cusing. She tidies papers, puts them away, closes a drawer with a bang.

'I see something in you, Nuala, I don't see in many students. My dad would have called it pluck, an old-fashioned word.' Her voice smiles. 'It's nothing to do with being clever and I don't agree with your assessment of yourself. Courage, spirit, grit, not sure how to explain it.'

'Yeah, well, it's too late. Thanks anyway.' I'm off the table. 'Thanks for the book. Hope the story's better than the naff title.'

'See what I mean, Nuala. Pluck.' Her voice follows me along the corridor, and I wave without turning.

Pluck. I like it and say it over. I start to read the book straight off. By the time I remember I was supposed to meet the others it's late and dark. I need a smoke, weed. Kelly and the like are moving on to other things, bigger stuff. I'm not interested, or so I tell them. No money – not yet. I settle for more book. Botched arms glare at me. Angry burn marks, marching to my elbow. The fourth one was messy, stank and oozed pus – good at the time.

I read the book in two nights.

'Mrs Leafe.' No one else is around. 'Thanks. I've read it, couldn't put it down. Christ, what happened – it's so unfair. Is it the same now?'

'I hope not, Nuala. What do you think?'

Lying in the dark trying to sleep I'm replaying our conversation. She wanted my opinion, listened while I rambled on. She'd asked me.

Joe

The cottage smelt of damp and unwashed clothes. Mud lay on the floor from my boots. I kicked at the ash in the unlit fire, knocking over a mug of cold tea. It pooled on the tiles. Clemmie licked at it. I pushed aside the debris of dishes on the draining board searching for her water bowl. Sour milk had congealed in a jug and dried food stuck to plates. I slept on the sofa many a night; Clemmie watched from where she lay on the blanket tossed across the floor.

I splashed my face with stinging cold water, leant against the sink and covered my eyes with my hands. 'Come on, girl.' I shoved open the door and went out.

I don't remember the steep climb or how long I sat on the cliff top near my cairn of stones. Clemmie nuzzled my hand wanting to be stroked.

Aoife. It was weeks since the funeral. My longing sliced me in two. I saw her in the wind-battered trees and the blowing sands. She laced my dreams. She'd been to the island more than once, to see Mary and bring her supplies. She avoided me and left without saying hello. For a while I hadn't seen her car in the yard and Mary evaded the question when I asked after her.

I tried to make sense of Aoife's grief and anger. Shouts filled my head. 'I didn't know. I knew nothing, I didn't mean it to kill him.' My stepdad lying against the fire fender, Jack in the tractor – confused images swarmed before my eyes.

She needs time, I kept telling myself, but I knew it was more.

A soft grey light drifted over the island transparent as smoke. Shapes, painted by the wind, rippled on the sea. 'I've lost her,

Clemmie. She's gone.' Clemmie pressed her warm body against mine. 'I've got to go too, Clems. Soon as Mary sells the farm.' The dog whimpered, her nose against my chin, a rough tongue licking my face. 'Not you, girl. You can't come, a farm dog, you'd hate the city.' I ruffled her ears. 'You've been my best friend.'

If you'm going to be a farmer you need a dog. Jack's words came back.

I pushed Clemmie away. 'Go home. GO HOME. Clear off. You're better off without me.' I balled a hand, thrust it into the black pain deep in my body. Clemmie stood, a pace away, quivering, her tail drooped between her legs.

I fetched the tractor, Jack's tractor. I needed it and it would sell with the farm.

'Knew you'd be over for it soon enough.' Art's hands were in his pockets, his hooded eyes giving nothing away. 'Got it ready for you, turned it over, engine sounds sweet. She's an old lady but good as new. He'd only had her a few days. Terrible thing, terrible. Broke Jack.' Art shook his head.

I walked slowly towards the looming tractor.

'Sure, he should have fetched it years ago,' Art hollered after me. 'If you have a problem – well, I'm here so I am.'

I mumbled thanks, appreciating Art's gruffly spoken offer.

Art had wiped the tractor. Streaks from the cloth patterned the bodywork. I squeezed past abandoned cans and sawn wood. The rope with its crude noose was where I'd hidden it. I slid onto the tractor seat, breathing fast, my heart slamming in my chest. For several minutes I sat and gripped the steering wheel, staring through the windscreen at the yard in front.

Go, take it home, Joe.

'What?' It was Jack's voice. I looked around. A sparrow flew in the open door and onto a roof beam. My hands shook as I eased the tractor from its resting place and onto the track. A watery sun flooded into the cab.

Art stood by the house. He touched his cap as I drove past.

'Married since 1945, just as the Emergency ended. I wore a purple dress. It belonged to someone else, wasn't the first bride to wear it neither. Had a little hat with a feather. Jack, a real dandy too, didn't recognise him, all scrubbed clean, his face rosy like a ripe apple.' Mary chuckled as she stared at the black-and-white photograph in her hand.

'Joe, take me to the grave, will you? There are things as I need to say to Jack.'

'Mary, it's cold. It'll be dark soon. I'll take you tomorrow.'

'No, now, while the mood's on me. I've lived here most of m' life, Joe. Bit of a sharp breeze won't put old Mary off.'

She shuffled around putting on her best coat and the hat she'd worn when she and Jack had gone off to Galway.

'Well, aren't you so smart?' I found a warm scarf on the hook behind the door and wrapped it round her neck.

'Looks like you could do with a bit o' laundering.' Mary's rheumy eyes peered at me. 'Right shabby you are an' all.'

I said nothing, hoisted her into the truck and drove as near as I could to the cemetery gate.

'This is more than a sharp breeze, Mary.' I helped her down and held onto her frail frame. 'You be quick, or Jack will be rearing up from his grave and having a right go at me for letting you come out on a day like this.'

I turned my back and stepped as far away as I dared when we reached the graveside, ready to catch her if she stumbled. I heard her tuts and murmurs. Sneaking a peek, I caught her wagging a finger over Jack's grave.

The tide was rushing in; white crests broke the wave tops. Over in the village lights came on in the houses. I hadn't been across to the bar for weeks. Afraid of the accusing glances, the spreading word.

Mary hung on my arm. 'It wasn't a day like this. It was a hot day, so hot even the clouds had fled. Pure blue, I remember, the sky a pure blue.' I had to bend my head to hear her.

'Come on. Let me get you home, into the warm.'

'Listen on, Joe. While I have the strength to tell you.

'He'd taken the new tractor. Daniel, I mean. Brand new an' all. Repairing a wall or something like.' She nodded towards her son's headstone. 'Been off for hours and Jack bothering, becoming more and more cross, other things needed doing – the animals and like. They didn't always see eye to eye, Daniel and Jack.'

Mary eased herself onto the worn graveside. I crouched in front and pulled her coat tight, took off my jacket and wrapped it round her shoulders. She held onto her hat with a gloved hand as the wind tugged.

'Daniel wanted to do newfangled things and his dad couldn't see why they needed to change the way things were. Both as stubborn as mules. Sometimes they didn't talk for days. I was that cross with the two of them, one night I didn't cook them supper. Presented them with empty plates and told them they weren't having anything until they stopped behaving like daft sheep. Well, it made them laugh – stupid buggers.

'Anyways, as I said. After he'd stomped around and called Daniel a few names he set off to find him. We owned half the island then. Only sold off the land … after. Jack lost heart. Lost interest.

'Jack was in a right mood after he traipsed around and found the tractor up in the top field. Daniel nowhere to be seen.' Mary pulled my hand onto her lap and covered it with her own. She stared beyond, at a point above my shoulder.

'Drove off, grumpy as you like.'

She stroked my hand, her other one covered her mouth.

'Ruts in the field, that's what he thought. Afterwards, it's what he kept on saying.'

I felt her shivering, could hear the sea crashing on the beach. 'Mary, tell me at home.'

'Theys both here, Joe. I want them to know I've told you.

'That's it. Daniel had gone to sleep … in the shade … under the tractor. Jack … he didn't know he was there, didn't see him.' She squeezed her eyes shut as a tear escaped. 'He drove right over him.

'Never forgave himself. Never talked of it. Flew into terrible rages or other times he wouldn't speak for weeks.'

I took Mary home and put a drop of brandy in her cup of tea, stacked the stove and opened its door, so the warm smell of smouldering peat seeped into the kitchen.

'For a long time, I couldn't cope with my own grief let alone Jack's.' Mary rocked, twisting her head from side to side. 'Oh, the pain, Joe, when I wanted to talk about Daniel, but Jack wouldn't have his name mentioned, not by me, not anyone.

'He'd killed his own son.' Mary moaned, hands plucking at the blanket I put round her knees. 'He got Art to take the tractor away, to hide it. Said he never wanted to see it again. He used to go there sometimes though – sit in the cab – like he had to keep on punishing h'self. Now them's together. Only me left. Don't seem much point any more.'

I pulled a chair next to Mary and put my arms round her.

'Only began to get better when Aoife started coming, just a little girl then. Someone to love, a child. They needed each other; they were special the two of them.' Mary held my wrist.

'It's why she's not coping. She's hurting bad, Joe.'

I held Mary until her breathing steadied and her head rested back against the cushion.

I felt Jack's presence the most when milking the cows, but not tonight. Bella restless, stamping her feet and the others, noisy, freaked, their eyes wide and scared. Shadows in the barn moved like ghosts, the wind shrieked abuse through the slats. My thoughts wouldn't let me be.

The crack as my stepfather's head hit the fender.

The stink of Bridget's body.

Nuala's eyes.

The noose in Jack's dead hand.

He killed his own son.

I squeezed my head between fists, sucked at the air with hungry gasps, tore into the yard and vomited over the concrete as dizziness engulfed me.

'Joe, good to see you, son. Missed you these past weeks.' Ronan the first to speak. 'How you doing?'

I acknowledged the question with a wave of my hand. I hadn't been across since Jack's funeral, guessed there'd been talk, knew what they were thinking.

'Funny, before you walked in, we were just saying as how old Jack over there farmed most of the island. Rented fields here on the mainland. Big landowner in them days. Employed a few men too as I remember.'

'Yeah, Mary told me.' I shrugged not wanting to talk.

I sipped my pint of Guinness listening to the surrounding conversation. Most of it rumours around a recession and all the newly built properties either half-finished or lying empty.

'The Celtic Tiger's biting back,' was Ronan's take. 'We've had it too good. Out on the lorry, I see it all over, desperate folk are trying to sell their houses. It's going to end badly, is my prediction. Very badly for a lot of people.' A hum of assent surrounded me.

'Them foreign investors pulling out.'

'You managing then?' One of the other farmers addressed me.

'Yeah. Till I move on.'

'Seems like all the young 'uns are going.' Arthur had a welding business by day and drank the profits at night, so the gossip went. 'Michael Ahern's boy, Finn, gone off to Dublin on his motorbike.' His slurred words came with a loud burp. 'Took that tasty piece with

149

him, his old flame so's I heard. Murphy's daughter. Aoife. Gone to the big city, to the bright lights. Shacked up together, the talk is. Old Murphy's spitting feathers. Got no one to fetch his beer.' He belched. 'On the rebound I reckon. Eh, Joe?' He guffawed into his glass spraying the froth over the bar top.

Eyes turned in my direction.

Ronan pushed Arthur off his stool. 'You've got a gob bigger than the Devil's Cave. Close it, you drunken fool. Don't jabber when you knows nothing.'

''Ere, what did you say? Who you calling ...?'

I downed the rest of my pint, banged the glass on the bar and fumbled through the door. The icy air took my breath away.

Nuala

Kelly's got so she's stuck-up. The blokes she hangs out with are shit. She's shooting, not big time, but enough to scramble her brains, enough to convince her it's the only time she's real.

'What are you like?' I yell at her because she's not listening. 'You'll kill yourself. Yikes, you were my friend, now you're scum. You don't even see me, you're grey, skin like a supermarket chicken.'

'Ooh, listen to fancy knickers. You're a skinny bitch with no breasts.' She throws an arm and thumps my jaw when I shake her.

I want to tell her, tell someone about the gun. Make her take notice of me. But the unwritten rule is we don't do betrayal not even on bastards like Jax. I keep shtum.

Kelly, me, a few others, we're in a basement, our new place. It's a hole. I thump the damp walls and my shoulder brushes against green mould. The smell … A memory, swift as lightning. Another room. Buried images.

Wake up, wake up. I'm shaking her. Who? A monster crouched in the dark corner is creeping across the room. Run. Banging on a door. Can't open it. Scream and scream. No one comes.

I screw up my eyes, grind my fists into my cheeks to make the pictures flee.

I'm not ready to go back to Falcon House. Narrow terraced houses crowd each other. The roads are wet, the streetlamps multiply in the puddles. People are leaving the station, glancing at the sky, stopping to open umbrellas.

Ted, his name is in my tears. The platform where we caught the train to the coast is empty, the flowers in the beds, brown and broken.

I try to remember. *Wake up, wake up*, It's a CD with no more words. 'MUMMY.' The shriek is mine. I want to remember. Nothing – crying – and a beach and big arms to hold me.

I'm back at the home. How? My shirt plastered to my shoulders, water drips off the ends of my hair. The night staff frown and point at their watches. 'Nuala, what time is this? You're drenched. Get those wet clothes off and go to bed.'

But I go into the kitchen instead. Make toast, pull margarine and jam from the fridge, slap it on in dollops careless of the spatters over the work surface. I pour Cheerios into a bowl and flood it with milk, spooning them frantically into my mouth.

'Don't take it away.' My arm stops them from trying. My mouth is crammed full; I splutter food across the kitchen floor.

Hands are on my shoulders.

'Nuala's hungry … she's always hungry.' I stammer. 'She … she was always … hungry.'

In my bedroom I am safe. I cry for her.

My head throbs. I can't stand the morning light squeezing through the gap in the curtain. My skin is shiny with sweat, eyes of glass, a tongue furred like a cat's tail, I can't swallow. The bedclothes are on fire, I push them off and curl in a ball clutching my knees to quell the shivering.

I dream, I sleep. Images fight with voices. Raised voices, soft voices, faces with no features. I'm on a fair ride, colours blurring, music blaring.

'Hey, how are you?' Martha is sitting on my bed holding a tumbler while I sip ice-cold water. Her purple jumper comes into focus, her hand brushes damp hair from my forehead. 'You had us all scared. Do you remember the doctor coming? We thought you had meningitis.'

I don't want to go back to remembering, I shut my eyes. Red lights bounce behind the screen of my lids.

'Do you think you could manage a shower? It might make you feel better.' Her hand is stroking mine and I want her to carry on doing it, stroking me back to sleep.

Three days, four days, a week, two. I can't tell how long it is. I venture over the side of the bed putting hot feet onto the cool floor. In the shower, I lather my body with perfumed gel, wash off the ripeness, turn the dial and a burst of scalding water punishes my head and neck. The water streams over me.

'You have a visitor,' Martha calls. 'Are you up to it?

'Who?' I croak, sinking into a clean bed with fresh pillows.

'She says she's your English teacher. She seems nice. Can I bring her up?'

'Suppose so.' A lurch of dread. The gun. Hidden in the drawer. Why is she here? My sparse room is dull. There's no sun to brighten it, a heavy sky presses on the window. I push Rabbit further down the bed and pull the covers around my chin.

Mrs Leafe's head pops round the door so all I see is her flaming hair half-tamed by two plastic combs. 'You poor old thing. You have been so ill. We were all worried.'

Who's all? I let it go. 'I'm feeling better, just wobbly.' It's strange talking to a teacher, one who's sitting by my bed. Her eyes flick around the room over the chest of drawers, searching, coming to rest on me.

She knows.

Shame crawls across my skin, and I stick my arms under the cover to bury the puffy burns, the red criss-cross slashes.

She flinches, she's seen, her voice catches.

'I have news. I've entered you for your English GCSE.' She fumbles in a cloth bag, pulls out a carton of grapes, a bar of chocolate and a card. 'I hope you're pleased.'

'Why? Me, take an exam! Why would I turn up?'

'Why wouldn't you?'

Because you've got me wrong. I'm not a girl who reads books, sits English exams. I'm a girl with a gun hidden in a jumper, who does drugs and has sex.

'Not to wouldn't make sense. A bit of work and you'll do well.' She's holding a card near her chin as though the truth has stopped its passage.

She means it. She really thinks I will take the bloody exam.

Suddenly I know I will.

My wracking cough is an excuse to say nothing.

'Open your card. It's from the pupils – your English group.'

Get well soon, multi-coloured letters sparkle with glitter. Inside, signatures and scribbled emojis. *Laura, Aran, Megan. Helen, Adam.* I can't read them all because the words become indistinct.

'Did you make them do it?' I squeak, swallowing hard.

'Nope. Claire's idea. She bought the card and got the others to sign it.'

'They don't like me!'

'They do, Nuala. But you must let them.'

Someone runs along the corridor, a door slams and music blasts.

'You're English, aren't you, not Irish? Why did you come to Ireland …?' I stop mid-sentence – too late because I've started. 'Most people go the other way.'

'I'm half-English. My dad was from Morocco. I never got to go there but I will one day.' Mrs Leafe chuckles. She leans on the quilt. 'I'll tell you why, if you promise not to laugh.' She squints at me and pours me some orange juice. 'Are you tired? I said I wouldn't stay too long. I lived near a seaside town. Blackpool, you will have heard of it.'

'Cool. A fun place, isn't it?'

'Well parts of it, but unemployment's high and it's tired. People want to holiday abroad these days. My dad was a school caretaker. It wasn't always easy being a different colour, but he never bothered, and I took my cue from him. He loved everyone and everyone loved him. I used to go to the sands, a favourite place. The seagulls would wheel over the sea, peeling from behind the clouds. I used to imagine they'd come from Ireland. I ached to fly, to hop on their backs so they would take me clear across the Irish Sea and into the mountains. I never forgot my longing, so when I qualified as a teacher, I took a ferry and came over to see if it was as good as I hoped it would be. After a few months I met my husband and here we are. My story in a nutshell.'

'I've done that too. Watched the birds and wished I could fly. Fly anywhere, a hundred miles away, a thousand miles.'

She smiles and pats my hand. We both stare at the wall like we're somewhere else.

'You need posters or some pictures.' It didn't sound like a criticism. 'At your age I covered my wall with posters of Justin Timberlake and Rihanna. My parents used to go mad because the Sellotape pulled the paint off the walls.

'Did you always want to be a teacher?'

She tears off grapes and hands them to me. 'I didn't know what I wanted to be. Because I'd always lived in a school, it's what I knew, so I sort of drifted towards it. I got into a college at Ormskirk near Liverpool and after my first teaching practice I knew it was what I wanted to do. I loved it, still do.'

'Did your mum and dad want you to be a teacher?'

'My dad was so proud.' Her nose wrinkles. 'He died the same month I started college. Had a stroke and died. I wanted to give up there and then, but Mum shoved me in the car, drove me back to college and told me to get on with life. Hated her for it at the time, but she did the right thing.'

I want a mum and dad.

A knock on the door stops me disgracing myself. A slim, half-girl, half-woman stands in the doorway. She's wearing black leggings and a black top stretched over her bust leaving an inch of white flesh above her waistband. Round her neck she wears a lime green, fringed scarf, bright against black hair and creamy skin.

'I'm absolutely not allowed to stay. They told me so downstairs. They said you've had flu, proper flu. That's grim. I'm Jess and I'm the lucky one who's got to be your new social worker. Nuala, it's lovely to meet you. Nicky told me what a super girl you are. And you must be Nuala's teacher. They told me you were here. Wow, great. My teachers wouldn't have bothered to come to see me if I'd been ill.'

Mrs Leafe and I exhale at the same time. 'Hi, Anna Leafe. Seems like we're both lucky to have come across Nuala.'

They're smiling.

You're not lucky. I'm a piece of shit. Wish I could think of something to say or do.

Jess unwinds her scarf and turns to Mrs Leafe, 'Your hair. Isn't it gorgeous?'

I've wanted to say it for ages but didn't dare.

'Sometimes I love it, at other times I curse its frizz!' They laughed. It sounded like a song in tune.

Wish I could be twenty something, have my life sorted like theirs.

'I wish mine was like that.' Jess runs her hand over her dead smooth locks. 'Straight as a dye. You and me the same, Nuala?'

I flick mine off my shoulders, hook it behind my ear and lie back against the pillows.

'I think we've tired you, Nuala.' Mrs Leafe says. 'Before I go, I've brought you another book I think you will enjoy. My dad gave it to me the day I left for college.' She places it on the table beside my bed next to the grapes. 'Nuala and I share a love of books. Bye, Nuala. Enjoy the read.'

A bubble of pride rises at being included.

'You get better, I'll be back to see you pronto.' Jess waves.

I shut my eyes, the door closes, their voices fade like music on the radio.

I read the signatures on the card again.

Later, much later, after I've slept, I lift the book to see what it is. *The Colour of Water.* Inside there's an inscription. *To our lovely Anna, for making us proud. Much love Mum and Dad. xx.* I tuck it under my pillow and lie in the faint dark of early night.

I wish I could make someone proud.

Joe

Arthur's words were a sentence delivered. I stumbled from the bar, crossed the road and kicked the sea wall until pain screamed in my head. I walked along the ribbon of tarmac that stretched into the distance, curving away from the coastline. The blackness of an inked-out sky stole around me, only the white shapes of grazing sheep gave definition. The occasional bleat of a new lamb broke the scrunch of my feet on loose gravel. Four miles, five miles. I didn't care how far. Aoife, her name on my lips.

I found myself beside the clock tower in the town square; sat for a while amongst takeaway cartons and cans, in a shop doorway, drank from a discarded bottle of whiskey, empty but for the last dregs. Cars passed and a refrigerated lorry hissed air as it moved off from a junction.

I read the streets. The car slowing on the corner, the bike against a wall, a figure emerging from the gloom. A brief exchange, the vehicle speeding off. The street empty again.

I walked that way and stopped to roll a cigarette, blew smoke, moved from the street lamp into the shadows. A youth in a black tracksuit, a hood pulled low over his head, his hands in his pockets, came alongside. No words. The two of us walked past a row of wheelie bins, then ducked into an alleyway.

'Skag? Crack?' Held notes between my thumb and finger.

The youth shook his head. 'Dublin only.'

I wanted to hit his acne-scarred chin.

'Weed.' He showed me a polythene package.

I swiped it to the ground and thumped the wall. The money was plucked from my fingers; I heard the flat slap of running footsteps as the black-clad figure sped off.

The alley smelt of urine and brick dust. I slid to the ground, my leg jammed against the opposite wall. The package lay beside a stinking puddle, rainbowed by petrol spillage. With cold and shaking hands I struggled to separate roll-up papers, to wrap the weed. The match a cone of light as I lit the joint. My lungs yearned. Dragging deeply, I inhaled the sweetness.

'Aoife.' Had I said it out loud? We'd been so good together. Her soft skin, how her hair slipped between my fingers. I was in a beautiful place, womb-like. Reflections from the shop lights danced in swirls of reds and blues. I pinched my skin, moaning with pleasure as I raked my arm with my fingernails. If I concentrated, really tried, I would feel when I passed from being awake to falling asleep. A breath, a beat of silence.

A rip of light stole in to where I lay. The cold had seeped through my cramped limbs. Violent shivers shook me awake. Half an hour, two hours, three hours, more. A minute, enough to wipe out the last few months and expose the lie that is my life.

On the edge of town, I found a lorry park with a café serving mugs of steaming tea. I was the only customer. A guy lolled on a stool behind the counter, his elbows spreadeagled on the worktop, his head resting on his arms. I warmed my hands on a small heater. What remained of the weed was a rock in my pocket though it weighed nothing. I kept touching it for reassurance.

'Time you were on your way.' The red-eyed café owner nudged me. 'It's not a bloomin' doss house.' He muttered more as he wiped the table with a striped cloth, but the words blurred into a jumble. Something fluttered at the edge of my mind, elusive, teasing, beyond my reach. Somewhere I should be, something I had to do. I sat on a kerb at the side of the road, trying to remember but gave up, it could wait.

The dustcart woke me as it clattered down the street. Men pulling bins bantered with each other. Loose paper blew along the gutter and collected against my feet. The sky a stretched grey cloud, rain spotted the pavement. I relieved myself against a wall and headed north, back the way I'd come.

Hours later I reached the island, fields pockmarked with grazing animals. In the distance a dog barked.

'Clemmie. God, Clemmie.' I ran towards my cottage.

She greeted me with excited yelps, jumping and turning in frantic circles to chase her tail. 'Oh, Clems. Clems.' The pungent smell of dog turd made me gag. Cooled pools of urine lay beside the mat. The dog dropped to her haunches, put her head on her paws, her tail between her legs.

'It's not your fault, Clemmie. It's mine, all mine. Joe McCurdy, Morgan whatever you call yourself, you're a swine.' My voice filled the small room. Clemmie whimpered, her dark eyes waiting, watching.

'Come here, girl.' I buried my fingers in the hair of her neck while she rubbed her nose against my knee and her tail wagged again.

I cleared the mess, filled her empty water bowl and gave her food. She pushed the bowl round the floor devouring every morsel.

Dirty pans, sour milk and congealed food littered the place. The mess, invisible to me before, bawled through my tiredness but had to wait.

The whitewashed walls of the cowshed hurt my stinging eyes. The cows milled around, the sound of their hooves too loud in my head. I retched over a pail, my guts in knots, throat burnt.

Dwarfed by the steaming flank of a cow, Mary sat on a crate. Milk flowed into a container.

'Mary.' I staggered forward. 'I'm ... I forgot ... I ...'

She struggled to her feet, her back twisted, her breathing laboured with the effort. Etched with pain, tiredness creased her face, her hair lay flat and damp across her scalp. She looked at me through blood-shot eyes. I held her steady, her head level with my chest.

She slapped me loud and sharp. I reeled, my hand on my stinging cheek. I grabbed Mary's thin wrist, shook her hand like an old cloth and held her away from me. She dropped her eyes and stumbled forwards, stopping to regain her balance. She walked away through the open door where daylight leaked.

Mary's slap, the mark of a branding iron spread to my neck and gouged my chest. I staggered against a stall, gripping a stanchion. The cows were restless, shit littered the straw. Plaintive mooing long and slow filled the shed with distress.

You'm a good lad. I lifted my head, spun round to see who'd said it. Nobody. I pushed aside the cows to reach for Jack's coat hanging on a hook by the door; I stroked the coarse tweed, lifted Jack's pipe from a pocket and cradled it in my hand. It smelt of tobacco, and I could see Jack puffing slowly, his face shrouded in smoke.

I finished the milking and turned the beasts into the yard; cleaned the shed, shovelling straw and excrement, sweating with the effort, hosed the floor, splashed cold water over my face to keep me awake. Only when I'd replaced the straw, refreshed the hay and could hear the contented munching of the animals did I allow myself to pause.

Then I started on the yard itself. Old Jess, Jack's dog, had died weeks ago, but the kennel remained. Mice and rats had chewed the bedding. I pulled at the rotting blankets, gagging at the smell. I moved the tractor and the truck into the lane. Chickens flapped at my feet pecking at the debris I piled into heaps. Old cans and pieces of mangled lead piping clattered where they fell. I restacked the woodpile and swept the areas in front of the barn and house. Time passed. I kept going. All the while Mary's door stayed shut but the hurt I'd seen in her eyes tore at me.

Weary and desolate I whistled to Clemmie. 'Come on, girl, there's something I need to do.'

I took the path to the cliff top. The fields, a spread of green. Sheep followed until they realised they wouldn't be fed. Clemmie dashed along the hedgerows, chasing smells. The sound of the waves grew loud. I clambered onto bare rock, transfixed by the white suds careering into gullies, only to be sucked out with wrenching force. Rain fell in straight lines from hanging clouds, dripped from my chin, soaked into my clothing.

My hand closed round the package in my pocket. I threw it as far as I could, saw it splash into the swell and disappear.

Nuala

Sixteen today. It should be special. The walls of my room are the same colour, my bed's in the same position, scars on my arms, a gun in my drawer. Just another day.

'My God! Mirror, mirror on the wall who's the ugliest of them all?' Skinny arms, knobbly elbows, sunken cheeks. I breathe in and count my ribs. Usual black trousers, black sweatshirt. hair into a bobble.

Jess appears, says she has a surprise. I still feel lousy from the flu. 'Put the window down and grab some fresh air. You are as pasty as an uncooked scone.' She said it last time we were in the car. Really made me feel better!

'How come you're not predictable like most social workers? Where are we going?'

She wrinkles her nose, excited. 'If I tell it won't be a surprise. You'll like it. Its special being sixteen. We have to celebrate. Sweet sixteen and all that.'

We sing to the radio as she drives, she waves to strangers. She makes people smile, me too.

'I'm going around once more and if I don't find a parking slot, I'll double-park! It's crazy. Everyone's gone bonkers. It's ages until Easter. All shopping for chocolate eggs and fluffy chickens!'

'There, quick. someone leaving.'

Jess nearly clips the nearest car in her haste to turn into the parking bay, 'Yeah, we made it. Come on. Let's go.' She bangs the steering wheel. We race across the street until she stops at a pink door and pushes it open. There's a buzz of hairdryers.

'Hi, we have an appointment – for a hair colour – the works.'

I'm in the doorway. 'What!'

'Here.' She hands me a purse and whispers. 'Pay for it with this. I'll come in with you but I'm not playing the social worker. Pretend I'm your big sister or something. I always wanted a sister.'

Jess flicks through magazines, looking at hairstyles while we wait. The voluminous gown swamps me. 'I feel a prat,' I say as I try to turn back the super-wide sleeves.

'Hey, what about this? "Shaved on one side, sultry-straight on the other". Or this, "cool sophistication". Here's the one, "Funky and fun for the trendy teen".' She holds a picture of a brooding teenage model with skin as smooth as wax.

'I wish.'

'You enjoy yourself. I'll come back in a while. Bet I won't recognise you.' She is gone, leaving an empty space.

'Pink or purple woven highlights will suit your hair colour. Feather the fringe, make it softer round your face. Take about two inches off.' A stylist with a blonde plaited bun on top of her head is lifting my hair, letting the strands slip between her fingers. She sweeps it back from my face. 'You have such fabulous eyes and fine bone structure.'

Have I?

'You know best. Whatever you think suits.'

Noise and chatter.

'...my daughter-in-law wears ...'

'Greece was fabulous ...'

'then he said ... and ...' 'No, wow, amazing.'

What to say? Keep quiet. Pretend. I'm on a different planet. Someone will notice and kick me out. Hideous purple paste wrapped in pieces of foil. 'Magazines? A drink?' I'm scared to shake my head. 'Comfortable?' No, I'm bloody not with my neck extended backwards over a basin, my hair a foaming froth of shampoo. 'Water hot enough?' I can tell they ask these questions all the time, I don't answer. I'm washed then she starts all over again.

'How many flippin' washes?'

'Shampoos, we call them shampoos.'

Pardon me. *Shampoos.*

Having my scalp massaged is so good I want to go to sleep.

'What do you think?' Melanie, it's on her name badge, runs her pink comb through my hair, removing the tangles. 'Touching your shoulders.' She scissors her fingers round my hair to demonstrate.

162

'Okay.' I nod, not sure it's me who sits in the chair reflected in the mirror.

Strands of hair drop to the floor; stray bits fall onto my lap.

'Scary, isn't it? It will look great.' Melanie grins. 'A new you!'

Someone's lit a happy flare inside me.

After two hours I'm waiting for Jess. 'Attractive, beautiful, gorgeous.' They mean me. I keep glancing in the mirror to see if it's true.

'Wow, bloody wow.' Jess gives me a hug. 'Happy Birthday,' she whispers in my ear.

I pay at the desk, shocked at how much it costs. Can something this good be happening?

I point to a card on the desk. 'Can I apply for the job?'

Saturday staff required. Ask within.

Neither the hairdresser nor Jess move.

'Are you interested in hairdressing? It's not the glamorous end. It's sweeping hair, making drinks for customers, stacking the shelves. We'll teach you how to shampoo hair and do massages. Not great pay, I'm afraid, but you can have your own hair done for nothing.'

'Sounds good,' I say.

'How old are you?'

'Seventeen.' I hope it's old enough. Jess doesn't blink, only the slightest tilt of a lip.

The manager must have been listening, comes across. Scissors in one hand a comb in the other, one raised, painted eyebrow. 'Okay, let's try it then. Start on Saturday and we'll assess it after a month.'

'Great, thanks.'

Outside Jess gives a little jump in the air. 'Nuala, I'm so proud of you. Not only do you look a million dollars you are a million dollars.'

'It's been my best birthday ever.' I don't care if Jess sees how chuffed I am. 'Thanks for this.' I touch my hair. 'And for not saying anything ...'

'Shh.' She puts a finger to her lips. 'Let's call it initiative. I like it.' Her laugh tinkles. 'We'll finish the morning with a burger and a milkshake.' We link arms and skip along the pavement.

Back at Falcon House, there's been an incident. A kid has kicked off, there's been a fight. Usual stuff. Tension fills the space like a bad smell. Baggage is what the staff call it. 'You're all strung tight as guitar strings,' Craig says. Often a string twangs and hits one of us in the face.

I retreat to my room, change my sweatshirt for a black lacy top – the label still attached. I don't remember 'acquiring' it and I wonder if it's one Kelly lifted. The purple streaks in my hair catch the light. 'You're passable.' I wink at my reflection.

I want to flaunt the new me, go somewhere, do something.

Ted, why aren't you here? I send him off a selfie.

His reply is the best.

SEXY. LOL xxx

At McDonald's there's a tribe of little kids traipsing in holding balloons. 'Come on, birthday girl.' A woman calls, I guess it's her mother. A kid in a pink party dress and glittery princess shoes giggles and pushes to the front.

Obviously, the only thing we share is a birth date.

They disappear inside, and the street is quiet again.

By the river the ducks are preening themselves on the bank. There's a half-eaten sandwich on the ground in the grit. I pick it up and throw it. 'Here.' They waddle over, necks straining, flapping their wings. 'Eeeee,' I run at them before they can reach it, sending them waddling in fright back into the water. A man with a dog walks past and throws me a look of disgust like I'm a pile of his dog's shit.

'What?'

I'm not going back to Falcon House yet. To broken furniture or a smashed window, loaded sighs.

I don't want to be alone either.

You don't have to join them. Walk, leave while you can.

'Hi, what goes?' They're huddled together, bunched for protection. Same faces, pinched, acned. Smoke gags me.

'Nuala!' Heads jerk in my direction. 'Hi, lover girl.' Kelly's spread over some guy. He's tall, black hair shaved short at the sides, two partings and a ponytail on top of his head. They're both glary eyed.

'Christ, Kelly, it's only early evening. You're a mess.'

'So? What's it to you?' She's posing like a model, gyrating her hips.

'What's so funny?'

'Ooh, get the fancy hairstyle. Too good for us, are you? Looks like you got striped pyjamas on your head.' They choke with laughs,

164

she kisses him, plays with his groin. I want to puke.

'Here.' It's Declan sidling up to me. 'Have a joint.'

'No, trying to give them up. Oh, go on then.' A long slow draw and the smell of new straw drifts round me.

'Where've you been?' he says.

I shrug. 'I've been ill.'

Declan looks at me blankly. 'Ugh. Take no notice of those two. That Kelly's something else. What did she say to you about striped pyjamas?' He's grinning.

We share the smoke till it's done.

'Another?' He lights it before I answer.

'Oi, you. Stuck-up cow.' Kelly's swaying over me, pulls my hair, I throw her hand off.

'Got Jax's … bap, bap, bap, bap. Well, have you?' Two fingers poke into my face. 'Think we don't know. Wonder who else might like to know? Wouldn't be a stuck-up cow then, would you? You'd be a locked-up cow.' Her bloke farts, they're in fits of giggles.

'Filthy piece of garbage,' I spit back at her. 'Bloody leave me alone.'

Then pain, like a burn. More pain. Hands in my hair. Purple and black twisted in her fingers. Teeth bared in a snarl.

Declan yanks me back before I kill her. He stands over me like a bodyguard while I sit on a broken wall, tearing at the brick, breaking my fingernails.

'Want to try some?' He balances two pills on his palm.

'What?'

'Acid. What do you think? Guarantee it'll take you some place you've never been. Higher than the sky.'

One swallow and a slug of water.

'It's my birthday.'

Declan cups his hands round my face. 'Lousy, friggin' shit that is.'

'Nothing's happening, Dec.'

'Wait. It will.' He's holding me, wrapped in his coat.

'Those stars. They're getting bigger, brighter, turning into moons.'

'Did you see?' My hand is waving in front of me. 'Whoosh, a falling star. Whoosh, whoosh. They're all falling, fireworks for free. Hmm, hmm.' I dance with the graffiti figures from the side of the derelict house. Slow smoochy steps in time to the cymbals in my head. Faster, whirling rainbows, feet tapping, thunderclaps. Every leaf on every tree is dancing, black against the sky, blacker than black, witches with fingers, pointing at us, pinching me. The wind is a thousand needles pricking, a scalpel shaving off my skin, peeling it inch by inch so I am bones and organs. In the palm of my hand my heart is beating. In out, in out, tick, tock, tick, tock. It stops. I shake it. Harder. 'Restart, you bugger'. It doesn't. 'I'm dead. Useless heart.' Throw it away. It drowns in the puddle where the stars have landed.

Much later Declan and I walk the streets, our arms around each other's waists. The lights flickering on and off in a shop window fascinate us. 'Poetry,' I say, 'that's what it is. A light show just for us.' Declan agrees, and we sit on the kerb, watch a while longer.

'We're an audience, Nuala, at a pop concert with no songs.'

'Do you believe in God, Declan?'

'Well, I used to go to church as a kid if that's what you mean.'

What's he saying? The words keep moving. 'Is that the same thing?'

'Maybe. Do you then?'

'Do I what?'

'Believe in God.'

'I don't know if I'm a Catholic or a Protestant.' A giggle gambols along the pavement. 'That's so funny.

'Today might not even be my birthday.'

Declan is studying his hands, turning them over to check they belong to him. 'Why is that then? My birthday is the twentieth of December. It's the same every year, not on the same day though only the same date.' He scans my face to make sure I've got it.

'That's because you know when you were born.' I smooth the frown on his forehead with the palm of my hand.

'I don't remember it; being born I mean.' His frown is back.

'Get this then.' I whisper in his ear. 'I don't … know when I was born. No one knows. My birthday is a made-up date.'

He takes my hand and puts it on his knee, strokes my fingers like they're fur. 'Tell me again in the morning 'cos it doesn't make sense to me.'

'Nor me, Declan.' I purr like I'm his cat, his big black and purple-striped cat.

Sunday, I want to die. My bedroom walls pulsate, knife flashes of light make me flinch. I stagger to the kitchen and drink. Cold water dribbles over my chin. Let it.

'Are you ill again?' Martha's all concern. I pretend. She's not fooled. 'Nuala, I've seen it all before.' Disappointment in her eyes.

She shows me the birthday cake they made for me – the one I wasn't there to eat – then she scrapes it off the plate into the bin. Pink icing, sponge cake, smashed candles all hit the bottom of the can.

Martha leaves me alone.

The gang scene. I won't be part of it. Never, ever, ever again I promise.

A sob whispers into the blackness butting my window. 'Thanks, Declan, for last night, for being kind. I mean it. Go well.' With a concrete head and sick in my throat, I ferret beneath my jumpers and lift the black metal from its grubby cloth.

It's not real.

It's cold. Stark when I lay it on my white skin. There's a smell of oil from the cloth and smears of grease shine in the light.

I grasp the handle, my palm like a glove.

Go on, do it.

I curl a finger round the trigger.

Go on. I dare you.

It's a voice dancing in my skull.

I press the barrel on my tongue, hear the click against my teeth, taste the tang of metal.

It is real.

'Fucking hell.' I throw it. The gun hits the skirting board.

I freeze. The room swims, my lungs in a vice.

Crawl across the floor. Fingers, not mine, shaking fingers, alien fingers, stretch for it, claw it closer. Hide it.

I bury it under the mattress.

Rabbit crushes into my chin, his button eye like a pebble in a shoe. His fur, soggy from my stifled breath and dribble.

I'm not dead. I'm not dead.

Sleep is somewhere else. Morning's hours away.

Joe

'The cows are going.' Mary stood behind me.

I wiped my arm across my face convulsed with the disgrace of yesterday. Before I came across to the cowshed this morning, I'd straightened my place, swept it, left dirty dishes to soak in hot water, taken the sheets off the bed, turned the pillow still bearing the dent of Aoife's head, set the fire ready to light tonight to warm the place again. I didn't want time to think.

'What do you mean, the cows are going?' It felt like she'd slapped me again.

'I need to talk to you, Joe. Things I have to say.'

I finished what I was doing with a sense of dread, knocked on Mary's door as a stranger might.

'Come in quick and keep the north wind out.' Mary sat in her chair, one swollen leg on a footstool. I stood by the table twisting my woollen hat, Clemmie by my knee with her head tight against my leg.

'Mary, I'm sorry. What I did … it was …'

'Aye and you'm right about that but what's done's done. Now are you going to be sitting. I'll be having the neck ache if you'm not. You can be putting me a log in the stove too before you do.'

I saw the old lady Mary had become. Her sagging skin, her head shrunken into her neck, dark rings around her eyes. Clemmie lay down by the fire at her feet.

'The cows …?'

'Aye, they're going tomorrow or next day. Whenever the truck's free and the paperwork is sorted.'

'Not to the abattoir. Don't …' I saw Bella's huge soft eyes.

'No, no. To Home Farm where we got your dog from. He said he'll take them.'

'But …'

'It's for the best, Joe. What you going to say against it then?'

I slumped in a chair, hands across my face.

'Right, well, one thing out the way.' Mary struggled to her feet and shuffled towards the dresser, paused to put cold hands on my shoulders. 'There's more, Joe. Hear me out.'

I closed my eyes. Didn't want to listen.

'I promised I would stay while you needed me, and I will.' I struggled with the words, could feel Jack in the room, hear him sucking at his pipe.

'You've been a mess since Jack died, Joe. It's been hard for all of us for different reasons. This won't make it easier for you.

'It came the other day.' Mary gave me a postcard. A glossy picture of a busy street dominated by an imposing statue. DUBLIN written in black letters across the bottom.

I held the flimsy card between rigid fingers. 'Aoife. I know. She's gone to Dublin. I heard it in the bar.' I put the card on the table, pushing the gaudy scene away.

'Read it, Joe.'

As though asked to read my own death sentence I stared at the neat writing.

Darling Auntie Mary,
I wanted you to be the first to hear – Finn and I got married at the weekend.
I want to be happy. I want a family.
Be pleased for us.
Love you
Aoife x

'Much too hasty if you ask me. Won't solve anything.' Mary's voice shook. 'But she's made her bed, she has to lie in it.' She squeezed my shoulder and I put my hand over hers. Only Mary's wheeze broke the tomb-like silence.

I let go of her, walked to the window and rubbed away the condensation. A cockerel perched on the step of the old broken tractor which I hadn't touched since the day Jack died. The bird's red cockscomb jerked as it crowed to the hens pecking in the yard. Through the gate, the track, the grasses lying flat, beaten by the rain. Seagulls swooped on the grain; their caws penetrated the silent room.

'There's more I need to say, Joe.' She was pulling at the dresser drawer that always stuck. 'Get me this envelope. These old hands are useless nowadays.'

I grasped the envelope for her.

'It's for you, Joe. Your eyes are better than mine, you'll have to study all them papers. Go on then. I'm hopin' it'll give you something else to think about.'

I read; my mind too dulled to make sense of the legal jargon.

'Mary, what is this?'

She pulled the kitchen chair nearer.

'We talked it over – he wanted it this way. "He's a good lad is Joe, make a good farmer when he knows a bit more," is what he used to say. Mary chuckled. 'Always knew better than anyone else, stubborn as they come, right to the end.

'You didn't kill him, Joe. Don't think it. He knew he hadn't got long. Remember a while back when we took off to Galway – it's when we sorted it. What do you think then, Farmer Joe?'

My hands shook. My name jumped at me from the thick paper.

'The farm is yours Joe, and a little money to start you off. Money for Aoife and enough for me. For a while we thought, hoped, you and Aoife … Sometimes you young things can't see what's good for you.

'Looks like you could be doing with a drop of my brandy. Have you nothing to say?'

'Mary, I can't. I don't deserve …'

'He loved you, Joe. As near to having another son as he could get. You made his last few years happy. He loved his farm too mind, wouldn't have entertained the idea if he supposed you'd mess it up.'

'I messed it up the other night. You don't have to do this, Mary. Tear it up. Pretend you've never shown me.'

'It's what I want too, Joe. Besides which, the old devil would come back to haunt me if I went against his wishes. Make it work, Joe. You can do it. It's not much. More a smallholding than a farm. Anyhows, it's yours. Put a brew in the teapot and stop sitting there like you're made of stone.

'There is one more thing.' Mary shuffled into her own chair, nudging Clemmie where she lay twitching, lost in dreams.

'As soon as she can come for me, I'm going to the mainland, my cousin lives there.'

'No.

'Mary, this is your home. No, you can't …'

'Yes, I must, Joe. Jack and I used to talk about it – if anything happened to him – I'd go to our Philomena's. That's an end to it.'

I crouched at her side, put my arms round her frail shoulders and pulled her head into my chest. I kissed the top of her forehead, her skin so paper-thin the veins showed through like contour lines on a faded map.

'Stop your blabbing,' she mumbled. 'Let's have some tea and strikes me you've got work to do then.'

I walked across to Jack's gate feeling flattened like barley after a storm. This both my worst day and my best. The wood, rough with algae, felt different. I saw the relief of the ground, the indent where the sheep shelter from the storms, the cliffs at the point. The grass an emerald green and the hedges leafing after winter. I rubbed a handful of dirt between my fingers and smelt it. My soil, my land.

'Help me, Jack, I'll make you proud.' I smiled, the smile became a laugh, the whoop set Clemmie barking. In the shabby farmhouse Mary stood framed in the window. She waved and I waved back.

I couldn't bear to watch the cows being loaded onto the truck.

'Going into beef instead then? It's rubbish, the price for milk. Lots of farmers doing the same.' The truck driver slapped the flanks of the animals not noticing my lack of response.

Bella turned on the ramp and bellowed. Frightened eyes rolled in her head.

'Go on, old girl. You'll be fine once you're there.' I rubbed her nose and turned away remembering what I owed her. The truck became smaller and smaller as I watched it disappear.

The cowshed had already taken on an abandoned look. My sense of loss echoed in its emptiness.

'For the best, Joe. Slate's clean. Do what you like now. Jack only kept them few cows for sentimental reasons. He always said farmers can't afford to be soppy but underneath his grumpiness he was soft as ducks' down.' Mary unhooked Jack's old jacket and put it over her arm. 'You'll not be needing it.'

'Leave it, Mary. I like it there. It's like Jack's watching me.'

'Aye and I bet he is an' all. Muttering away to himself and choking on a dirty old pipe.' With a sigh she hung the jacket back on the hook, lifted a sleeve and let it fall.

'I've a mince tart in the oven. We could both do with the company tonight, I'm thinking.'

Nuala

Morning comes at last. My decision made. I climb out of a window and drop soundlessly onto the flower bed. Crouch, listen, my hand against the rough brick wall. Nothing. Run, past the bakery, across the car park of the supermarket and into the streets of terraced houses and closed curtains. Lights flicker on as people waken. The gun knocks against my hip. I slow when the river is in sight, clutch my side to relieve the burning.

'Good morning to you. Promises to be nice later.' A man in a suit, an anorak thrown over the top raises his hand as his black Labrador sniffs at my feet, nudges at my jacket with its nose, tail wagging fast. 'He thinks you've got biscuits. You haven't, have you?' He points at my pocket, laughs and walks on whistling.

I'm sure he knows.

The river at this end of town is more of a wide stream. The path alongside is easy to follow at first but it narrows, and there's fallen trees and tangled branches with brown, clinging leaves.

We came here, Ted. I wonder if you remember it like I do. Our second date but we didn't call it that. It didn't work, did it? We were like two nervous deer, scared of each other.

Remember this? I text him a photo. He won't remember.

The stream is fast flowing, the marsh boggy. Birds with witches' cries startle into flight. The noise of the waterfall is loud, but I can't see it yet. A white smash of water hurtles over a deep crevice in the rocks, the spray wetting my feet. A tree branch teeters on the brink before launching itself into the fury. I toss a stone; it disappears into the pool beneath the fall.

At the water's edge I stand on a flat boulder and put the gun at my feet. I kick it as far as possible into the stream. A splash. Some ripples. The stream never falters, keeps pouring its load over the rocks.

As easy as that.

My hand dangling in the flow is like a punishment, icy cold, so numb I can't feel it hurting. There's sunlight at my feet, rainbows in the water. A beetle scurries from the undergrowth into daylight.

Here, Ted, for you. I blow him a kiss, send him a selfie, me and the waterfall. All the other lads have pictures of their girls on their phones, he says – would I mind? He'll be well pleased, two pictures in one day.

The ache in my stomach has gone, I've stopped shivering. I realise I'm hungry.

It's belting hot when I go back to school after Easter, too hot for sweaters. I keep mine on.

'Thanks for the card,' I mumble. We're on a bench under a tree on the playing fields. It's weird, sitting with them.

'Ooh, I like your hair. Where'd you have it done?' Claire (or is it Megan?) brushes it with her hand. I yank away from her.

A boy asks, 'Are you better?' I expect he's sorry I am.

Mrs Leafe shouts 'Hi,' a wide smile on her face.

'What's this, Nuala? Homework? You've been ill.'

'The essay you set before the holidays. Some books too, those you lent me. I've read them.'

She's running her finger along the spines.

'I'll find more. Did you enjoy them?

'Well done by the way.' She's handing me a previous piece of work from a pile on her desk. 'Good mark, well deserved. You've grasped the meaning behind the question.' I stuff it in my bag. 'Do similar in the exam and you'll pass easily.'

She must be talking about someone else. 'Ugh.' I pull a face. like an idiot? 'I'm only taking English, no other fucking exams. Sorry,' I mutter, 'didn't mean to be stroppy.'

She grins at me. 'Okay. You can study in the future. I think you should – you are perfectly able. Standing before me is a determined young lady who will succeed at whatever she puts her mind to. I hope it's on the right side of the law!'

She's laughing at me, poking fun. I don't mind. 'Here's hoping.'

*

The smell of the hairdressing salon is delicious. I love the sweet mixture of shampoo, spray and colour products.

'Hi, Nuala, we're busy today. A bride is coming in later.'

Gemma's always nice. Nearest my age. Sandie is too.

'A coffee for Mrs Drury, then will you shampoo for me? Lots of hair to sweep up when you have a minute.'

Others think it's boring. It's my favourite job. Hair, different shades and textures like fairy gossamer.

All the time there's chatter, laughter, noise from the hairdryers.

'You're good at this.' An old lady swathed in a lurid lime green gown peers at me from where she sits, head back over a bowl. 'Your hands must smell gorgeous.'

'They do, but they look like wrinkled prunes at the end of the day and my feet ache. Sometimes I think I'm too tired to walk home.'

'You'll get used to it. I remember when I started as a nurse. The first week, back of a shift, I stood at the end of the ward thinking no way could I walk down it one more time.'

She's laughing. 'A long time ago. I'm eighty-seven now.' I help her from the chair, a towel wrapped round her head. She's tiny and holds onto my arm until we reach another chair. 'Thank you, dear. I like to have my hair done each week – it's lonely when you're on your own. I'll ask for you to wash it every time, yours is the best and I enjoy the massage.' She's smiling with watery eyes, pats my hand. 'You're so kind.'

I make an excuse, disappear into the restroom and sit on the loo until I can breathe again.

Books scattered all over my bed. Tomorrow is the exam. 'Why can't I remember anything?' It's all marching out of my brain. Under my quilt I bury my head in the pillow and kick the textbooks off the covers.

I am by the stream again. Warm, the sun like a hundred torches waving in the trees. There is someone coming towards me – Ted. Not Ted, a gun with legs and a grinning head, chasing me. Bramble thorns hook into my skin, tear me to pieces. My scream jolts me awake. I push at the window for air. It only opens a fraction, reminding me who I am, where I am. 'You forgot, didn't you. You're Nuala McCurdy. IN CARE. Not Nuala McCurdy who sits exams.'

Jesus, what am I doing?

'Good luck.' You'll do us proud. Martha's driven me to school. 'You're a star, Nuala.'

It's not too late to run. Running's what I'm best at.

Mrs Leafe is there. She sweeps me up with the rest, shepherds us along. 'Best of luck, best of luck, you'll be fine.' She has a word for each of us as we pass single file into the hall. Her hand touches my arm. She mouths 'thank you' and I'm in the exam room.

Silence swallows me. Fuck.

The paper – a fuzz of words. My shaking hand. Sit on it, make it stop. Sighs and shuffles, backs of heads lean towards the desks. Everyone's writing. Someone is standing by my desk. I want to leave. It's not a teacher. It's Big-un, he's smiling, pulling a funny face to make me laugh. He lifts a pen and together we begin to write like we did that first day.

'Celebration cakes for the end of term!' Mrs Leafe unwraps chocolate rolls and cupcakes. 'Some of you are leaving and some won't take English in the sixth form, but I wanted to be the one to tell you I won't be here either next term. I'll be back though. You may have guessed. I'm having a baby so will be off on maternity leave.'

'Oh, Miss.' Oohs and aahs from the girls, the boys joke with each other behind closed hands.

A thump in the gut for me. A hole has opened, another great yawning pothole.

'Nuala.' She pulls me aside as the bell rings. 'Sorry if it's a shock.'

'Makes no difference to me.' Swallow the truth. 'I'm never setting foot in a school building again.'

'We're thrilled about having the baby and things.'

'Yeah, well good luck.' I shrug off her arm. 'I wanted a baby once. Gutted when I wasn't pregnant.'

Shouldn't be telling a teacher this.

She's nodding. 'Yes, I saw your face. I'd like you to come and see me, see the baby when it comes. I'm not far away.' She's holding books against her chest. She wants me to say yes.

Turn away, look somewhere else.

'Not my style. Easy come, easy go, that's me.'

God, I'm cruel.

'It doesn't have to be. It can be different.'

'Not for me it can't. It's how we do it. Kids like me.'

I take off before she says more. 'Never need and never be needed.' I fling it over my shoulder to hit her where she stands framed by the window.

The town centre sucks. People going nowhere. End of school.

I won't go back. At the river I sit on the grass surrounded by duck poo.

'First day of the rest of my life and all such bumf.' The ducks aren't fucking listening.

'Great.'

Not.

Next morning. Haven't slept. Something's eating me up, a maggot in my brain. What is it? I remember – something I've got to do. Something to put right. The bedroom window's misted. I write sorry in the moisture. It's early, there's not much traffic on the road. It's raining.

The car park, the ugly school, grim like an army barracks. Bang my arms, wish I'd brought a coat. So much for summer. Cars arrive but not hers. Hers is a blue Fiesta, a small bump in the back where she said she'd hit a post.

Just leave it. Who cares anyway? You do. That's who. Boxers slugging it out in my head. 'Shut up, shut the fuck up.'

She backs into a parking spot and opens the boot to retrieve her bag.

'Miss.' She jumps, pushes back against the car door.

'Nuala!'

'I wanted to say … thank you.'

Cottonwool stuffs my mouth.

'For lending me the books and stuff.' Kick my foot, cough. 'Congrats – about the baby – I mean.'

She hugs me, right there in the car park. Christ, anyone can see. Her arms tight around my shoulders, her bag against my back. She's not saying anything. I turn when I'm halfway down the drive, before I duck under the bridge.

She's standing by the car watching. 'Twenty-fifth of August, GCSE results. Remember the date. I'll be at the school,' she calls and waves goodbye.

Back in bed, Rabbit is tucked in beside me, his soft fur against my lips. I'm warm.

Joe

'Mary, why don't you let me take you?' Mary had been sitting in her coat for the past hour, the remnants of a lifetime in a shabby brown suitcase beside her. 'I'll not be needing anything more,' she said. The room looked like it always did except for the absence of the photos and a pipe of Jack's cold on the table since he died.

'No, Joe. Philomena's coming for me. I want you to drive us back across the causeway. See us safe on the other side. Trouble with inland folk they don't understand the sea and the tides.

A car bumped into the farmyard. A thin stick of a woman eased herself out, holding onto the roof as she straightened her back. The cousin was as old as Mary; her silver hair wound in a bun at the back of her head, loose strands escaping from a tortoiseshell comb.

'You keep away, mind. Don't come bothering her. She needs to settle.' Philomena grasped her walking stick and tapped my chest with a blue-veined hand. 'There's not everyone agrees with what they've done. Others could have benefitted if the farm had been sold.'

I bit my lip to hold back a knot of grief and followed the muttering woman into the house.

'Don't think much to driving across soft sand, can't trust it,' she grumbled. 'We'll go straight off, soon as I've been to the toilet.' Philomena's stick clattered onto the kitchen floor. 'We can stop off at the tearoom on the way back. Never liked this old place.' She dismissed it with her hand. 'Needs modernising so it does.' She shut herself in the bathroom.

'You don't have to go. Mary, please let me look after you.' I held her sagging shoulders.

She put her fingers against his lips. 'Put the case in the car, Joe.' She glanced around the room one last time. 'Aye,' was all I heard her say.

I drove them back across the causeway, then helped Philomena into the driving seat when they reached the other side. 'Who'd want to go living on an island?' She shook her head, banged the door shut and started off with a lurch, her bespectacled eyes peering over the steering wheel. I ached to give Mary a hug but could only wave. 'I'll come and see you.' She never looked round.

The car disappeared. I stooped to pick a small pink flower poking through the grass, left it on the wall like a memorial. Trudged home tasting the salty air, the island a stark silhouette against a colourless sky, the sand concertinaed into ridges, flat seaweed stranded in pools. Today the trek seemed endless. I climbed the steps from the strand to where the gravestones stood proud on the headland.

'Not today, Jack. I can't face you today.' I turned for home.

The sheep were sheared, and a warm June sun had shone all day. Thomas the shearer had been reminiscing.

'Can't believe it's near on eighteen months since Jack went.' Thomas looked around as though expecting him to appear. He told lots of stories about Jack in his younger days, had me laughing.

'Wish I'd known him then. He must have been a lad, Daniel too.' I was glad of the company and the refreshment when we finished the work.

'I went to school with Daniel. He always wanted to work the farm. Had big ideas but Jack would have none of it. Bit of a traditionalist I reckon.' Thomas chuckled. 'You should have heard them going at it sometimes, like fisher wives they were. Tragic it was – the accident. Changed Jack for sure.' He drained his glass. 'He'd be pleased you're carrying it on. Had a lot of time for you. Jack wasn't one for praise but it's what he used to say.'

After Thomas had left, and the sheep moved to a new pasture, I walked around the outhouses of the farm. I'd spent weeks repairing leaking roofs and preserving wood with a lick of paint. The old tractor was still there but I couldn't shift it, promised myself I'd try to sort it. I'd got used to it in the yard, the hens roosted there and Clemmie lay in its shade. The other tractor I kept in the cowshed. At first I hated sitting in the cab. Too many memories. But I'd become used to it, proud even. I'd ploughed a field and resown it with grass. I recounted my achievement to Art. 'I reckon I've watched it grow inch by inch.' He'd pursed his lips and almost smiled.

I was accustomed to my own space. Through the spring I'd kept the fire in the house going – in case Mary returned, I told myself. I knew she wouldn't come back but I couldn't bring myself to think of the bigger place as mine. I liked my cottage, though sometimes Aoife seemed to fill the room, reminding me she'd once been there.

Aoife, a cut, healed on the surface, tender and bruised beneath.

In the months after Mary left, I was busy. The paperwork floored me. I would spread it over the kitchen table, then crawl into bed hours later, head full of questions, the table littered with half-completed forms. Word had spread about me taking over, more gossip when Mary left. All had an opinion as to who should have had the farm. I heard the snatches of talk, aware of the sudden ending of conversations when I entered the local shop or at the cattle market. How could I tell them I missed her? Missed her clucking to the chickens, telling me off for my muddy boots, seeing her dozing in her chair.

I found the bar difficult too. Felt as conspicuous as when I'd first set foot in the place. The regulars acknowledged me with a silent nod over their beers. The talk loud around me of the country's economic crash – angry voices, strained faces. Ronan wasn't there. 'On a driving job,' they said.

'I need advice.' I addressed the man sitting next to me at the bar. The place fell quiet like they'd all been waiting for the moment. Even Seamus stopped serving to listen.

'I've a sheep that's coughing.'

A collective drawing-in of breath from the farmers. The others lost interest and resumed their drinking.

'Lungworm most like.'

'Eaten a thistle and regretted it.'

'Gobbling the nuts, over-excited.'

'Hope I'm wrong but could be ovine pulmonary adenocarcinoma.'

The babble of voices made me raise both hands.

'Hold on, I'm a beginner remember.' In the future I would say this was the moment the locals took me under their wing. Afterwards they would always enquire after the farm, eager to share their knowledge, remind me of what I needed to be doing, moan with me over the stifling regulations. I listened to them. They liked me for that.

'Ask three farmers and you get three different answers.' I laughed with them.

Art was the same. Came over to the farm for a beer, or we'd meet on the track and talk sheep.

'Need a couple of teaser tups to set the ewes going next year. 'Tis expensive though.'

'Art, you frighten me with the language you use. What the hell is a teaser tup? Got myself a second-hand computer and I spend hours checking these things on the internet. Some of it makes sense.'

Art harrumphed. 'You can't learn farmin' from a machine. Don't understand these newfangled things. Waste of time, seems to me.'

We got on best when we had our heads over the engine of a car. After months of tinkering we fired up the old Morris Minor and Art drove round the island going no faster than ten miles per hour.

'You're as proud as a new dad you are,' I laughed at him. Art tipped my cap over my eyes and biffed me.

I was making sheep pens the day Ronan showed up. I'd seen a car and presumed it to be a tourist on the island for the afternoon.

'Joe, how are yer?' I recognised the voice but squinted against the brightness to determine its owner.

'Ronan. What brings you here? Can't believe you're taking a walk.'

Ronan patted his paunch. 'It's what I should be doing, but no – came to see you in your place.' He studied the yard. 'Better than when Jack and Mary lived in it. Bit tidier like.' He ran his hand along the painted windows of the farmhouse. 'Moved in here, have you?'

'It got too much for the old 'uns.' I leapt to defend them, didn't like it when people made comment.

'Yep. Salt of the earth, old Jack, but farming's no easy job.'

I found cold beers and we sat on a seat outside the empty house.

'How are you finding it then?' Ronan ran his finger round the top of his glass. 'I mean, are you making it work?' I liked Ronan, believed I owed him after the night the gardai showed up.

Wary of his question, I whistled to Clemmie, she came over and I rubbed her ears.

'I'm learning. Why do you ask? Does it look like I'm not or do folk think I'm too green, waiting for me to fail?'

'Whoa, I come as friend not foe.' Ronan offered his hand. 'These are not good times and the country is sinking into its own stinking mess. The Celtic Tiger has lost its roar. Only ones with any money, it seems to me, are the bankers who caused the bloody mess in the first place.' Ronan emptied his glass and was up for another. 'However, I didn't come to talk politics, interesting though it would be.'

I fetched two more beers and pulled off the caps, sipping at the head of my own before it overflowed. How much did I want to confide?

'To be honest, the farm, it's fair to middling but it's not easy. Vet's bills and the like, they're the killers. I don't need much when there's only me.' I stared at the sky turning the colour of old gold. 'It's not really big enough to be profitable. I never want to leave.' I said it almost to myself.

'Okay, straight to the point. There's a driving job going on the timber lorries. Not full-time, only when we're busy, short distance. I know you have a licence. I wasn't meaning for you to give this up, extra income that's all. Lots of farmers diversifying these days. Send me away with a flea in my ear if you like – no hard feelings, mate. Think on it. You can be lonely in places like this, Joe, a young man like you.' Ronan hesitated and coughed.

'Did you know? Aoife ... has had a baby, a son, grand little lad, so it's said.' Ronan patted my arm. 'Better you hear it from me. Women, eh, fickle as fireflies and as hard to find.'

I was restless after Ronan left, my head scrambled like a plate of eggs. I set off with Clemmie across the fields. She barked with pleasure, scrabbling at rabbit holes, her nose brown with soil. I reached the ruined church. I hadn't been there since Aoife left. I still saw her face, in the crowds in town, amongst the tourists, at the auctions. Always someone else.

Here her laughter rang amongst the tumbled stones.

'Be happy.' I threw my wish across the sea and over the mountains to Dublin.

'Beautiful, isn't it?' A hiker with a hand-hewn pole was speaking to me. The English accent sounded strange.

'It is. I live here – at the farm in the distance.' I pointed to where it blended into the landscape.

'Lucky you. Guess it's hard in winter. Must see some fierce storms.' The man pulled two cereal bars from his rucksack and handed one to me.

'Used to it, I guess. Those are my sheep.' They were like polka dots on green material. I didn't mean to sound smug. 'Thanks for the biscuit.'

The man looked at his watch. 'Five minutes and I need to go – before the tide comes in – I wanted to stay on the island but there's no accommodation. Someone needs to do B & B or something. Don't you ever yearn for the opportunities the bright lights could bring? It's remote for sure.'

'Exactly why I like it. It's those opportunities I don't want, don't need.'

'Right. Nice to talk to you. Good luck. I envy you being contented with your lot. Few people are.' The man set off towards the shore.

Contented? Mum, my brothers, Bridget, Nuala, Aoife, Jack and Mary. A parade of people stretching back. You're a survivor. I played with the idea and liked it. Told Clemmie, 'It's a new chapter. A brand-new chapter.' We loped down the hill, jumping over the stones, me trying to keep my footing.

Nuala

I'm bored of thinking of Mrs Leafe and her growing baby. Were you pleased about having me, Mum? Did you tell Dad and dance round the room excited? Why haven't I even got a picture of you?

Visit Debbie. A sudden idea. Her baby must be seven, eight months old. She'll say, who the hell are you?

I paint my fingernails black and wear a rainbow friendship bracelet round my wrist. It's only Debbie. Don't need to show off. With my hair pulled back and my old leather jacket on I feel okay. 'No breasts,' it's what Kelly called me. I stick them out. 'Yeah well, you're right but I don't care a monkey for what you think any more.' I grin at the thin girl reflected in the window glass; she grins back.

A blue and yellow rattle, cute. The shop girl is young like she should be at school. She puts the rattle in a pink-striped bag, fiddles with her earing and shouts, 'Next.' She's bored too.

New Street. Sounds right. Scruffy houses posh once. Multiple numbers on the doors. 1, 1a, 1b, 2, 2a, 2b, 2c. Christ, how many people live here. I think Debbie's crumpled bit of paper says 32b. It's a house with a red door. A torn ball is half-buried beside a bicycle wheel on a dried patch of grass. I'm never living in a place like this. If this is what Jess means by 'leaving care arrangements' she can keep them. The main door opens with a squeak into a square hallway with black-and-white tiles. I knock where there's a baby crying, thinking I may be at the right place. Knock again louder. Perhaps she can't hear over the racket. The lock rattles from inside and the door opens a fraction. This is such a mistake. The top of Debbie's head appears, I see the dark roots of her hair.

'Debbie, it's Nuala.' My heart has stopped; an unwashed smell wrinkles my nose. We stare at each other. 'Hi, I … came to say hello.' She lets me in and flops onto a sofa.

'Big room.'

'No furniture you mean.' She strikes a match then blows it out.

'Nice rug. Shall I pull the curtains back?' As well as the sofa there's a semi-decent chair and a set of shelves with nothing on them. Cigarette smoke itches my throat.

'Why are you here? What do you want?'

'Is that the baby crying?' Daft question but the noise is getting to me.

'He's in the bedroom.' She nods towards a door. 'Never stops yelling. Never sleeps neither.' She's relighting a fag.

'I bought him a present.'

She pulls the rattle from the bag and puts it on the coffee table beside her smokes and a rolled-up dirty nappy. 'Thanks.'

She's in her pyjamas and it's past lunchtime.

'Shall I grab him?'

'If you like.'

The baby's strapped in a pushchair, snot running from his nose. He stops screeching and puts his arms up. Wants lifting. I wipe his face with my sleeve. 'Come on, mate.' How do I undo the bloody clasp? I can't fathom it so pull him out the top. 'You are stinky.'

'I had a bad night.' Debbie's in a ball, her legs tucked under her. 'Ryan, cut it, won't you.'

He's only whimpering. 'Hey, what's this?' I jiggle him on my knee, give him the rattle. He holds it in a chubby little fist and tries to stick it in his mouth.

'Sorry, I haven't been before.'

She shrugs.

'Jesus, Debbie, you look awful.' I want to hug her. 'Look, don't take this the wrong way. I know nothing about babies, but I know you shouldn't be smoking, not in the same room anyway.'

'Right. You know nothing about babies, so shut the fuck up.'

'Here, have him. You're right. I'm going if that's how …'

Tears are rolling down her face, her chest caved in with sobs. Her cigarette shakes in her fingers, ash drops onto the carpet.

'Oh, Debbie,' I hug her like she's a piece of precious china with Ryan squashed between us. 'Shush.' I rock them both, squeezed together on the sofa until she's quiet, and the baby falls asleep. My arms ache.

'Right, I'll make us both a drink and you a piece of toast.' It's odd taking charge. 'When's the last time you ate?'

Another shrug. Answer enough.

The kitchen's a gloomy beige like the other room. Someone's stencilled ivy round the window. By the sink there's used baby bottles, a blue and yellow Linfield F.C. mug and another with BEST MUM written on the side. Both have cold coffee in them. I fill the bowl with hot water, add lots of washing-up liquid and plunge my arms in. For just a minute I'm a little girl again. Bernie is laughing as I squeeze froth and bubbles between my fingers and blow them into the air. I shake my head to stop remembering. A pan with a few dried baked beans is on the stove. Somewhere there must be a cloth to clean the work surfaces with. Use a tea towel instead, brush the crumbs onto the floor and leave the dishes to drain.

'Tea or coffee, Debbie?' No answer, so I make tea. The bread is mouldy. It'll have to do. I dig at bits with my fingernail, and it's better toasted. Margarine? Jam? In the fridge there's a slice of pizza and two filled baby bottles. Jesus, Debbie!

'Here you go. At your service, madam.' I stop dead, the toast slithers off the plate. She's fast asleep, dried tears smudge her face. 'Debs.' She makes a little whistling sound. At least she's alive.

'It's you and me then, mate.' Ryan's awake again, watching me with dark brown eyes, sucking his thumb, a damp curl plastered to his forehead.

'Do you enjoy having your tummy tickled?' He wriggles but keeps on sucking. 'Shall we open the window, let out some of Mummy's smoke?' The window doesn't budge. 'No joy there. Suppose you're used to it.' I find a nappy in the bedroom and lie him on the unmade bed. 'I've absolutely no idea how to do this so please will you co-operate.' He's trying to suck his toe and smile at the same time. 'Yuk, Ryan. That is so stinky.' I wipe God-knows-what off his bottom, holding my breath as I do it. There's white cream in a pot which I smear on hoping that's what it's meant for. 'Better? At least you smell sweeter.' I take him to the window; he giggles when his feet touch the glass and he pushes off with them. In the street, a woman is holding a mountain of coats while three children run ahead of her. Between the clouds I can see swipes of blue sky.

'Come on. We're going out. Leave your mum to sleep. What do you think?'

I grab a bottle and wheel the pushchair through the lounge and into the stairwell. Can't find a key so just close the door quietly behind me. Debbie's not going anywhere. Pushing Ryan along the road I pretend he's mine.

'Is this good? Look, Ryan, there's a doggie. Woof, woof.' Lucky there's no one to hear. 'Woof, woof.' He chuckles. He's gripping the rattle. 'You like it, don't you?' I'm chuffed. 'Shall we go to the river, see the ducks?' I think babies like ducks.

In the corner shop I buy a packet of biscuits and break one in half. 'Yummy, yummy.'

'Meets with approval.' The shopkeeper leans over the counter. 'Don't stuff it all in at once, little man, or you'll choke.'

Soggy bits dribble from his mouth. Maybe he's too young for biscuits. He looks fine, not blue or anything.

At the pond a little girl is feeding a fat white duck with bread, but she runs squealing back to her dad when the geese waddle over. 'Let's take you out of your pushchair.' Ryan's little padded bottom is like a cushion on my knee.

The sun appears and I extricate my arms from my coat. 'Do you want yours off too?' Do babies catch cold? By the bandstand there's a clutch of young mums with their kids. One of them says something because they all turn in our direction. 'None of them look older than sixteen, do they, Ryan? All dressed the same, strappy white tops and leggings. Like it's a uniform.' I pull his thumb from his mouth. 'You don't say much, do you?' He puts it straight back in. Can't believe I'm talking to a baby. 'Does Mummy bring you here?'

Great. Ryan's sleepy after I give him his bottle and put him back in the pushchair.

The child-mums go quiet when I walk past them. Up yours, little shits.

Too soon to go back yet. Give Debbie a long sleep. I wonder if Kelly or some of the gang are around. So long since I've seen them. It would be a laugh – give them some gossip – they'd play guess the father. The shopping mall is hot and busy. 'I don't miss them. Well, only sometimes.' Ryan's not interested.

I've enough money for a chocolate bar. I eat it sitting on the concrete seats beside a planter with no plants, more like a bin with a Starbucks cup, a pink dummy and a glove.

Ryan's awake, rubbing his eyes with his fists. Kissing his dimpled knuckles chokes me up. Swallow hard, don't blab like an idiot.

'Try this.' He sucks my chocolaty finger. 'Mmm, good, isn't it, Mister sweet tooth? Now what shall we do?'

I want to look after this baby forever.

'How about we go somewhere I used to like. Up high, to the sky, where you can breathe. It's called a multi-storey car park. Big words, aren't they? You're so serious.'

The lift comes, I bang people's ankles with the pushchair wheels. 'Really.' A woman in a red suit has a loud voice. I put a finger up and she turns away.

'Bye.' I bawl when she gets out at level four.

I love this place like it's the top of the world.

'I came here when I skipped school, Ryan. Don't you be doing the same, mind. Can you see the cars, and motorbikes, the tiny people? Best of all, can you see the trees, way over there?'

Trees. The ripple of the wind. Fairies playing in the pines.

'Big-un taught me to love trees. Him and me, we used to sit on the bed, and he'd tell me the best stories ever. He'd like you, baby.'

I should have visited him. Nicky gave me a phone number. Bernie's card with the new address is still tucked in a drawer. I wanted to see him I really did but couldn't face it after the hospital and everything. Too pig-headed to admit it. Did he learn to walk again? Is he alive? A knife stab in my chest. Too late now, too long ago. Wishing something different, a niggle that won't go away. You blew it, Nuala McCurdy. All because you're a selfish cow.

'Out you come and see the buses then.' His hot little neck catches my tear.

'There's a bus. It looks tiny from here but it's not. Someday I'll take you on one. We'll sit right at the front and press the bell. Ting-a-ling, ting-a-ling. And see, there's a lorry, a bin lorry. You can see the orange flashing lights, can't you?' We lean over the rail, my arms around him. He waves his hands and feet, a bundle of movement.

'What do you think it'd be like to fly? Imagine it, Ryan – to get away from all this crap, never be sad again. Never know what losing your mummy feels like, never have to go into care, miss out on what other kids have and be some sort of freak. I'll hold you tight, I promise, all the way down. We'll float and float, you and me.'

I close my eyes and try to breathe. Jesus, for a minute it was happening. I'd wanted to do it. The wind rushing, me and Ryan gliding into a pool of light where I won't be me, he won't be him.

'Sorry, sorry, sorry, Ryan. I didn't mean it. I wouldn't do it, not for real. Oh God, good job you don't understand. I had my chances. Things nearly worked out. You deserve some too. Don't make a muck of yours like I did.'

He's exploring the stud in my ear, his small hand warm on my neck. I grab his fist and nibble his knuckles in a mess of kisses. He giggles. 'Come on, let's take you home.'

He presses the button in the lift, wants to press them all. 'Don't squirm or you'll go back in your pushchair.' We head for the shopping centre exit.

'Nuala.'

Who said that?

Police officers everywhere. More, running this way past shoppers who press themselves against the shop windows. The sound of sirens. The bench I sat on, the pink dummy. Nothing else the same.

'Nuala, it's all right. Give me the baby. Give me the baby, Nuala.'

Hot and cold make me dizzy.

'Step away, Nuala. Stay calm. No one's going to hurt you. I'm going to walk slowly towards you. Let me have the baby.'

I'm holding Ryan so tight he whimpers.

My feet are blocks of concrete.

'What are you fucking doing? Get away from me.' My scream bursts my head open. Ryan's screaming. 'Look what you've effing made him do.'

'The baby, Nuala.' A policewoman is holding out her arms.

Fucking police. 'What have I done?'

Ryan's piercing yells are shaking his body, he's kicking me.

'You've done this – made him fucking cry.' He's dangling like a doll in front of me.

'Good, Nuala. Give him to me. Well done. He's safe. You're safe.'

There's a space where he's been. I feel him there.

Ryan's crying a long way off.

'I didn't abduct him, steal him, kidnap him, none of the idiotic things you're saying. Can't you hear what I'm telling you? Debbie was asleep. Tell them, Debbie. The kid was awake. We went for a walk that's all.'

'It's not helpful to get hysterical.' The woman police officer shakes her head at me.

'How do you expect me to bloody be?' The throbbing in my head is a ball of red and black and green.

We're all squeezed in Debbie's shabby flat with its shabby furniture and essence of smoke. Jess is sitting next to me, her face blanched, as if it's her in trouble.

'It scared Debbie, Nuala. When she woke the baby had gone.'

Her perfume, which I like, today is making me sick.

'She thought you'd taken Ryan ... out of spite. Revenge, the word she used.'

'God, Debbie!'

It doesn't matter what I say. They'll think what they like anyhow. Hands over my eyes, the pinpricks of light I see are better than accusing faces.

No one's talking, only waiting.

'Okay. I've not seen Debbie since she left Falcon House. She gave me her address. I came to see her today, to see her baby. She was a mess, Ryan was crying. I made her some toast and tea, I even bloody washed up, cleaned the kitchen. When I came back in here, she'd gone to sleep. I took Ryan into the fresh air, out of this stink. We watched the ducks, walked into town. I took him to the multi-storey to show him the cars and buses and the … trees. Oh, and by the way I gave him a bottle and some biscuits.'

Debbie sniffs, plays the victim. She sneers in my direction and wipes her eyes with the back of her hand until her social worker gives her a tissue.

'I WAS GOING TO BRING HIM BACK.' Heads jerk. Jess rubs my hand. Ryan yells and Debbie grabs him from where he's sitting on the floor and rushes from the room.

'Can I go?' I close my eyes. Ribbons of colour. Fuzzy voices. Murmurs fading.

'Nuala, a baby was missing. The police had to act. Were right to act.'

'And yes, Nuala McCurdy is an unstable, self-harming, drug-user capable of kidnapping a child and dropping it off a multi-storey car park. Thanks for the character reference.'

'People saw you from the pavement, Nuala. It frightened them, what you might do. The police, they accept you meant no harm.' Jess chews her lip, waiting for something.

I can't be bothered. I want to sleep, quit the talking.

'You've done well, this past six months. Turned things around. Grown up, matured. A hiccup, this is a hiccup. Put it behind you, Nuala.'

'What's the fucking point of anything? When I try to do something right, it goes bloody wrong. I'm sick of it all, sick of all of you, sick of me.' I slam the car door on Jess' pale face as she leans across the passenger seat, lowers the window but changes her mind and waves a hand instead.

*

189

Sleep must be somewhere else because it's not anywhere round here. If I shut my eyes, I hear Ryan chuckling, open them and the dark's a strangler.

You don't have to stick around. No one will miss you. Cut the place – like Ted. It's worked for him. Go find him. Disappear, vanish, run.

Putting on the bedside light doesn't stop the voices. They get louder. A fire is catching, burning below my ribs, crawling through my veins, twitching my arms and legs, swelling, forming itself into an idea. Filling my head like a headache.

Over there. Why not? Be anyone you want. A job, money. None of this shit. I'll find Ted. I laugh out loud.

'YEAH, why not? WHY NOT. You're coming too, Rabbit. Where I go you go. Don't tell a soul. Got it. A big secret. You, me and a great new world.'

Joe

I stood in Jack and Mary's house. Despite my best effort to keep it aired a mustiness was creeping in. It used to be the heart of what they were: Mary, never happier than when stirring a pan at the stove, Jack, sitting dozing after a day in the fresh air. Now the place looked unlived in, unloved. Loss hurt like cramp. I righted a china horse. The clock with its comforting tick had stopped, the hands stuck at 7.20. I opened the door of the bedroom. Daniel's room, it hadn't changed since I slept there after Bella kicked me. Tools scattered on the chest of drawers alongside a small stack of postcards. The rubber band holding them disintegrated as I pulled one out. A picture of boats and the sea, the colours bright.

> *September 1958*
> *Alexandria is a busy port in Egypt. Tomorrow I am*
> *sailing through the Suez Canal.*
> *Hope you are being a good boy and looking after*
> *those new piglets.*
> *Uncle Amos xx*

Jack's brother. I leafed through the cards with their exotic foreign stamps imagining how exciting it must have been for the young Daniel when the postman delivered them. Sighed and stacked them where I'd found them, dismayed to have to clear all this away – someone else's family life.

I opened windows and left the door of the house ajar while I collected the hen's eggs and boxed them. There are new chickens coming next week and lots of repairs still needed doing.

Mary and her chickens. Some were so tame they would fly onto her knee when she sunned herself beside the front door. I smiled remembering.

Mary, she'd been lurking in my head for the last few days. On impulse I decided to go and see her, the address on the table still where she'd left it under a mat. 'Just in case mind,' she'd told me. 'Don't you be coming over bothering and such. You'll be having enough to be doing here.' At the time I'd acknowledged her with a grimace, not trusting myself to speak.

'Come on, Clems. Let's have a day out.' I closed the farmhouse door and jumped into the truck. Clemmie bounded in after me, sat on the passenger seat panting with excitement, her pink tongue protruding.

I stopped on the mainland to buy supplies and a bunch of flowers to take to Mary. The morning mist lifted as we travelled inland from the coast and an early autumn sun tipped the trees with lemon. I sang snatches of Beatles songs, remembered from my childhood. 'Liverpool's own if past their heyday,' I informed Clemmie. Words and cigarette smoke streamed from the window.

The countryside was full of houses for sale or building sites with no one working on them, proof of what everyone was talking about in the bar. At the recent cattle auctions the mood had been gloomy, prices falling, uncertainty pooling like a blocked drain. Desperate times, recession, austerity, I heard it all the time. I'm cushioned, living on the island, only myself to bother about. How had Aoife fared?

The sign told me I'd reached the place. A small nondescript town of terraced houses with drab doors, a few shops, shabby and desolate in the middle of the day. I wanted to push the buildings apart, make space. Two women with trolleys stood talking and a group of men leaned against the wall of the pub.

'Oh Mary, you must hate this.' The yellow bunch of flowers beside me the only colour around.

The road lay off the main street, but I couldn't find the house number.

'You seem lost. Can I help?' A woman walked by, her coat held closed in her bunched fist.

'I'm looking for number 23.' I showed her the piece of paper.

'Yes. The Cedars. The care home. That drive there. The house is hidden by the trees.'

'No, I think it's a private house.' I looked around confused, raking the nearby bungalows for a number.

'Who are you visiting?'

I saw the woman's green uniform under her coat.

'Her name's Mary O'Shea. Her cousin is Philomena.' I didn't know Philomena's surname.

'That's right. Mary, she's a dear old soul. Come with me. I'm going on shift. I'll show you where she is. She's in Red Wing. I'm a carer. Nice she's got a visitor. Follow me.'

A gardener knelt pulling out geraniums from a tub in front of a low modern building. There were benches on a patio but no one sitting on them.

I wanted to shout at the woman. 'A dear old soul? Don't talk about her like that. She's Mary. She's feisty, independent, the kindest person in the world.'

'I think there's a mistake. Mary O'Shea, from Connemara – from the islands.'

The woman stopped. I read her name badge, pinned above her pocket: Sue. She put her hand on my arm. 'I think this is a shock to you. Come and see her. It's a nice place. She's well cared for. Been here over a year. We love her loads.'

Warm air mixed with the smell of cooked food and urine engulfed me as the door closed in my wake. A cleaner washed the floor with a soapy mop, I stepped around signs warning me not to slip. Sitting rooms spread from a central hub like spokes of a wheel. A man with a serviette tucked into the neck of his shirt fluttered a hand in my direction.

'Mary, someone here to see you.' Sue bent close to Mary's ear. 'He's a handsome young man so he is.' Sue smiled and winked as she fastened the top button of Mary's heather-coloured cardigan and eased down the wrinkled skirt where it had risen above the old lady's knee. 'There, now you're smart for your visitor.' She dragged a red plastic chair across so I could be close to Mary. 'I'll be pushing on with the drinks then.'

I perched on the edge of the seat. In front of me Mary slept. She smelt of laundered clothes and talcum powder. Her neck arched sideways, her chin resting on her chest. A soft wheeze accompanied each breath.

I touched the almost transparent skin of Mary's hand with my finger. Veins stood like rivulets.

'It's Joe,' I whispered, my mouth dry.

Eight seats were arranged in two rows from the chimney breast where a fire with artificial coals glowed orange. A row of birthday cards, some with 90 on them, decorated a mantlepiece. Three other residents sat in the chairs. Two lay asleep, the other fingered the newspaper spread open on her knee, turning a page back and forth.

Sue appeared with coffee for me and a beaker with a spout for Mary.

'She may take a sip or two. Sleeps most of the time.' She gently shook Mary's shoulder.

'Are you a relative?'

'Yes – no. Well – sort of.'

'She had a small stroke six months ago, not really ever recovered.' Sue mouthed the words. 'I think she hears you though. You just talk to her.' Sue and another carer bustled on with the trolley, calling names as they distributed the drinks.

'I've increased the flock. Right made-up with them I am. I think Jack would approve.' I felt foolish, but no one paid me any attention. I held Mary's hand between my own. 'You'd be right proud of the yard too, clean as a whistle if it wasn't for those pesky chickens of yours. Thinking of getting some pigs. I know you used to have some.' I talked on, told her about the island and how a thunderstorm had caught me over the far side, drenched me to the skin. 'I miss you and Jack, go to the cemetery when I need to ask him something. Miss Aoife too. Wish …' I could admit it to this silent Mary. I wanted her to scoff at me and make one of her cutting retorts.

'I better go. Only thirty miles but you know those tides.' Mary's eyelids flickered open. A tear held for a moment spilled onto her cheek. I wanted to believe I'd detected the faintest squeeze of my hand. A cushion had fallen to the floor and I placed it behind her neck, kissed the top of her head and fled.

Back in the truck, Clemmie stretched and yawned on the front seat. She licked my face. I stared at the yellow chrysanthemums lying in the seat well, took them into the home.

'For Mary O'Shea.' I told the person typing behind a desk. She nodded.

'We'll see she gets them.' She gave me a half-smile.

I drove home, crushed into silence. Still on the mainland, I parked the truck in a lay-by, took Clemmie along a path onto the cliff top and sat on a stile from where I could see the north coast of the island, framed by a mauve-blue sky against the dark horizon. A thin curl of smoke came from the chimney of Art's farm. His cattle, small as toys, dotted the shore. Over the hill my own sheep would be grazing, moving as a group around the field, the grass a brighter green after the summer. The urge to be there spread into my belly like a hot drink.

'Come on, Clems. Jack and Mary trusted us with something special. We must make it work. Let's go home.'

'If the offer's still on the table I'd like to give it a go.' I'd been waiting for Ronan to come in. Sunday lunchtime, regulars and a few late autumn visitors filled the bar with conversation. Raucous laughter from three young lads in the corner had heads turning in their direction.

Ronan took a long swig from the pint I bought him. 'Don't you wish you were that age again?'

'No, I don't.' I pulled a face. 'I was a mess.' A spiral of fear leaked from the depth where I'd hidden it. I shook my head. Ronan eyed me.

'Some things better left buried, eh. Let's talk about driving lorries, shall we?'

Nuala

Money. I need money, if I'm to escape.

A red purse with a broken zip. Twenty-five pounds and a load of cards. Too easy. Shouldn't have left it on top of her bag. Deserved to lose it. 'Let it be a lesson to you madam.'

But sod it. I feel bad.

I want to do this right. 'Last time, I promise.' The bloke with the beanie is staring 'cos I'm talking to myself. Time to get off the bus.

I pocket the cash and dump the purse in a bin for dog waste. 'Sorry.' I whisper to the load of plastic bags. 'I truly promise. Won't do it again.'

'Can I work more days; I've left school and that?' The salon's teeming. Kids without appointments waiting with their parents. Jill the manager's waving her scissors.

'You are sent from heaven, Nuala. I'll sort something. Can you stay? The juniors are at college and Annie's off sick. Help!'

At the end of the day I count my haul, the nicked notes and the legit.

A few weeks of extra days and I'll have enough. And it will be mine, all earned, not nicked.

I feel grim about the purse but this new feeling – it's sort of different. Nice.

'Why don't you get a tattoo, Nuala?' We're shampooing clients' hair at adjacent basins. 'I've had a second one.' Gemma brushes off bubbles to show me the vine twisted like a bracelet round her wrist.

'Doesn't it hurt?' Mrs Carter asks, her chin in the air, water dripping onto a towel.

'A bit. Not for long though.'

'How much?' Why am I asking?

'I've got a friend. Just started his own place. He'll do you one. Cheap like. Spread the word.'

'When you're as old and wrinkly as I am, will you like it then?'

Gemma's laughing. 'Live now. My motto, Mrs Carter. Go on, Nuala, it'll be fun. I'll take you.'

Wet paint. The cardboard notice hangs on the knob of a bright purple door propped open with a Buddha's head.

'You the tattooist?' Gemma's friend is bald, wears a white T-shirt and purple corduroy trousers the same colour as the door. 'Expected you to be, you know, trendy.'

'Take me or leave me.' He's picking at his teeth, a half-eaten apple in his hand.

He must have practised on himself! His arms are a mess of blue, black and red swirls. A wolf, or maybe it's a dog, bares its teeth above his elbow.

We flick through a book of patterns.

'What! You want that. I could do you one like Gemma's or a bird or something.'

'No. That one'll do. Quit glaring at me, Gemma.'

I stare at the images of tattoos plastered on the wall. He's a moving piece of graffiti in front.

'If it's what you want.' He's lost interest.

'Sorry if you were hoping to show off.'

He cleans the area with something cold, feels for a smooth bit of skin on the inside of my arm. His gloves are black like bin bags.

'Seems I'm not the only one to be creative here, baby.' Hooded eyelids hide his eyes, but I hear his smirk.

If he makes more snide comments or says anything else about anything, I'm going.

He talks to Gemma.

I'm a piece of meat. Jesus, it hurts. Same but different to burning or cutting.

A mini-drill scratches the skin. *Zzzz.* Close my eyes. Boring, boring through the tissues, into muscle, past the veins and arteries to places where hidden thoughts are buried, the seal cracking like eggshell.

'Done. Finished.'

'Nuala.' Someone's working my shoulder. Gemma's eyes are inches from mine. 'Are you asleep. Like it?'

'Signature colour.' He fills the silence, wraps my arm in a bandage. 'Take it off tomorrow. Keep it clean.'

Only Martha around, thank God, when I reach Falcon House. 'Tattoo.' I brandish my bandaged arm and grin as she clamps her hand over her mouth. 'I'm good. It's not me you need to worry about.' I nod towards the kitchen. 'Ask those two newbies in there what they're about.' She shakes her head then attends to the huddle of boys and I escape to my room.

Twenty-four hours he said but I pick at the bandage on my arm.

The skin's red and puffy but purple ink picks out the word. It's sore.

'What do you think then, Dad?'

No response. Like always.

Wash off the oozing fluid. The water's too warm. Make it hotter. 'Ouch, ouch, ouch.' Can't feel the ache in my chest.

'Did you get a tattoo, dear?'

'I did.' Mrs Carter's remembered. I like she wants to see it. I push out my arm.

DAD in purple ink, two purple lines snaking below it.

'Ah, that's nice.' She's peering over the top of her glasses. 'He must be a special dad. What did he say when you showed him?'

My shame, bare, stuck in front of her face.

Why did you go, Dad? Was I so bad? A screaming, smelly, ugly kid. I would have kept out your way, not been a nuisance.

'Are you all right, dear?'

'Yeah, well, he's not seen it yet. Never will neither.'

'Oh. Oh.' She's tugging at the ties on her gown, pretending they need retying.

'Dead itchy, for a week or two, like a cat with fleas. You mustn't scratch it though. Ruins it. Drove me mad. Here. Have *Hello* magazine. Just your thing, Mrs Carter! Catch up on the gossip! Stylist won't be long.'

I sound like an idiot.

She pats my shoulder.

*

My room is desolate. A rumpled bed. The chair and wardrobe stare accusingly. A few belongings stuffed into a rucksack. Nothing worth anything except Bernie's card saying: *Come and see us when you're ready. We love you.* Reflected in the window, a girl in black leggings and a tracksuit top with a purple-lined hood. I hug myself to trap the whizzy feeling,

I stash the card and my money in my bag, including Jess' twenty pounds – more cash than I've ever had. Some squirrelled away from my allowances, some saved from my wages. Over a hundred. Lots.

How much'll I need? Anyone's guess. Train, ferry, food. Bit extra. No hitching lifts until I'm across the water. Don't give some snitching lorry driver the chance to say, 'Yes, I took her in my cab.' He'll tell the police, but not what he demanded as payment.

When I get to England, I'll do what I want.

'Hey, Rabbit, we're on our way.'

Joe

'I have plans but I need capital to invest. Pigs and tourists.'

'An unusual combination,' Ronan mused. 'Not sure which would be the most trouble.'

'If I do up the farmhouse, and it needs lots doing, I can move in there. Good to be closer to the animals. I'll renovate the cottage, then let it to visitors. There's nowhere for them to stay on the island at present – a man, a hiker told me that. And pigs – Jack used to have pigs. I read it on a postcard I found. Came from Jack's sailor brother to young Daniel. Hope you're looking after the piglets, it said.' I stopped. The other drinkers were all listening, amusement curling their lips.

'Good on you, Joe. Go for it, man.' Seamus pulled a pump handle. 'Optimism makes a change, what with all this gloom around. Bad times for the economy mean bad times for me.'

'Nah, we'll not stop drinking. Buy more to drown our sorrows more like.' The banter flew around. As near to friends as I'd ever had. I tapped my glass, planning the new pig pens I would build in the shed.

'It's why I want the job on the lorries – part time only. Not give up the farm, never do that but the extra money would fund some of my plans. Problem is I'm constricted by the tides.'

'We'll sort it. Welcome on board. It's only when we're short or there's a driver off sick.' Ronan slapped me on the back. 'Welcome aboard, Joe. Let's drink to it.'

I walked home across the causeway whistling, took the cliff path past the cemetery. A strong westerly wind scudded clouds across a heavy sky and tugged at my hair, its energy my own. At the two graves I weeded the tufts of encroaching grass, then sat for a time on Jack's edge stone.

The wide expanse of sea stretched unbroken to the horizon. 'Think you'd say I'm doing grand, Jack. I'm in for a good lambing. Lots of ewes with twins. The ram you bought is top class, but I'll need to be swapping him next year perhaps.'

My mind drifted back to those first few days on the island when I lived in a tent, desperate and in a mess. I remember wanting to surrender to the sea, to disappear beneath the clawing waves. At best I wanted to flee to America. Now I can't imagine living anywhere else but here.

They sent me on a course to get my HGV licence. I'd driven lorries before but not big beasts like these. I liked the familiarity of sitting in a cab learning about the dials, the technology, hearing the purr of the engine, the power beneath my hands, even the smell of the diesel fumes. My first assignment meant travelling south, near Cork. Ronan sent another driver along to show me the ropes. The narrow roads were challenging but I got there and back. Proud of myself.

'You new here? Not seen you before.' The man sat in Ronan's office reading a newspaper. 'They reckon these fires were started deliberately. Think it's a kid.' The man gave a low whistle and I peered over his shoulder at the headline. ARSON SUSPECTED.

'Yeah, I've read it.' I remembered the times I'd set fire to fences and garden gates, stuck a burning cloth through an old guy's letterbox once. It had been a laugh, something to boast about with your mates.

'Bored kids. My name's Joe, by the way. I'm a part-time driver, part-time farmer. Hard to fit it all in sometimes. Not seen you before either.'

'Hi, I'm Derek, brought a lorry over from England. I used to come a lot but spend more time at the Shropshire yard these days – managing. More logistics than driving for me now. How does it work then, two jobs like? Isn't farming a full-time occupation?'

'It's tough …' I grimaced. 'I make the driving work fit alongside the farm with all my earnings allocated to ongoing projects.'

I laughed when old Art called me a juggler. 'All these things you'm doing. What's wrong with farming, I say. You youngsters, never satisfied, that's your trouble.'

'Oh, I am satisfied, Art, I really am. Diversify is the name of the game.' My days on the farm were long, the weather often rough. I fashioned pig pens from a design I found in a book. Needed money to buy a breeding sow.

I understood the rhythm of the farm, knew the pattern of the seasons. They mocked me in the bar when I said I could smell a storm coming – as I used to laugh at Jack when he made predictions about the weather.

'You have to feel things, Joe.' I heard Jack say. 'Not listen to damn weather forecasts – feel what the land and the sea are telling you.'

You've been gone over two years, Jack, and there's never a day passes you're not telling me something.

'Not a born and bred Irishman then.' Derek's voice pulled me back from the island. 'Liverpool, Wigan, somewhere that way I'm guessing.' He was swarthy skinned, dark hair, flecks of grey at the temples; a hint of an accent I couldn't place suggested a different ethnicity. I said nothing.

'Sorry, mate, too many questions. Pleased to meet you. We all have reasons for being somewhere other than home. Maybe see you over at my place sometime.' He laughed somewhere between a scoff and an apology.

Exhausted I made a bed for myself in the corner of the barn, spread my sleeping bag on the fresh straw, glad this year's lambing was almost over. I slept with Clemmie beside me listening to the ewe's snuffling sounds, alert to any sign of distress. Times like this reminded me I was still a novice and doubts and fear would creep in. In the months after Jack's death, I panicked when Jack's voice grew faint, but it passed. I learned to talk to him again, to walk the fields, to stand in the yard, share my plans, my worries and sometimes my loneliness. Give Jack time to answer.

Many nights I saw the sun set and the dawn break. I lost two lambs and a ewe. On bad nights the cold made my arms and legs rigid, I wore weariness like a hair shirt. The feel of the limp, lifeless bodies stayed through the day and only the birth of more new lambs and their mother's tender attention dispelled my gloom.

'How's the lambing? Guess it's why we haven't seen you for the past weeks.' Seamus moved to where I sat at my usual end of the bar.

'You're not wrong. Full-time job, night and day. Only a few more to give birth. Time enough for a quick pint.' I enjoyed a long mouthful of the black liquid. 'Tastes good. How are things over here? Anything going on?'

Seamus coughed, straightened the towel and shifted the beer mats, rearranging them in a line. He poured a whiskey and set it in front of me.

'What's up?' I sensed the man's awkwardness, saw indecision flutter across his face. 'What's going on?'

'I don't suppose you've heard. Not sure I should say,' Seamus whispered in the empty bar.

'Someone's been looking for me,' I answered for him. Anguish brushed me like a cloud of smoke. 'Bloody well tell me. You're going to anyway.'

'Aoife Murphy – you and she, once, I think ...'

'What about her?' I stretched across the bar and gathered Seamus' shirt in a fist at his neck. 'What's happened to her?'

'Fuck you, Joe.' Seamus pushed my hands away. 'Finn, her husband. Killed in a motorbike accident, on the motorway round Dublin. Doing over a ton, in the early hours of the morning. Hit the central reservation and went under a lorry. Mad for bikes and speed from being a lad.'

I collapsed onto my stool.

'Christ.' Aoife's face flashed before me, the sound of her laughter, the way she used to tip her head back and smile.

'When?'

'Three, four weeks ago I reckon. The funeral was a while ago. Church packed so I heard. Sorry if ...'

The vein in my temple pulsed. The door opened and Arthur, a regular, walked in. I didn't want to speak to him or anyone else so pushed money across to Seamus and nodded, hoped it would stand as an apology for my behaviour.

Over the next few weeks I tried to write Aoife a letter but always screwed it up, bought a sympathy card but didn't have an address even if I'd wanted to send it. None of my business I kept reminding myself. She has a life in Dublin. I hoped she had friends to see her through this tragedy.

I hadn't seen her since the day of Jack's funeral. At first, I refused to believe she'd left for good; acceptance came with news she'd gone to Dublin, married Finn. I worked hard to forget her. Sometimes a voice in the breeze, a laugh on the waves, a white flower beneath a hedgerow caught me unawares and I would have to begin all over again, learning not to care.

*

The new sows came. On advice I bought two. They rooted around in the straw in the pens and turned the side area into mud. On warmer days they wallowed in the shallow pond I'd dug. I spent too long watching them, fascinated by their behaviour. It got so they knew me, pushed my hand looking for pig nuts. They wouldn't farrow yet, but I fussed over them like a father.

'Come on, Clems.' I whistled to the dog who had her nose buried in a pile of logs, her tail wagging furiously. We tramped the fields to check on the sheep and lambs. The spring had been wet and cold, I worried for the lambs.

It had rained all night, drumming on the roof, battering the cottage windows. The ruts of the track were muddy puddles and the stream an angry torrent. Debris piled against the stone bridge and the water level was rising behind it. I waded in, feeling the suck against my wellies. I pulled at broken tree branches and clods of grass torn from the bank. A log hit me on the back of the legs almost toppling me over. Clemmie ran backwards and forwards on the bank barking.

'It's all right for you, dog,' I screeched as the ice-cold water flowed over the top of my boots. 'Your feet aren't sopping wet.'

I saw the ewe as I walked home to change my clothes, knew it was in trouble. Two lambs bleated beside her; the rest of the flock grazed over the far side of the field. I leapt the gate and ran. The ewe was on her back, legs in the air, froth around her mouth. I pulled her onto her side, tried to get her to stand but she was too weak. She wobbled and fell. I tried again.

'Come on, old girl, stay upright.' Her lambs butted their heads against her abdomen seeking reassurance and a feed. I knew she wouldn't make it, her eyes wild, each breath bubbling from rigid jaws. I sat on the wet grass and watched her die. Helpless, guilty, like it was my fault. What else could I have done? Had I been careless? If I'd found her sooner? My questions remained unanswered.

'I'm not cut out for this, I'm a fraud, Clemmie, just playing at being a farmer.' The dog's warm body lay against my leg. The cry of the lambs roused me, I lifted them by their hind legs and carried them over to the shed. I'd use the tractor to move the mother. Five orphaned lambs to feed by hand. One had been a triplet, two from a ewe lost in lambing. Now these. I put the two wet lambs in a pen of their own while I made up bottles and took off sodden boots, emptying them of water.

'Whoa there.' The biggest lambs greeted me with loud bleats jostling to be fed. 'You three have to wait.' I loved the fierce tug as they pulled on the teats of the bottles, the rich liquid devoured in no time, only remnants dribbling from their mouths.

'Joe.' My name dropped into the vastness of the barn.

I turned like a wheel slowing.

She was standing inside the door, a small child in her arms. The pompom on his hat matched her red coat.

'Aoife!' I stood rigid, hands by my side, gripping the lambs' bottles, cold seeping into my unclad feet. I saw the shiver of her shoulders, her face white and thin, her eyes afraid to meet mine.

'I had nowhere to go. I couldn't take it any longer. The only place I wanted to be was here.' Her faint voice wilted to nothing.

I dropped the bottles and took a step towards her. Disbelief made me stumble, the barn walls blurred, my legs too heavy to move. She came into focus as I reached her. The child made sucking noises on his thumb and studied me with steady blue eyes. I wrapped my arms around them both and rested my head on top of Aoife's, willing her not to pull away.

The years, the months, the days she had been gone fell to the ground like snow off a roof. Her hand rested on my chest.

'This is Fergus.' Aoife said as the child squirmed to the floor and pulled off his hat. 'He's two.' She turned from my gaze. 'He's … he's mine and Finn's child.'

'I know, Aoife. I heard.'

Fergus tugged at my jacket, pointing at the lambs.

'Do you want to see them?' I ruffled Fergus' hair, relieved as my tension found expression. 'Come on then.'

Unsure at first, the little boy hid behind my leg while the lambs scrabbled against their metal pen. Their loud bleats made him jump.

'They are greedy, aren't they? They can't have any more milk because they've just had a feed.' I crouched to be at Fergus' level. He copied, making me smile.

'No,' Fergus said in a loud voice and wagged a small finger at the noisy lambs.

'Are you hungry, Fergus?' The little boy nodded.

Aiofe watched us, her arms crossed. 'The cows. There are no cows?'

I shook my head, feeling Mary's slap as fresh as if it was now.

I walked across to Aoife and held her by the shoulders. 'You are so thin,' I looped stray hair behind her ear, 'and … tired.'

'I am, Joe.' A glisten in her eyes suggestive of tears.

I pressed her head against my chest and rocked her. 'Come on, let's get you into the warm.

'Right, I'll need to light this fire for a start, put dry socks on, then I'll make porridge.'

Fergus squealed when Clemmie licked him, he sat beside her on the floor stroking her ears. Aoife on the edge of the sofa, stared at nothing, her coat pulled round her.

'You'll stay?' A tentative question to Aoife as she stirred her porridge in her dish, not eating it. 'At least for a while?'

'Maybe for a day or two until …' She stopped. 'You can tell me to go, Joe, if you'd rather. I would understand. Why would you want me here, us here?' She put down her spoon. 'I said horrible things to you. I haven't forgiven myself.'

'Another day, Aoife. I think we have a lot to tell each other. You're here. I want you to stay. I hope it's enough?'

I laced my fingers with hers.

'It's the same, Joe – but empty.' Aoife and I stood in Jack and Mary's kitchen; a wash of sunlight filtered into the room through grubby windows illuminating the stone floor. As though remembering, Clemmie curled on the rug in front of the cold range.

Aoife walked to the other side of the table and ran her hand over the pitted surface. Fergus opened the doors of the dresser and banged them shut again.

They had been here for a week. Aoife had few words. She was always cold despite the warmth from a big fire. She wore one of my sweaters with the sleeves rolled up, sinking into it like a child in adult clothes. I slept on the sofa so Aoife and Fergus could have the bed. One morning she'd slept beyond the time I rose. Fergus had padded through and I made breakfast for us both. We peeped round the door at Aoife, curled on her side, only the top of her head visible. In her sleep she puffed, her eyelids fluttering disturbed by a dream.

Fergus giggled as I dressed him and put on his bright red wellies. 'Two conspirators going on an adventure.' I put my finger to my lips. 'Shh.' Fergus held my hand in the misty, new-day light but soon he ran ahead, jumped squealing into puddles.

He grew confident with the lambs and loved to feed the smaller ones. 'Naughty lambs,' he told them as the big ones tried to take the bottles from his hand. I laughed at his serious little face, and the way he copied my every action.

Aoife found us in the barn, clearing straw from a pen, me with a spade and Fergus using a small shovel I gave him.

'I think these strong ones need to go in the field soon. Eat some grass. What do you think, Fergus?' The little boy climbed onto the rungs of the pen and we leaned over, watching the orphan lambs butt heads and gambol in the clean straw.

Aoife smoothed Fergus's hair and her arm crept through mine. I squeezed her hand and we shared a smile, her first since her return.

'Aoife, were you happy?' Here in Mary's kitchen I asked the question.

She was dusting Mary's ornaments on her sleeve. 'Was I happy? What's happy, Joe? Finn was good to me. He provided for us. Worked hard. We both knew early on we had come together for the wrong reasons. He, lured by city life, me, because …'

'Aoife, you don't need to tell me. I shouldn't have asked.'

'You deserve an explanation, Joe. I want to tell you.' She sat in Mary's chair. 'I could never compete with his bike. Always his first love. Even after Fergus came. On light evenings he and his mates would be in the backyard tinkering with their bikes. They rigged a tarpaulin, attached it to a wall so if it rained, they'd be dry.

'Often at bedtime, he would grab his helmet and take his bike for a spin. I wondered if he went somewhere else – to someone else. I don't think so though – he just loved the dark, the opportunity for speed. It gave him a buzz he never found with me.

'I'm sad Fergus is too young; he won't remember his daddy. Finn loved him in his own way. Perhaps as Fergus got older, they would have become friends.

'Was I happy? The gardai knocked in the early hours of the morning. I woke to them banging on the door. Even before I answered, I knew who it would be. I knew what they would tell me. I think I expected one day it would happen, only a matter of when. They said he died at the scene without ever regaining consciousness. They said I could see him but advised me not to. I can't remember if he said goodbye, if he kissed me or Fergus before he left. I can't remember, Joe. It's like watching a recorded film end too soon, the screen going blank.'

I yearned to hold her, to warm her, to trace the dark smudges beneath her eyes, touch her sunken cheeks. A figure in a glass dome.

Aoife stretched her legs, placing them on Mary's stool. 'She wouldn't want you to leave the house like this.'

'I know. Can't bring myself to clear their stuff. One day I want to renovate. I have plans. Feel awkward, like it shouldn't be mine, that's the truth. The cottage has been enough for me; if I have any money, I put it into the farm.'

'Joe, let's go to the old church. Remember how we used to?' Her voice dropped to a whisper as though in fear of being chastised.

I carried Fergus on my shoulders, galloped along pretending to be a horse. The boy clung on squealing to me to stop but as soon as I slowed to a walk the little legs beat against my chest. 'Faster, horsey. I like it.' We tumbled into a heap on the grass and waited for Aoife to reach us.

Agony clawed at my throat. Nuala – a beach – like a flitting shadow, the memory gone before it formed.

The sun was warmer, but a grey curtain of cloud crept from the horizon. I watched Aoife as she walked amongst the ruin, touching the blocks of stone as though trying to reconnect. She stood where the altar would have been, a breeze lifting her hair.

'Why don't you have the house, you and Fergus?' It was like someone else had said it. Her head jerked, she put her hand to her eyes. She didn't reply, just stared.

Rain began to fall, large drops splattered on the grass. The breeze increased.

'Let's run for it.' By the time we reached the cottage we were soaked. Water trickled off our hair and into our eyes. Clothes clung to our skin. Aoife stripped Fergus; he ran around the room freed by his nakedness. I threw her a towel, pulled off my own sodden shirt and rubbed myself dry. I caught her glance, but she turned and disappeared into the bedroom to change her clothes.

I lay awake uncomfortable on the sofa, afraid to toss around too much lest I disturb them. Clemmie slept on her blanket, one ear twitching.

What were we to do? I cursed myself for being clumsy again, telling her she could have the house. She would go back to Dublin. Pick up her life as best she could. In her grief she'd come to the place that had been her escape as a child. Foolish of me to hope it was for any other reason.

'Are you awake?' Aoife stood in the doorway. 'I couldn't sleep either. I heard you moving around.' She came and sat on the floor in front of the sofa. 'You've been so good to us, Joe. You can't go on sleeping here.'

I stared at the fire, the glow of the embers in the darkness.

'You made a kind offer earlier.' She said it softly. 'But it's not what I want. You said you had plans. What are you going to do, Joe?'

I closed my eyes wishing I could close my ears to her words, tried to swallow the constriction in my throat. 'I might move in there eventually, let this place as a holiday cottage. A crazy dream, but the income would be useful.

'Where will you go, Aoife? Back to Dublin?'

She didn't seem to hear my question. 'Me in the farmhouse, you here. It wouldn't work, Joe. I think we both want something else.'

She faced me now. Moonlight through the open curtains reflected in her eyes. Her finger smoothed my eyebrow, traced a line across my cheek.

'Always wanted something else – but too stubborn and scared to admit it. I ran away once, Joe. I don't want to do it again.'

I swung my legs to the floor and slipped down beside her. 'I'm the one who runs away. Do you mean …? Are you saying …?'

'Yes. If it's what you want too.' She put her finger across my lips. 'Don't say anything, Joe. You must take time – it's not just me, it's Fergus too, a big ask. I'm reeling from all that's happened. I'm a bruise only beginning to change colour.'

I lifted her onto the sofa and pulled the quilt over us both, held her in the crook of my arm, her breath warm on my chest as she drifted into sleep. I dared not move for fear of waking her, for fear of finding this wasn't for real.

Nuala

Tomorrow I will be gone.

'Sure, now that's a sad face. It's your first time to England, I'm guessing?'

A man is standing at my shoulder, shorter than me, his bare head wet and shiny. He battles the swirling wind and the drizzle, pulls the collar of his jacket round his ears.

'*Gaoth na mara.* Wind of the sea. Gentle as a maiden's touch. Cruel as the devil's breath.'

'Are you a friggin' poet or something?' I swipe at my hair whipped wild by the rain.

'It's warmer inside.' His eyes are green-grey pools of oil, pulling me in.

'So? Go inside then.' His face is transparent like a boiled sweet. 'I didn't ask for company.'

'Always do an ending before a new beginning.' A shrug, half a smile, his hand is on my wrist, but I can't feel it. 'God bless you. Let luck be a friend.'

He weaves his way back across the throbbing deck, a shadow framed by the light of the door. 'Farewell.'

'Weirdo.' The insult drowns in the waves.

I hold on to the rail as the ferry squeezes from the estuary. The lights retreat and blur. I want to be soaked, for the wind to tear the clothes from my body. I want to feel pain, feel something.

BIG-UN AND BERNIE; Maisie my kitten as lost as me; Ella, we were going to be best friends forever; Nicky and Jess – I think they liked me or at least bits of me; Kelly, Declan, the others with names I can't remember. Mrs Leafe, pluck is what she said I had. She noticed me. Debbie, Ryan, all that horrid stuff finally made me leave. A queue of people. Me, walking away. Their names and faces tumble in the violence of the ferry's wake, a white path stretching back to Ireland, breaking up, growing faint.

Mum, Dad …

Colder than ice, I stay to see the land dissolve in the mist, sink below the horizon. 'Goodbye.' The wind whips round. Ahead there is only grey sea and an arc of opal sky littered with black clouds and arrows of light.

Ted. One name I hold on to.

I go inside.

The light's white-bright, conversation and the sound of a coffee machine do my head in. Discarded coats, bags and pushchairs. People eating, scrunched serviettes; empty paper cups roll across the tables. A baby sleeps in her mother's arms, oblivious to the chaos. A scab to be picked. I move where I can't see them.

Where's the weirdo? Nowhere. Tired faces, laughing, sleeping faces but not his. Outside, black shutters the doors and windows. Goosebumps pimple my arm and dive inwards. Let luck be a friend he'd said. It never has been, but the words keep buzzing. He spoke to me. He spoke those words. I heard him. Eejit, who's the weirdo, me or him? Hunch in a corner, out the way. Hood over my face. Stop thinking. Lie low.

Liverpool. England. 'Don't disappoint. Please let it be good.' The ferry drones on.

Docking. Cranes, a skyline of bleak warehouses. Gulls screeching, hanging in the wind. An ungodly time of the morning, barely light. Feel like shit. Washed up, discarded, like the rubbish floating on the water.

I don't want to get off.

Move. Follow the herd. Disappear.

Joe

'I need to go back to Dublin, Joe – for Fergus's cot, his toys, our clothes. I have to clear the flat.' Aoife sounded weary and defeated.

'Let me come too. Let me help you. You'll come back here?' I was cautious with her. Take it slowly, I kept reminding myself.

'It's not fair to ...'

'Aoife.' I held her arms. 'I want you to.'

She closed her eyes and swayed against me.

I followed her through the cramped dark hallway of her flat to a sitting room with a kitchen at one end. Fergus's pyjamas and a rolled nappy were strewn on the floor beside a blue baby cup. A mug of undrunk tea sat on the fireplace. Aoife stood motionless on the rug. I wanted to turn around, go back, leave this other man's home. I drew back the curtains. In the street below a woman in an orange anorak struggled with shopping bags and a pushchair; a small child running behind stopped on the kerb to watch the cars as they queued at traffic lights. A white van revved its engine sending a cloud of black smoke rolling across the child. A man on a bike wove between the vehicles, cars tooting at his recklessness. The sounds of the city, too relentless and loud in my ears. All those people sharing the same air.

'I left in a rush. Twelve weeks since the accident, Joe. I'd been awake all night. All I could think of was coming to the island. In the end I lifted Fergus and we left.' She slumped onto the sofa, twisting a yellow teddy in her hands. Fergus was pulling toys from a box by the fireplace and tossing them across the floor.

'What do you want me to do?' I tried to break her reverie, my splintered voice making the question more abrupt than I intended.

'I'm sorry, Joe, I shouldn't have let you come. I ... I didn't want to face it on my own.'

'Let's collect what you need. I wouldn't have let you do this by yourself.'

I was cleaning out the fridge, tipping waste food into a bag when I heard Aoife's gasp from the bedroom. 'What? What's the matter?' I shouted.

She was staring into a wardrobe. I could see leathers and a scratched motorbike helmet.

Aoife collapsed onto the bed. 'All his gear.' She sobbed.

I led her into the sitting room, handed her the wet cloth.

'Here, you finish cleaning the worktops. I'll sort the wardrobe.' I struggled not to upstage her emotions with my own. I took a bin liner and lifted all the clothes from the shelves, tearing the black plastic in my haste to have the job done. A vague whiff of oil or petrol came to me as I lifted the helmet. I ran a hand over its dome and around the padding of the lining.

'Finn,' I whispered the name.

There wasn't a lot. We packed clothes into holdalls and tins into bags. I dismantled the cot and loaded everything onto the back of the truck; it took little space.

'Not much to show for a marriage, is there?'

I put my arm across her shoulders and gave her a gentle squeeze.

'Are we done ...? The furniture?'

'All the landlord's.'

I strapped Fergus into his car seat before Aoife came down the stairs. She'd stayed for a few minutes, to say goodbye or to say hello again, I wasn't sure which. She climbed into the cab, clutching a small wooden box and a photo frame, a shredded tissue in her hand.

'Mum's.' Aoife opened the empty box. 'She used to keep jewellery in it. Nothing much, she had nothing special, but as a little girl, I used to love putting on rings and necklaces and prance around in her high-heeled shoes.'

'How old were you when she died?'

'Eight. She was ill for a long time, but I always told myself she would get better. They didn't let me go to the funeral, so for ages I wouldn't believe she was dead. I had terrible tantrums because they wouldn't let me see her. Without Mary and Jack's care I don't know what would have happened. It's why I loved them so much.'

I reached across, turned over the photo frame. A young man sat astride a motorbike grinning into the camera. 'Finn.' I said for the second time that day. 'Fergus has his smile.' I placed it picture side up on Aoife's knee. 'Don't hide him away.'

We left the bin liner of clothes in a charity shop on the outskirts of Dublin and later broke the journey at a roadside café. Fergus made us laugh, clambering onto the red plastic seats, excited with his cone of chips and his drink with a straw. I tipped Aoife's nose with my finger. 'It will all work out.' She nodded, her eyes troubled and dull.

We were learning to be together, sometimes dancing in tune, sometimes clumsy.

'How much space does one small child need?' I grumbled, tripping over a row of cars snaking across the carpet.

'I'm sorry. You must hate us invading your space.' Aoife rushed to tidy up.

'No, I don't hate it. Having you here tells me how lonely I was on my own. Aoife, I've been thinking – should we move into the farmhouse?'

'I think Jack and Mary would be pleased. And let the cottage like you planned, Joe?'

'The extra money would be useful. Buy more pigs.' I twirled her round in a circle both of us grinning with excitement.

'We'll paint it yellow, nice and bright. Decorate the back room for Fergus. I'll build some new kitchen units …'

We began to sort the farmhouse, finding ourselves hushed by the task. Aoife giggled. 'Why are we whispering? It's not like Jack and Mary will jump out the cupboard.' She stroked a small ornament, a ginger dog with a pink tongue. 'I remember Mary saying Daniel gave her this one Christmas. He'd saved all his pocket money. These things are worthless but they're so much a part of the house, part of them. Let's wrap them in paper and decide later.' She wore one of Mary's pinafores over her jeans. Wayward strands of hair escaped from a red and white headscarf tied around her head. 'Where do you think she is now, Joe?'

I put aside the stick I was using to stir the paint and wrapped my arms round her waist. Aoife had been with me for ten months, ten months of discovering each other again.

'I think she's with Jack, setting him to rights and luring the angels into her kitchen where she's baking wonderful cakes and scones.' I breathed deeply. 'Can't you smell them?'

We had brought Mary home at the end of summer, as the leaves were turning to copper and the autumn storms rolled in from the Atlantic. Mary was with Jack and Daniel, back on her island. She lay beside them in the cemetery overlooking the bay. A sad day, another exit, another shifting of the order of things. She would be telling them not to be fussing. She would say, 'I've had a good life.'

'If we want to move in here soon after Christmas we'd better stop dreaming and get painting.' I let Aoife go with a quick kiss on the back of her neck. 'Fergus will be back tonight and he's very willing but not much help.'

The first time Fergus's grandparents, the Aherns, had visited, we'd both been nervous. 'They are nice people.' Aoife kept telling me and reminding herself. 'They've lost their son, so their grandson is all they have left of him.' I felt like an interloper, clumsy, too big for the cottage. Would they think me and Aoife – all too soon? Fergus called me Daddy-Joe, but I willed him not to say it in front of Finn's parents.

They were quiet – anxious too. Fergus and I had taken them to see the animals whilst Aoife finished cooking the lunch. Afterwards we all climbed to Joe's point as I called it, a mild winter's day, a wind off the sea curled waves onto the rocks below and the seagulls bobbed on the swell. We rebuilt the cairn of stones.

'I'm glad Fergus has such a beautiful place to grow up in.' Finn's mother Anne brushed my arm. Her eyes betrayed her grief and I covered her hand with my own in a moment of acknowledgement for us both.

'Race you down the hill.' I ran with Fergus in pursuit. Squeals turned to giggles when I faked a stumble and fell headlong onto the grass with Fergus landing on top of me.

Since then Anne and Michael have fetched their grandson once a month and taken him back to their place for the weekend. He loves to go with them and for us it's precious time together.

I watched Aoife, on the highest rung of the stepladder, stretching to reach the top of the wall. She sang to the song on the radio, her body gyrating in time to the music.

I loved her being here, I loved her. I'd dared to tell her, to use the words, only a short time ago.

We'd been sitting, the two of us, on dry sand, our backs to the rocks sheltering from a chilling wind, the day full of sky stretching to the horizon and beyond.

'Nothing's changed, everything's changed.' I pulled Aoife close.

'What's changed, Joe?' Her voice was muffled behind her scarf.

'I love you. And I can say it.'

Our silence more binding than any words.

'Aoife, I don't know what love feels like, but this is special.'

She hadn't laughed or teased me, appreciating what it cost to say it. She hugged me and kissed away the furrows on my brow.

'Your family – love was there?' The question hung.

'Possibly – from my mum. But I only saw it in the cuff round the ear or the shared bag of chips. Best was when she'd say, "Fetch us some tea, Micky Joe." I'd make her sit on the sofa and take it to her – then I'd get a smile, sometimes she'd hold my hand – for a moment. She wouldn't ever talk about things like love but I can see loving us meant exhausting herself, working at as many cleaning jobs as she could, not eating when there was only food for us children and … taking the abuse from my stepfather so when he was sober she had a husband and we had a dad.'

'And Nuala?'

I held my breath. Aoife had never used her name – I'd only spoken of her once before.

'If we are to go on, we have to know about each other, Joe. I used to be so hurt; whenever we got close you would turn away. You retreated to some private place. I didn't understand who or what you were hiding from, but you went far away like a receding tide.' She threw her arm towards the breaking waves.

'I loved Nuala, but I tried not to. All my energy went on getting through each day getting enough … drugs to … survive.

'I took her to a beach one time.' I cried, talking through my tears. 'I loved her then. One afternoon. It's all I gave her, all I've got.'

Aoife stroked my knuckles, finding the soft skin between my fingers.

'I keep telling myself she's been adopted. She'll have a new home, a loving family. I try to think of her at school, growing up, becoming a young lady, but I can only see her jumping the waves with me feeling her hand in mine.

'She used to come to me – I could feel her – talk to her, tell her things.' Aoife's pressure tightened on my hand urging me to go on.

'Then she came less and less. I told myself I was stronger; it was me letting go for the best, she had to move on with her own life. It felt like she was the adult and I the child.' I closed my eyes to recall the little girl in her yellow knickers dancing on the sand. Aoife massaged the back of my neck with cold fingers.

'Sometimes I have this dream. She's calling me, I don't hear her voice, just a long scream – but it's her. I can't get into the room because it doesn't have a door. When morning comes, it all seems ridiculous and I try to forget.

'Aoife, what if something bad has happened to her?'

Aoife kissed the skin below my ear and wrapped her arms around me; my breathing calmed, and we watched the waves break and creep closer as the tide came in with the dying day.

'Get painting, woman. Two walls to finish.' She blew me a kiss in reply. She's less fragile, the colour's back in her cheeks, the hollows in her face filling.

When I find her crying silent tears that need to fall, I don't ask her why – just hold her.

Nuala 2016

England. I've made it.

Follow the crowd. Act confident. No one's bothered. Swallow the nausea. Walk away from the quay, far from the yawning ferry spewing cars and people all rushing somewhere. Where? A guy in overalls carrying number plates is standing by the perimeter fence. London, his cardboard notice reads. A van stops, and he disappears.

Boarded shops, pavements spotted with chewing gum. Grey roads and a grey wind. Town, head for town. I jump at the rattle of metal.

'Sorry, love, opening up. Have a good day.' A man in a turban and a striped jumper is lifting the gate of his shop. The sky is brightening and for a moment a patch of sunlight spotlights us both. 'Lovely morning.' He pauses and smiles.

I run like a chased cat. Along the street, around a corner, over some traffic lights, cars hooting as I dodge between them. People on their way to work let me pass.

Get a grip, get a grip. Stop behaving like an airhead.

I rest against a wall mounted with iron railings and take deep breaths. It's a park, a few trees and a path. A patch of scruffy grass, a McDonald's bag – and me.

Welcome to England. This is what you wanted. You're here. The little voice grows louder, shooting like blood into my arms, my legs. It escapes as a giggle.

'Ted, I'm in the same country as you, not so far away.'

I want to ring him. Right now. Wish I could. I *need* my phone. I'm hungry but food will have to wait.

There's a brick building scrawled with graffiti. *Red scum. Up the Superwhites.* Beats faded pictures of men in balaclavas with guns. Toilets. Open 9 – 5 p.m. What if you need a pee at five past five? Another fence with a padlocked gate. Easy. Hop over, give the door a hefty shove. Does anyone ever test these things? I'm in.

A wild girl glares from the mirror. I have to do it, but it's hard. My hair clings to my scalp like it anticipates what's about to happen. I cut off chunks with the hairdressing scissors I brought from the salon. Black strands fall into the sink like a dead rat. A dead Nuala. The pulse in my neck throbs.

I should have let Gemma do it, but she might have told. I'm like a punk, hair sticking out at angles. The razor finishes the job, a few nicks where it's hard to reach, they sting like mad. I'm back in the salon smelling shampoo, colour and coffee. My arms ache, inside the ache's worse.

'Who are *you*? Who the hell are *you*?' My eyes are too big for my face and a mole on my cheek's as big as a crater on the moon. I run a hand over the bristles of my near-shaved head. 'I don't recognise you, so fat chance anyone else will.'

The stubble turns pink when I spray it with the fancy-dress paint I bought. 'Okay, it won't last but it'll be good for a few days.' Like hairspray it catches the back of my throat. My cough echoes loud as thunder. 'There you go, Nuala McCurdy. Transformed. A new you.' I pull my hood up, feel less naked. Christ, there is a load of hair. Some goes into the smelly bins by the toilets, but it takes for ever swilling the short bits down the sink.

A jogger in black lycra and an orange vest runs past as I vault back over the fence. Music on, the slap of his steps, he takes no notice.

The bus station is heaving. I guess it's rush hour. They all seem to know the form.

A guy in a uniform has been watching me. He's walking this way. 'Where to? Can I help?'

'Chester.' The first name I see on the stand in front of me.

'Then you're in the right place. Bay 8. Bus should be along in ten minutes. Safe journey.' He walks on leaving a trace of tobacco in the air. Didn't give me a second glance.

Okay, Chester it is. Sounds as good as anywhere else. I buy a ticket, stand in the queue kicking at the kerb with my boot.

Words jump at me from the billboard beyond the kiosk.

25th August. It punches me in the gut.

'Don't miss it, Nuala. 25th August. I'll be at the school.' What Mrs Leafe had said in the car park.

I hear her saying it, can see her red hair.

I'd promised her I'd come.

Did I pass? I'll never find out. No point wishing.

She'll be waiting, watching for me. She will for certain. I've spoilt it all.

Sorry, miss. For not being there. I wish I could tell her why.

I mean it. She was great. I liked her. Feel sick letting her down.

The bloke behind me is munching on a sausage sandwich. How not to grab it straight off him? I can almost taste the meat. I try not to watch. The tosser bins what's left as the bus arrives. I want to retrieve it, I'm starving. The bus is hot and smells of disinfectant. Grab a seat near the back; my backpack beside me will stop anyone sitting there. Pull a face at my reflection in the window. Houses, shops, fields, factories are a blur. Where's Chester? Perhaps it's near Blackpool.

It's not like Belfast. Loads of black-and-white buildings, groups of people following guides waving flags on sticks. This is the best bacon sandwich I've ever bought, and I sit on a bench and eat it with my feet on the rails of the old walls. People like stick figures walk in all directions below me. A man in a suit weaves his way along the street on skates. Weird. I'm not staying here. It's too posh. Move on, tomorrow maybe. But where to? I hum a tune, walk away fast, to squash the lump of panic. I want to ask how far away the sea is but maybe it's a daft question. Might make people notice me.

I'm tired. My eyes sting, my feet hurt like there are stones in my boots. I've passed a few dossers preparing for the night, spreading their cardboard and sleeping bags like their doorway is a fucking hotel. A black dog with hair over its eyes wags its tail, 'Hey there.' It sniffs my hand and I ruffle its head. It lies next to a guy and a girl. The guy's got a pointy beard, a yellow scarf round his neck. She's holding a blanket to her chin. Spaced-out the pair of them.

Bloody summer. It stays light too long. I want to sleep. I'm in a bay round the back of a supermarket. Place is shut, car park empty.

One night. That's all. One night. Find somewhere tomorrow. I so want to believe it.

'Do you want a lift? Can I take you somewhere?' The car has flattened me against the hedge.

A woman, unusual. 'I missed my bus.' I think she buys it. Anything to sit for a while, stop walking.

'Where are you going?'

'London.'

'London! You're a long way from there. Are you sure?'

'Drop me wherever.'

Wish I hadn't got in the car. She keeps throwing me glances. Her legs are so short her boobs are crammed against the steering wheel; she's peering through thick glasses.

Pretend to be asleep.

'I used to hitch-hike when I was your age. All over the country me and my friend went. Different today though. You don't often see it now, especially girls. My mother used to have kittens. Made me carry a safety pin on my belt.' She giggled like she was young again. 'Not sure a safety pin would have been effective. Had no trouble though – people were kind back then.'

I can't imagine her hitch-hiking, can't imagine her young. She's sitting on a flowery cushion, eyes on the road. We travel along at a steady slow pace. There's a long stream of cars queueing behind us. She doesn't notice.

'Six of us – overland to India, in a VW van. Kept breaking down but Peter always got it going again. He's the man for me I decided – married for forty-eight years. Still miss him.'

Don't sleep. Her voice hums like a bee in flowers. Open the window. Nice breeze on my face. I'll shut my eyes, for a minute, only for a minute.

'Hello. Would this be a good place for you? I'm turning off here, into Wales.'

The light's so bright I shut my eyes against it. Why am I in a car? They've found me.

'A nice little sleep? Travelling always makes you tired, I was the same I remember. Sorry to wake you but … well, London's in that direction.'

'Thanks for the lift. It's been great. Sorry to have gone to sleep.'

She's smiling. 'I've enjoyed having you there. I miss company. Good luck.'

The little silver car butts back into the traffic and disappears.

It's a wide roundabout. Lorries are parked in a lay-by beside a mobile café. There's a kiosk selling flowers, cheerful bunches in buckets.

I have no idea where I am. What a fool for taking a lift. She'll be onto the police right away. Yes, officer, a young girl, pink hair. Dropped her at …

Three options on the signpost. Wolverhampton, Shrewsbury, Chester. Not back to Chester so two options. Eeny, meeny, miny, moe … Right sorted. Big-un used to sing the rhyme, to make me laugh, whenever I couldn't choose. I'll text him in a few months when I've got a job, a place – and a phone. Tell him I'm good. He'll be pleased. I'll do that when I'm sorted – not like I *need* him any more. Say I'm in England. Make him proud of me like he was of his own two sons.

A drink of Sprite from the kiosk then I'm off. The verges are uneven and the grass long. Bloody hell the cars and lorries are so close.

I've been walking for ages. Jesus, there must be some place somewhere.

Sirens. Louder. Coming this way. Dive into a lane, squeeze behind a field gate, crouch behind the hedge.

An ambulance screams along the main road, blue lights flashing. Breathe again.

'Is this how it will be? You'll jump, hide when someone talks to you, whenever you see a police car. You're an idiot, Nuala McCurdy. Is this what you left Ireland for? So you could be a pathetic, frightened creature.

'Aargh, Jesus. Sneaking up behind me. You great oaf of a horse, you frightened the life out of me. Were you earwigging? You've got a lovely soft nose.' He lets me stroke his brown, smooth neck. 'What do you think then? Fuck the world. Right, I agree. Sorry, I don't have anything for you but thanks for listening. See you.' His snort is the same as my smile. 'Need to clean your teeth by the way. They're yellow.'

Fuck the world. It's always worked before.

Joe 2016

'Into Liverpool. First drop in Birkenhead, then on south.' Ronan pointed to a map in his office at the yard. 'Okay?' I froze at the sound of Liverpool and didn't take in the rest of what he said.

I'd been covering longer journeys for a while, but never yet to England. Liverpool – a quiver of excitement – or fear. I loved being on the road, the order of pine trunks loaded in regular ranks on the trailer, the presence the long lorries commanded on the highway. But back to England. Could I deal with it?

'As much work as you want, Joe,' Ronan had said. 'I can rely on you. None of the hassle some drivers give me.'

The farm was thriving, but I worried. Aoife told me I spent too long studying the prices. Government austerity measures meant volatile markets, the price of pork and lamb fluctuating wildly. I increased the number of pigs I kept. The animals had accommodating natures and did well on the light soils of the island. It was my own venture; something I had introduced to the farm and the animals Fergus loved best.

We had ambition. We needed more fields. Art was struggling with his workload and had offered to rent us some of his, but the extra expenditure was a risk.

'It's what I mull over in the night.'

'I can manage the animals, Joe, when you're driving.' Aoife massaged my shoulders as I pored over a spreadsheet.

'I know you can but … I hate being away from you and being away from here. You've got the cottage to look after too, all those bookings, the cleaning, sheets to change and beds to make.'

'Joe, stop worrying. I've never been so happy. You love the occasional lorry-driving jobs; you've often said so. If the extra money lets us do things, then a day or two apart isn't so bad, is it? It needn't be forever. Besides, when you're back …' She twisted my hair in her fingers and kissed the top of my ear.

I pulled her onto my knee not quite able to believe we were living this life. I would watch her sitting on the rug playing with Fergus absorbed in a game. Or dressed in wellies, huddled into her coat and hood, sloshing through mud to feed the animals, returning with red cheeks and droplets of rain on her eyelashes, her laugh tinkling like crystal. We sometimes argued about things but when the brittleness, the temporary turning-away, had run its course we would realise whatever had sparked the fire in the first place didn't matter. We would find each other again, remember the joy of being lovers. Emerge like birds after a storm. Other times doubts niggled, and we sought each other's reassurance.

'You've been grand with Fergus. I don't want …'

'I love him like he's mine, Aoife. I don't remember he's not.' Then the past would leak into the present and I'd see Nuala and remember what kind of dad I'd been to her. 'Sorry' was a useless word. All too late. Be happy, my silent cry.

'We're mates. He's my little farmhand. Clemmie loves him more than she does me. The traitor has transferred her affections.' True, Clemmie was Fergus's constant companion and the two of them would take off across the fields on some childish adventure. The baby had grown into a confident little boy.

I liked to lean on the gate surveying the farm – talk to Jack, feel the old man's presence. Now Fergus climbed up too. 'Like two old codgers you are,' Aoife would laugh.

'Are you sure you're happy, hidden away here?' Always my question and I asked it as she sat on my knee, her fingers distracting me as they crept inside my shirt.

'Joe, what's all this? Is it because Ronan's asked you to go to England, to Liverpool? You once told me this place was a cotton-wool island. I don't want it to be. I want it to be home – like you've made it for me and Fergus.

'Tell me more about your family, your mum. You never speak of them.'

'I never think of them, Aoife, that's why.' Not true. Sometimes a place, or a first name, is mentioned on the radio and they flash across my mind. I keep them away as if shrouded in a sea fret.

'Don't you think your mother must wonder about you? She must miss you.' Aoife's eyebrows knitted in a concerned frown. 'You don't ever stop loving your own child.'

Her words lanced like a scalpel.

'I was the youngest by a few years. Probably the result of a drunken brawl, even rape. My dad left. My stepdad was ruthless especially when he'd been drinking. He used the language of the belt. Did Mum love me? She never said. Maybe she did, maybe she didn't. I only remember her always being tired, thin, worn out. She shouted a lot, clouted me if I got in the way.

'Don't look so stricken, Aoife. You asked. I didn't feel sorry for myself then and I won't now. I knew nothing different. The same for lots of kids. We stayed out of the way of the adults as much as we could – amused ourselves in whatever way we wanted, often in ways we shouldn't. I only saw her cry once. She screamed lots of times when he hit her, but cry, I only saw that once.

'It was when Dean, my eldest brother, was sent down. Six years for aggravated burglary – for carrying a knife. He used to show off, wave it around in my face. Didn't give over until he had me in tears. I guess he was her favourite, her firstborn. I suppose she must have wanted kids, maybe Dad and she liked each other back then. Dean said he forgot he had a knife when he broke into the house, but the jury didn't believe him. Why did she cry? I can only think she saw it all happening again. The same cycle of deprivation handed through the generations. She may have hoped it would be different for her family. Then she knew it wouldn't be. Dean slammed the truth into her face.'

'Do you want to go and see her?' Aoife asked, her head curled into my shoulder.

The shabby terraced house in the shadow of the football ground. The brown front door, its glass panel fixed with gaffer tape. Clear images in my head. Inside, the narrow hall cluttered with bikes, shoes and discarded coats. Mum, sitting at the stained table, her hands red-raw and cracked, streaks of blood between her knuckles where she was forever scratching. A smell of burned fat under layers of old smoke, dry and rancid so it caught the back of your throat and made you cough. The kitchen at the back of the house opening onto the yard. *Make us a cup of tea*, Micky Joe. She would light one cigarette after another, a fug as thick as a November fog trapped within the walls. No, I don't want to see her.

'There's no point in dragging up the past. Long gone – let's leave it there.' I shook my head to dispel the memory.

'Well, if you ever change your mind, I'll come with you – if you want me to.'

'You are the best thing that ever happened to me, better than crumpets with cheese or chocolate cake or ...' Aoife's kiss stifled my words.

On that first journey over to England a long-forgotten fear had nagged like gut pain. The loud clang of metal ramps as I drove off the ferry announced my arrival. My hands were ice-cold. Would one of my brothers be among the workers on the dockside? I found myself searching for a thin woman hurrying home after a night's work wearing a grey coat with a red scarf, trainers on her feet scurrying along the pavement. I saw only tired, anonymous faces preoccupied with their own lives. Family ties that trap like flypaper. My childhood, my youth, lost between the terraced houses, buried on the wasteland and hidden in dark alleys.

A signpost to the city centre and hospitals had me fighting to concentrate. Red traffic lights blurred through amber into green and I moved off swallowing the bile that burned my throat. Headed for the tunnel, put the Mersey between me and memories. In a lay-by I'd opened the cab window and sunk my head onto the steering wheel.

'Damn it all.' A cry whipped away by cars and trucks speeding by. Birkenhead, then on through Cheshire into Shropshire. Only when green fields and trees took the place of the industrial heartland had I relaxed.

Now months on and several trips later the fear I'd felt that first time across felt like it belonged to someone else. Today I stood on the ferry deck watching Liverpool's docks emerge from the horizon's haze. How long since I had fled the city? Seventeen, eighteen years. A lifetime – a winter night when I took a bag stuffed with nothing of use. When I dodged through the back streets avoiding anywhere where those I didn't want to meet hung out. Then I'd caught the first boat available; the dark and biting wind my only deck companions. A long time ago. I'd changed, like Liverpool itself had changed, both of us evolving into something to be proud of.

A heavy sky turned the city streets to dull ribbons with puddles lit by overhead streetlights. The weather deteriorated, the rain becoming heavier. Flashes of lightning. Spray from the roads made driving difficult. Some villages I passed through were tight to navigate. With no pavement, the sides of the road were rivulets sweeping leaves and debris down the hill. One hell of a storm.

Through the windscreen, I saw a figure flattened against the stone wall of a country estate, the tree above giving scant shelter. I slowed, not wanting to soak the huddled form though I couldn't make the situation worse.

Christ, it's a girl.

Nuala 2016

Rain, it only rains like this in Ireland. 'Come on, sun, where are you?' Flashes of lightning streak the sky against black, black clouds. Need to find a shelter. There's no pavement, no houses, no bus shelters. The sides of the road are rivers. My feet are wet. There's nothing around. Shivery and soaked, clammy and cold at the same time. Bury my head in my arms, tuck against a stone wall, seek cover from a tree. The rain is bouncing off the leaves and trickling down my back.

What have you done? You haven't got the right clothes. No place to go. No real plan. Loser as always. Give yourself in. Go back. Warm bed. Food.

'NO, NO, NO.' Lightning flashes, crazy sheets of colour. An answer.

A truck. Spray arcs like a fountain. Quake of brakes. Stops only feet from me.

'Are you trying to shave my skin off, arsehole?' My bellow is sucked into the judder of engine noise.

Nowhere to run.

A guy is shouting through the cab window. 'I'm only going to the next town. Can I give you a lift there?'

A timber truck, as familiar as toast. Trunks stacked on the trailer, piled high. Green algae on the bark, bright in the rain. Feel them, breathe them in, Big-un's work smell. I'm seven or eight. Is it one of the drivers who used to play with me? Matt, Lee, Ivor – I remember their names. Course it's not them. Why would it be?

'Well, what do you want to do?'

Can't speak. Shake my head. Never seen the guy before. Hope

he'll piss off.

'Hey, I didn't mean to frighten you, just it's filthy wet out there and there's nothing between here and where I'm going – about ten maybe fifteen miles.'

A great clap of thunder and I'm pulling at the door. I'm in there, backpack first, like a shield between me and him.

'Here, this might help.' A towel lands in my lap. It smells musty but dries my hair and face.

The windows of the cab steam up, bits of paper and a sandwich wrapping clutter the seat. A smell of engine oil and coffee. Like I remember. I've only got in because of what it is, a feeling of 'home'. Not telling him that. Hide in the towel, wipe my face pretending it's wet from the rain.

He's going on about a timber yard somewhere, wants to know why I'm here, where I come from. He's got a scouse accent. Shrug to show him I'm not listening, try to stop shivering.

'I live in town, work there. I've been visiting my grandma. Yeah, I've been visiting my grandma. She's been ill. She's old.' Hope it'll satisfy him.

'Right.'

He seems okay. You only think so because he drives a wood lorry. Why's he keep looking at me? Creepy.

I wriggle out of my jacket and wrap the towel round my shoulders like I'm at the hairdresser's. He's prattling about Liverpool and stuff.

'Do you sleep in here?' Rubbish thing to say – give him ideas.

'Sometimes. Depends on the journey.'

I can't keep my eyes off the chocolate bar in the front pocket – just like the one Matt always kept for me in the same place – an invisible link pulling me backwards. I want some of it. Must have some.

Reach for it, pull back the silver foil, breathe in sweetness. I break off a row of creamy brown squares, snap it in two and flick a piece across. He says nothing, just takes it.

Then, 'Help yourself.' He sounds all choked like he wants to cry. Oddball.

'Thanks. I will.' And I take more, licking the flakes from the tips of my fingers.

It tastes so good; I eat it all. 'Oops, I'll leave you the wrapper then.' I chuck it into the space and then burrow in my seat. I put my feet on the dashboard. I begin to warm up.

'Enjoy it?' He's laughing at me, but nicely.

I could like this guy.

'What does your dad think to you hitching lifts?' He's pointing at my forearm. He's seen my tattoo.

'Nosy bugger, aren't you?'

My face gives something away because he says, 'Sorry, didn't mean to pry. I'm Joe. And you?'

Ah, ah. Not falling for that one, mate.

He's staring at the FUCK and OFF Declan painted on the toe of my boots ages ago.

'So? What's it to you,'

'Okay, okay.' He grins, hand up in mock surrender.

The sound of the wipers is hypnotising. I gawp out the window, he gets on with driving, leaves me alone. Seems like a sound bloke. But not going to tell him my name, no way.

'I'll drop you here. Top of the High Street. Buy yourself a hot drink or something, dry off. There's a café along there on the left.'

Wow. He's tossed a twenty quid-note on the seat beside me. No favours asked.

'There's a bunkhouse too. Up the hill. Cheap but clean. Take care.'

So much for the story about my grandma. He's not daft. I like he doesn't pretend.

Push open the cab door, a draught of air cools my face. It's stopped raining

What the fuck, lift the money. It's there. He's offered it.

'My name … it's … it's Jess.' I owe him something.

Sorry, Jess, for using your name.

Red hair, a beard. Cool. Same sad expression like he's fighting something.

'Thanks.' I mean it.

The truck pulls away up the hill, the familiar low throb rooting me to a place, a time, a million years ago. I watch until it's hidden by the bend.

I'm hollow as a dead tree.

This feels like a place I might hang around.

Nuala 2017

One year and twenty-one days since I last smoked weed. It's not like I'm counting but I've known forever that only this day, the one you're in, is the one to get through.

It's my treat to myself coming up here to the timber yard. I found it 'cos of what that guy said about it, the one who gave me the lift. The smell of the cut wood, the bits of curly bark scattered on the ground. Sometimes deer come to graze at the top of the quarry. Mostly it's just me and an owl that hoots when it begins to get dark.

Today I have a purpose.

Lean against the log pile, music on, book to read. And wait.

'What the fuck? You scared me half to death.' I jerk myself awake,

A man's brown eyes, and swarthy pockmarked skin are inches from my face. Hot breath and the smell of liquorice swamp me.

'Scared *you* half to death,' he says, his lips shape words he can't get out. 'I thought you were dead, slumped like that. You kids, always messing around up here these days. Drive me mad.'

'I've seen them. I'm not one of them. They're idiots. They'll learn.' My heart is thumping in my ears.

'If I'd moved those logs,' he says jabbing towards a forklift truck that wasn't there before. 'I might have killed you.'

'Yeah, well you didn't.'

He's panting hard, sits down beside me with his legs outstretched. The end of one finger is missing and he covers it with his other hand when he sees me looking.

'You're trespassing.'

'I know. So? It's quiet. Peaceful when the workers clock off.

231

That's why I come. And besides I came to see you.'

'Me?' He stops kicking at the gravel with the toe of his boot.

'You're the boss, aren't you? I've seen you around. Doing things, after the others have gone.'

His voice is hesitant. 'Why do you want to see me? I don't know you.' Suspicion is reddening the tops of his ears.

'I want a job.'

'You want a job. Just like that. You think I'm that crazy?' He pulls up one leg and rubs at the side of his knee. 'Go on then. Talk. Tell me why you want a job. I admire your gall if nothing else. What kind of job do you want exactly?'

To stop him laughing at me I hand him a tissue. 'Here, you've got sweat running down your face.' He's embarrassed now and I watch until he's wiped it.

'Seeing as you ask, I want to learn to drive a forklift like you and a timber truck. Then when you retire having taught me all you know I'll take over the business.'

He rumbles a laugh. 'The heck you will. How old are you?'

'Eighteen.'

'Eighteen. I wish I'd had your cheek when I was that age. I wouldn't have said boo to a goose. Go on then, tell me about you.'

'Nothing much to tell. I'm a waitress in a café, in town. I can get a reference. Been doing it for well over a year now. Crummy job, nice people. Coming up here is my present to myself because … Well, for reasons. I want a job and I want it on the yard. That way I make someone very proud.'

His silence is filled by the cawing of birds returning to the trees to roost under a pink and turquoise sky. He's rubbing the stump of his finger like he wished he hadn't lost it.

'I love this place,' I say to remind him I'm here.

'So do I.' He's looking sideward at me. My striped leggings look like crayons in a box and I trace a purple band with my finger.

'I know more about timber yards than you might think.' He looks like he needs convincing. 'Do you have a map on the wall of all the places the trucks go to and a kettle with mugs where the drivers make their tea?' I sound stupid. I cover my mouth to stop hope escaping.

'I don't do things like this. Ever.' He's shaking his head, a white scar on his cheek disappears into the crease of a grin. 'And why does it feel like I'm not going to regret it?'

'Yes.' Slap. I high-five him so he can't change his mind.

'Not quite so fast. You're too young to learn to drive a truck. You start in the office, at the bottom, learn how things are done. One day at a time. We'll see how it goes, shall we? What's your name anyway?'

'Nuala. You absolutely won't regret it, I promise. Can I start at the beginning of next month?'

'Given your eagerness, I'm surprised you don't want to start tomorrow.'

'There's something I need to do first.' I pull a face. 'There's another thing. Who's the driver that comes across from Ireland and when's he next over here?'

'Strange question. What's this about? There's more than one.'

'The guy with the red hair and a beard.'

'Joe. That'll be Joe. Why? Do you know him?' He says it slowly his eyes narrowing to slits.

'No, but he gave me a lift. Oh, ages ago. It was shitting rain, I was soaked. Decent I remember. He told me about this place.'

'He's due in back end of this week, Thursday or Friday, I think.

'Which though? Thursday or Friday. It's important.'

'Thursday. But I'm warning you one hint of trouble and you're out on your neck. Got it.'

'Got it.' I give him a mock salute and we both laugh. 'I must go. I'll come again. We can talk some more. Promise I won't play dead next time.' I sprawl my arms and stick out my tongue pretending. Makes him laugh. 'Thanks. I won't let you down.' When I turn and wave, he's still sitting by the stack of timber staring straight ahead.

Thursday, its dead busy in the café but at least it makes the morning pass quickly. My head's that stuffed with thoughts I keep forgetting if the customer wants coffee and walnut cake, a cheese scone or teacake with jam. All the regulars know I'm having a week off, but I haven't told them where I'm going.

Standing here on the side of the road all the what-ifs line up like an identity parade. I shove them out of the way and try to look like I'm waiting for someone. Which is what I am doing, only he doesn't know it and it could all go so horribly wrong. At every sound of an engine my heart skips a beat.

Then I hear it. The hiss of compressed air, the clang of an empty trailer, the truck I've been waiting for, coming slowly around the corner. I step into the road, raise my thumb with my arm outstretched forcing him to shudder to a stop. He lowers the window.

'Can I have a lift?' I can see he wants to shout at me, a series of expressions flit across his face.

'That was a bloody stupid thing to do. Where are you going?'

I pull open the door and jump in while he's not saying no. I remember it all from before, stuff sprawled across the seat, a packet of sandwiches for later.

'Ireland – please.'

'Not far then!' A car driver behind blasts his horn. We pull off and I dare to breathe again.

'How's your grandma?' He's looking ahead but I can hear his smile.

'What? Oh that. You remember me then?'

'Sure I do. You look different.'

'Yeah. Hair doesn't grow back in pink.'

'It looks better. Why Ireland? You're not running away, are you? Not in any trouble?'

I throw my rucksack onto the floor and fold my arms.

'Not this time. Running back more likely but only for a few days.'

'Who you going to see?'

'People.' Just saying it makes my voice croak. 'My mum and dad for starters. At least my *nearly* mum and dad.'

'Sounds like there's a story there.'

'There is. A long one.'

'Well, it's a long journey, plenty of time.'

'Yeah. You got kids?'

'I have a stepson. Fergus. Love him to bits. And … I had a daughter once … love her too but …'

'You had your fun and buggered off.'

'A bit more to it than that, but yes, I guess the truth is I buggered off as you so nicely put it. Do you always talk like this to people you don't know?'

'I do know you. We've shared this cab before, remember. And that money you gave me. I'll buy you a coffee this time. Besides I'll soon know you a whole lot better. I've got a job in the timber yard back there. Start next month.'

'You?' He's pointing a finger at me. 'That's you. Derek, the boss was telling me about a girl asking for a job. He was properly taken with you.'

He was tapping on the steering wheel then grinned.

'You seem like one amazing young woman.'

234

'I am. The best. Hey, have you got any chocolate stashed away in here like before?'

Acknowledgments

It is said that writing is a lonely occupation. That may be so, but turning a manuscript into a published book is most definitely a team effort. My thanks to Wenlock Writers on the Edge for their patience and careful scrutiny of the early drafts. Especially to Maggie Bardsley and Brenda Carter who have read and reread it almost as many times as I have. To my editor Susan Davis and copy editor Colin Taylor for their professionalism and to Olga Levitt and Margaret Canonn for being fresh eyes at the end of the process.

As always thanks to my family for being there and showing me what is really important.

ALSO AVAILABLE BY JO JACKSON

TOO LOUD A SILENCE

It is 2011, Egypt is in the grip of the Arab Spring. There is no room for outsiders.

Born in Egypt but raised by her adoptive parents in England, journalist Maha Rhodes recognises a growing desire to touch her roots. Despite her mother's unexpected resistance, finding out who she really is becomes important.

The turbulent political events in Cairo are a catalyst but when she travels to her birthplace she is completely unprepared for the devastating secret she will uncover.

Events draw her into the mayhem. She experiences the abuse and the violence of the revolution and is moved by the Egyptian cause and the passion of the demonstrators. She meets people who fight for change. She faces up to her own naivety and finally understands what it means to belong.

Too Loud a Silence will take you to Egypt. It is a beautiful, poignant, sometimes brutal story of cross-cultural identity, of a mother's love and guilt.

This is a truly wonderful story, a multi-layered novel handled with insight and sensitivity.

Sarah Vincent